EVENINGS
near the Village
OF DIKANKA

NIKOLAI GOGOL

EVENINGS
near the Village
OF DIKANKA

Stories edited by Beekeeper
RUDI PANKO

FREDERICK UNGAR PUBLISHING CO.
NEW YORK

Translated by Ovid Gorchakov

Illustrated by A. Kanevsky

Printed in the United States of America

Library of Congress Catalog Card No. 60-13980

CONTENTS

Page

PART ONE

PART TWO

PART
ONE

PREFACE

🌸 "What oddity is this: *Evenings near the Village of Dikanka?* What sort of 'evenings' could they be? And thrust into the world by a bee-keeper! Mercy on us! As though geese enough had not been plucked for pens, or rags enough turned into paper; as though folks enough of all classes had not covered their fingers with ink-stains! The whim must take a bee-keeper to follow their example! Why, so much stuff gets into print nowadays that one has more wrapping-paper than one can use."

A month ago I had a foreboding in my heart that there would be this kind of talk. For a villager like me to poke his nose out of his hole into the great world is just like what happens if you go into the apartments of some great lord: they all come round you and make you feel like a fool. It would not matter so much if it were only the upper servants, but any wretched little whipper-snapper hanging about the back yard pesters you, too; and they begin stamping at you and shouting: "Where are you going? What d'you want? Get out, muzhik!" I can tell you—But what's the use of talking? I would rather go twice a year to Mirgorod, where the district court assessor and the reverend Father have not seen me for the last five years, than show myself in that high company; still, if you do it, you must face the consequences, whatever they may be.

At home, dear readers—no offence meant (please don't be annoyed at a bee-keeper like me addressing you as if I were speaking to some old friend or crony)—at home in our hamlets it has always been the peasants' habit, as soon as the work in the fields is over, to climb up on the stove-couch and rest there all the winter, and we bee-keepers put our bees away in a dark cellar. At the time of year when you see no cranes in the sky nor pears on the trees there is sure to be a light burning somewhere at the end of the hamlet as soon as evening comes on; you can hear in the distance laughter and singing, a balalaika playing and at times a fiddle, talk and noise. Those are our evening parties! They are like a ball, though not altogether so, I must say. If you go to a ball, it is to prance about or yawn with your hand over your mouth; while with us the girls gather together in one cottage, not for a ball, but with their distaffs and carding-combs. And you may say they *do* work at first: the distaffs hum, there is a constant flow of song, and no one looks up from her work; but as soon as the lads burst into the cottage with the fiddler, there is noise and bustle, the fun begins, they break into a dance, and I could not tell you all the pranks that are played.

But best of all is when they crowd together and start to guess riddles or simply talk. Heavens, what stories they tell! What tales of old times they unearth! What creepy things they describe! But nowhere are such stories told as in the cottage of the bee-keeper Ginger* Panko. Why the villagers call me Ginger, I really cannot say. My hair, I fancy, is more grey nowadays than red. But, you see, when a nickname has once been given in our parts, it sticks to a man all his life. Good people meet together in the bee-keeper's hut of an evening, sit down to the table—and then you have only to listen! And the guests, let me tell you, are by no means of the humbler sort, mere muzhiks; their visit would be an honour for someone of more consequence than a bee-keeper. For instance, do you know Foma Grigoryevich, the sacristan of the Dikanka church? Ah, he has a head on his shoulders! What stories he can reel off! You will find two of them in this book. He never wears one of those homespun coats that you so often see on village sacristans; no, if you go to see him, even on working days, he will always receive you in a gaberdine of fine cloth of the colour of cold potato jelly, for which he paid almost six rubles a yard in Poltava. As for his high boots, no one in the hamlet has ever said that they smelt of tar; everyone knows that he polishes them with the very best fat, such as I believe many a peasant would be glad to put in his porridge. Nor would anyone ever say that he wipes his nose on the skirt of his gaberdine, as many men of his calling do; no, he takes from his bosom a clean, neatly folded white handkerchief embroidered on the hem with red cotton, and after putting it to its proper use, folds it up in twelve as his habit is, and puts it back in his bosom.

And there's another one. Well, he is such a fine young gentleman that you might easily take him for an assessor or landreeve. When he tells a story he holds up his finger and studies the tip

---

* *Rudi* in Ukrainian.—*Ed.*

of it, and he uses as many tricks and flourishes as you would find in a book. You listen and listen and begin to get puzzled; you find that for the life of you you can't make head or tail of it. Where did he pick up all those words? Foma Grigoryevich once got back at him for this. He told him how a lad who had been having lessons from a deacon came back to his father such a Latin scholar that he had forgotten our own tongue: he put *us* on the end of all the words; a spade was "spadus," a grampa was "grampus." One day when he was with his father in the fields, he saw a rake and asked: "What do you call that, Father?" And without looking what he was doing he stepped on the teeth of the rake. Before his father could answer, the handle swung up and hit the lad on the head. "Damn that rake!" he cried, clapping his hand to his forehead and jumping half a yard into the air. "May the devil shove its father off a bridge!" So he remembered the name after all!

The tale was not to the taste of our ingenious story-teller. He rose from his seat without a word, stood in the middle of the room with his legs apart, craned his head forward a little, thrust his hand into the back pocket of his pea-green coat, took out his round lacquer snuff-box, tapped the face of some Mussulman general, and, taking a good pinch of snuff powdered with wood-ash and leaves of lovage, crooked his elbow, lifted his hand to his nose and sniffed the whole pinch up with no help from his thumb—all without a word. And it was only when he brought out a checked blue cotton handkerchief from another pocket that he muttered something—I even think it was a saying—about not casting your pearls before swine. "There's bound to be a quarrel," I thought, seeing that Foma Grigoryevich's fingers seemed about to make a long nose. Fortunately my old woman chose that moment to put hot rolls and butter on the table. We all set to work upon them. Foma Grigoryevich's hand, instead of forming a rude gesture, stretched out for a hot roll, and, as always happens, they all began holding forth about my wife's skill as a cook.

We have another story-teller, but this one—better not even think about him at night—has a store of terrible stories that make your hair stand on end. I have left them out on purpose: good people might be so scared that they would be as afraid of the bee-keeper as they are of the devil. If God spares me to live to the New Year and bring out another volume, then I may scare my good readers with some of the ghosts and marvels that were seen in the old days in this Christian country. Among them, maybe, you will find some tales told by the bee-keeper himself to his grandchildren. If only people will read and listen I have enough of them stored away for ten volumes, I daresay—if I am not too damned lazy to rack my brains for them.

But there! I have forgotten what is most important: when you come to see me, gentlemen, take the high road straight to Dikanka. I have put the name on the title-page on purpose so that our hamlet may be more easily found. You have heard plenty about Dikanka, I have no doubt, and indeed the bee-keeper's cottage is not a patch on the houses there. As for the park, I don't suppose you would find anything like it in your St. Petersburg. When you reach Dikanka all you have to do is ask any little boy in a dirty shirt minding geese: "Where does Ginger Panko, the bee-keeper, live?" "Over there," he will say, pointing with his finger, and if you like he will lead you to the hamlet. But there is one thing I must ask you: don't swagger with your hands behind your back, for our village roads are not as smooth as the drives going up to your mansions. The year before last Foma Grigoryevich, driving over from Dikanka, fell into a ditch, with his new trap and bay mare and all, though he was driving himself and had on a pair of spectacles, too.

But, when you do arrive, we will give you the best melons

you've ever tasted in your life; and, take my word for it, you will find no better honey in any other hamlet. When you bring a honeycomb, the scent in the room is something you can't imagine—clear as a tear or a costly crystal such as you see in earrings. And the pies my old woman will feed you on! What pies they are: simply sugar, perfect sugar! And the butter fairly melts on your lips when you begin to eat them. Bless my soul, they can do anything, these women! Have you ever tasted pear kvass flavoured with sloes, or raisin-and-plum vodka? Or frumenty with milk? Heavens, what dainties there are! As soon as you begin eating them, you know it is a treat and no mistake. Last year—But how I am running on! Only come and see us—as quick as you can; we'll give you so many good things that you will talk about them to everyone you meet.

GINGER PANKO, bee-keeper

THE FAIR AT SOROCHINTSI

I

I am weary of the cottage,
Oh, take me out of here,
To where there's noise and bustle,
Where the girls are dancing gaily,
Where the lads are making merry!

FROM AN OLD BALLAD

How intoxicating, how magnificent is a summer day in the Ukraine! How luxuriously warm it is when midday glitters in stillness and sultry heat, and the blue expanse of sky, arching like a voluptuous cupola, seems to be slumbering, bathed in languor, clasping the fair earth and holding it close in its ethereal

17

embrace! In it, not a cloud; below, not a sound. Everything seems dead; only in the airy heights above a lark is trilling and the silvery notes tinkle down upon the adoring earth, and from time to time the cry of a gull or the piping of a quail sounds in the steppe. The towering oaks stand, lazy and care-free, like aimless wayfarers, and the dazzling gleams of sunshine light up picturesque masses of leaves, casting on to others a shadow black as night, but flecked with gold when the wind blows. Like sparks of emerald, topaz, and ruby the insects of the air flit about the gay kitchen gardens topped by stately sunflowers. Grey haystacks and golden sheaves of corn are ranged like tents on the plain and stray over its immensity. The broad branches of cherry, plum, apple and pear trees bending under their load of fruit, the sky and its pure mirror—the river set in a green, proudly-erect frame—how full of voluptuousness and languor is the Ukrainian summer!

Such was the splendour of a day in the hot August of eighteen hundred... eighteen hundred... yes, it was about thirty years ago, when the road ten versts beyond the village of Sorochintsi bustled with people hurrying to the fair from all the farms, far and near. From early morning waggons full of fish and salt had trailed in an endless chain along the road. Mountains of pots packed in hay moved along slowly, weary, it seemed, of being shut up in the dark; only here and there a brightly painted tureen or crock boastfully peeped out from behind the hurdle that held the high pile on the waggon, and attracted longing glances from the lovers of such luxuries. Many of the passers-by looked enviously at the tall potter, the owner of these treasures, who walked slowly behind his goods, every now and then carefully tucking his clay dandies and coquettes back into the hay they detested.

On one side of the road, apart from all the rest, a team of weary oxen dragged a waggon piled high with sacks, hemp, linen and various household goods, followed by their owner clad in a clean linen shirt and dirty linen trousers. With a lazy hand he wiped from his swarthy face the streaming sweat that even trickled from his long moustaches, powdered by that relentless barber who comes uninvited to the plain and the handsome alike and has for thousands of years forcibly powdered all mankind. Beside him, tied to the waggon, walked a mare, whose meek air betrayed her advancing years.

Many of the passers-by, especially the young lads, took off their caps as they met our peasant. But it was not his grey moustaches or his dignified step which led them to do so; one had but to raise one's eyes a little to discover the explanation of this deference: on the waggon sat his pretty daughter, a girl with a round face, black eyebrows arching evenly above her clear brown eyes, and merrily smiling rosy lips. Red and blue ribbons were twisted in the long plaits which, with a bunch of wild flowers, crowned her charming head. Everything seemed to interest her; everything was new and wonderful, and her lovely eyes raced all the time from one object to another. Well might she be interested. It was her first visit to a fair! A girl of eighteen at a fair for the first time! None of the passers-by knew what it had cost her to persuade her father to take her along, though he would have done it even earlier but for her spiteful stepmother, who had learned to drive him as cleverly as he drove his old mare, now, as a reward for long years of service, being taken to be sold. Oh, that tiresome woman! But we are forgetting that she, too, was sitting on the top of the load dressed in a smart green woollen jacket adorned with little tails, to imitate ermine, though they were red in colour, a gorgeous skirt checked like a chess-board, and a flowered chintz cap that gave a particularly majestic

air to her red round face, which betrayed so unpleasant and
savage a nature that everyone hastened to turn from it to
the lively face of the daughter.

The river Psyol came into our travellers' view; even from
afar they had felt its cool freshness, the more welcome after
the exhausting, scorching heat. Through the dark and light
green foliage of the birches and poplars, carelessly scattered
over the plain, there were glimpses of the cold glitter of the
water; and the lovely river exposed its shining silvery bosom,
over which the green tresses of the trees drooped luxuriantly.
Wilful as a beauty in those enchanting hours when her faithful
mirror so nicely framed her proud, dazzling brow, her lily-
white shoulders, and her marble neck shrouded by the dark
waves of her hair, when with disdain she flung aside one orna-
ment to replace it by another and there was no end to her
whims, the river almost every year changed its course, picked
out a new channel and surrounded itself with new and varied
scenes. Rows of water-mills tossed up great waves with their
heavy wheels, flinging them violently down again, churning
them into foam, scattering froth and making a great clatter.
At that moment the waggon with the persons we have described
reached the bridge; the river lay before them in all its beauty
and grandeur like a sheet of glass. The sky, the green and
dark blue forest, the men, the waggons of pots, the water-
mills were all seen upside-down, yet, somehow, not sinking
into the lovely blue depths.

Our fair maiden mused as she gazed at the glorious view, and
even forgot to crack the sunflower seeds which she had been
busily eating all the way. All at once the words "What a girl!"
caught her ear. Looking round she saw a group of lads standing
on the bridge. One of them, dressed rather more smartly than
the others in a white jacket and grey astrakhan cap, was jauntily

looking at the passers-by with his arms akimbo. The girl could not help noticing his sunburnt but pleasing face and glowing eyes, which, it seemed, were striving to look right through her, and she dropped her eyes at the thought that it might have been he who had uttered those words.

"A fine girl!" the young man in the white jacket went on, keeping his eyes fixed on her. "I'd give all I have to kiss her. But look at that witch sitting in front!"

There were peals of laughter all round; but the overdressed spouse of the slow-moving peasant was not pleased at such a greeting: her red cheeks blazed and a torrent of choice language fell on the head of the youth.

"Plague take you, you rascally bargee! May your father crack his head on a pot! May he slip on the ice, the accursed antichrist! May the devil singe his beard in hell!"

"Just listen to her!" said the young man, staring at her as though amazed at such a sharp volley of unexpected greetings. "And she can bring her tongue to utter words like that, the hag! She is a hundred if she is a day!"

"A hundred?" the elderly charmer countered. "You heathen! Go and wash your face, you worthless scamp! I've never seen your mother, but I know she's dirt. And your father is dirt. And your aunt is dirt! A hundred, indeed! The snotty-nosed pig!"

The waggon was drawing away from the bridge and the last words could not be heard; but the lad apparently did not want to let it end there: without stopping to think he picked up a handful of mud and threw it at her. The throw achieved more than one could have hoped: the new chintz cap was spattered all over and the guffaws of the rowdy scamps were louder than ever. The buxom charmer was boiling with rage; but by this time the waggon was far away, and she wreaked her vengeance on her innocent stepdaughter and her slow-moving husband, who, long accustomed to such onslaughts, preserved a stubborn silence and listened undisturbed to the harangue of his spouse. In spite of that, her indefatigable tongue went on clacking until the waggon reached the house of their old friend and crony, a Cossack named Tsibulya, on the outskirts of the village. The meeting of the old friends, who had not seen each other for a long time, put this unpleasant incident out of their minds for a while, as our travellers talked of the fair and rested after their long journey.

II

> *Good gracious me! what isn't there at that fair! wheels, window-panes, tar, tobacco, belts, onions, all sorts of haberdasher shops... so that even if you had thirty rubles in your purse you could not buy up the fair.*
>
> FROM A UKRAINIAN COMEDY

You may have heard a rushing waterfall, where the air is filled with a roaring, and a chaos of strange, vague sounds whirls round you. Are you not instantly overcome by the same feelings in the turmoil of a village fair, when all the people are melted into one huge monster whose whole body is stirring in the market-place and the narrow streets, with shouting, laughing, and clatter? Noise, swearing, bellowing, bleating, roaring—all blend into one discordant clamour. Oxen, sacks, hay, Gypsies, pots, peasant women, cakes, caps—everything is bright, gaudy, discordant, and rushing and bustling about before your eyes. The different voices drown one another, and not a single word can be caught, can be saved from the deluge; not one cry is distinct. The smack of hand against hand—the sealing of a bargain—is heard on all sides; a waggon collapses with a crash; there is the clank of iron and the thud of boards thrown on to the ground. Your head is so dizzy you do not know which way to turn.

The peasant whose acquaintance we have already made had been for some time elbowing his way through the crowd with his dark-eyed daughter. He went up to one waggon-load, fingered another, inquired the prices; and his thoughts kept revolving round his ten sacks of wheat and the old mare he had brought to sell. From his daughter's face it could be seen that she was not too pleased to be brushed against by waggons of flour and wheat. She longed to be where red ribbons, tin ear-rings, crosses made of copper, and "ducats" were displayed attractively under linen awnings. But even where she was she found many objects worthy of notice: she was much diverted by the sight of a Gypsy and a peasant, who smacked hands so violently after a bargain that they both cried out with pain; a drunken Jew slapping a woman on the backside; two fishwives bandying abuse and crayfish; a Russian stroking his goat's beard with one hand, while his other hand— But at that moment she felt someone pull her by the embroidered sleeve of her blouse. She turned and saw the bright-eyed young man in the white jacket standing before her. She started; her heart throbbed as it had never throbbed before at any joy or grief; something strange and delightful—she could not make out what—was happening to her.

"Don't be frightened, my lovely one, don't be frightened!" he said to her in a low voice, taking her hand. "I'll say nothing to hurt you!"

"Perhaps you won't," the girl thought to herself; "but

there's something strange—it might be the Evil One! I know it's not right, but I haven't the strength to take away my hand."

The peasant looked round and was about to say something to his daughter when he heard the word "wheat." That magic word instantly made him join two corn-dealers who were talking loudly, and he had no ears for anything else.

III

Do you see what a fellow he is?
Not many like him in the world.
Tosses off vodka like beer!
KOTLYAREVSKY, "THE AENEID"*

"So you think, neighbour, that our wheat won't sell well?" asked one of the dealers, who looked like a townsman, in tar-stained trousers of coarse homespun.

"I don't think—I know," said the other, a man with a big swelling on his forehead and wearing a dark blue jacket patched here and there. "I am ready to put a halter round my neck and hang from that tree like a sausage in the cottage before Christmas, if we sell a single bushel."

"Come, come, now, neighbour. No wheat has been brought except ours," retorted the man in the homespun trousers.

"You may say what you like," thought the father of our beauty, who had not missed a single word of the dealers' conversation. "I have ten sacks in reserve."

"Well, you see it's like this: if there is any devilry mixed up in a thing, you will get no more out of it than out of a hungry

* Kotlyarevsky—Ukrainian poet and Gogol's contemporary. *The Aeneid*—a comical version of Vergil's epic poem.—*Ed.*

Muscovite," the man with the swelling on his forehead said ominously.

"What do you mean by devilry?" asked the man in the homespun trousers.

"Haven't you heard what people are saying?" he of the swelled forehead went on, giving him a sidelong look out of his morose eyes.

"Well?"

"Well may you say 'well'! The assessor—may he never wipe his lips again after the gentry's plum brandy—has set aside an evil spot for the fair, where you may burst before you get rid of a single grain. Do you see that old tumbledown barn over there at the foot of the hill?" (At this point the inquisitive peasant went closer and was all attention.) "All manner of devilish tricks go on in that barn, and not a single fair has been held in this spot without trouble. The district clerk passed by it late last night and all of a sudden a pig's snout looked out at the window of the loft, and grunted so loudly that it sent a shiver down his back. That Red Jacket will be seen again, as likely as not."

"What red jacket?"

Our attentive listener's hair stood on end at these words. He looked round in alarm and saw that his daughter and the young man were standing with their arms round each other, murmuring soft nothings to each other and oblivious of all the jackets in the world. This dispelled his terror and restored his equanimity.

"Aha, neighbour! You know how to hug a girl, it seems! I had been married three days before I learned to hug my poor Khveska, God rest her soul, and I owned that to a friend who was my best man: he gave me a hint."

The youth saw that his fair one's father was not very quick-witted, and he began planning to win the man's favour.

"It seems you don't know me, good friend, but I recognized you at once."

"Did you, now?"

"Yes, and if you like I'll tell you your name and your surname and everything about you: your name is Solopy Cherevik."

"That's right—Solopy Cherevik."

"Well, have a good look: don't you remember me?"

"No, I don't. No offence meant, but I've seen so many faces of all sorts in my day, how the devil can I remember them all?"

"Too bad you don't remember Golopupenko's son."

"Why, is Okhrim your father?"

"Who else? If he's not, then maybe it's old Bald Grandad himself."

At this the friends took off their caps and proceeded to kiss each other; and Golopupenko's son made up his mind to attack his new acquaintance without loss of time.

"It's like this, Solopy: your daughter and I have so taken to each other that we are ready to spend the rest of our lives together."

"Well, Paraska," said Cherevik, laughing and turning to his daughter; "maybe you really might—you and he—graze on the same grass, as they say! Come, is it a deal? And now, my new son-in-law, stand me a drink to seal the bargain!"

And all three found themselves in the famous pot-house of the fair—a Jewess's booth, adorned with a numerous flotilla of stoups, bottles and flasks of every kind and description.

"You are a smart fellow! I like you for that," said the slightly tipsy Cherevik as he saw his intended son-in-law fill a pint mug and, without batting an eyelash, toss it off at a gulp, flinging down the mug afterwards and smashing it to bits. "What do you say, Paraska? Haven't I found you a fine husband? Look how he downs his drink!"

And laughing and staggering he went with her towards his waggon, while our young man made his way to the booths where fancy goods were displayed—where there were even dealers from Gadyach and Mirgorod, two famous towns of Poltava Province—to pick out the best wooden pipe with a smart copper band, a flowered red kerchief and a cap, for wedding presents to his father-in-law and everyone else who was entitled to them.

IV

> *If a man wants one thing*
> *And his wife wants another,*
> *You know who gets what.*
> KOTLYAREVSKY

"Well, wife, I have found a husband for my daughter!"

"This is a moment to look for husbands, I must say! You are a fool—a fool! It must have been ordained at your birth that you should remain one! Whoever has seen or heard of a decent man running after husbands at a time like this! You had much better be thinking how to get your wheat off your hands. A nice young man he must be, too! I expect he is the shabbiest beggar in the place!"

"Oh, not a bit of it! You should see what a lad he is! His jacket alone is worth more than your green blouse and red boots. And how he takes his vodka! May the devil take me—and you, too—if I have ever before seen a lad toss off a pint without winking!"

"To be sure, if he is a sot and a tramp, he is a man after your own heart. I wouldn't mind betting it's that very same rascal who pestered us on the bridge. Too bad I haven't come across him yet: I'd give him a piece of my mind."

"Well, Khivrya, what if it was the same. Why is he a rascal?"

"Why is he a rascal, eh? Just listen to the old addle-pate! Where were your stupid eyes when we were driving past the mills? A man's wife is insulted right before his snuffy nose, and he doesn't care a hang!"

"I see no harm in him, anyway; he is a fine fellow! He just plastered your ugly face with dung, that's all."

"Aha! I see you won't let me say a word! What's come over you? You must have managed to get a drop before you sold anything."

Here Cherevik realized that he had said too much and instantly put his hands over his head, doubtless expecting that his wrathful spouse would seize his hair in her wifely claws.

"Damn it! There goes our wedding!" he thought to himself, retreating before his wife's onset. "I shall have to refuse a good fellow for no rhyme or reason. Merciful God, why didst Thou send such a plague on us poor sinners? With so many nasty things in the world, Thou must needs go and create women!"

V

Droop not, plane-tree,
Still art thou green;
Fret not, little Cossack,
Still art thou young.
FROM A UKRAINIAN SONG

Sitting by his waggon, the lad in the white jacket gazed absent-mindedly at the crowd that milled noisily about him. The weary sun, after blazing tranquilly through the midday hours, was withdrawing from the earth, and the daylight was going out in a bright, seductive glow. The tops of the white booths and tents stood out with dazzling brightness, suffused in a faint rosy tint. The panes in the window-frames piled up for sale glittered; the green goblets and bottles on the drinking-booth tables flashed like fire; the mountains of melons and pumpkins looked as though they were cast in gold and dark copper. There was less talk, and the weary tongues of hucksters, peasants, and Gypsies moved more slowly and lazily. Here and there lights began gleaming, and savoury steam from boiling dumplings floated over the hushed streets.

"What are you grieving over, Gritsko?" a tall sunburnt Gypsy cried, slapping our young friend on the shoulder. "Come, let me have your oxen for twenty rubles!"

"It's nothing but oxen and oxen with you. All you Gypsies care for is gain; cheating and deceiving honest folk!"

"Ah! You are quite worked up, I see! Are you vexed at having tied yourself up with a girl, maybe?"

"No, that's not my way; I keep my word; what I've done I stand by for ever. But it seems that old gaffer Cherevik has not half a kopek's worth of conscience: he gave his word, but he has taken it back. Well, it's no good blaming him: he is a blockhead and that's all there is to it. It's all the doing of that old witch whom we lads jeered at on the bridge today! If I were the Tsar or some great lord I would hang all the fools who let themselves be saddled by women."

"Will you let the oxen go for twenty, if we make Cherevik give you Paraska?"

Gritsko stared at him in wonder. There was something spiteful, malicious, ignoble and at the same time haughty in the Gypsy's swarthy face; any man looking at him would have recognized that there were great qualities in that strange soul, though their only reward on earth would be the gallows. The mouth, completely sunken between the nose and the pointed chin and for ever curved in a mocking smile, the little eyes that gleamed like fire, and the lightning flashes of intrigue and enterprise constantly flitting over his face—all this seemed in keeping with the strange costume he wore. The dark brown coat, which looked as though it would drop into dust at a touch; the long black hair that fell in tangled wisps on his shoulders; the shoes on his bare sunburnt feet, all seemed to be part and parcel of him.

"I'll let you have them for fifteen, not twenty, if only you don't deceive me!" the young man answered, keeping his searching gaze fixed on the Gypsy.

"Fifteen? Done! Mind you don't forget: fifteen! Here is a five rubles for you as a pledge!"

"But if you deceive me?"

"Then the pledge is yours."

"Good! Well, let us shake hands on the bargain!"

"Right!"

VI

> *God help us! My husband is coming; he'll be here in a minute and give me a drubbing; and you, Pan Khoma, will not get off with a whole skin, either.*
>
> FROM A UKRAINIAN COMEDY

"This way, Afanasy Ivanovich! The fence is lower here. Put your foot up and don't be afraid: the old fool has gone off for the night with his crony to sleep under the waggon to see that the Muscovites don't steal anything."

Thus Cherevik's formidable spouse encouraged the priest's son, who was faint-heartedly clinging to the fence. He climbed on to the top and stood there for some time in hesitation, like a gaunt terrible phantom, looking where he could best jump. At last he came down with a crash among the rank weeds.

"Heavens! I hope you haven't hurt yourself? Please God you've not broken your neck!" Khivrya faltered anxiously.

"Hush! I'm all right, I'm all right, dear Khavronya Nikiforovna," the priest's son brought out in a painful whisper, getting on to his feet, "except for being afflicted by the nettle, that serpent-like weed, to use the words of our late archpriest."

"Let us go into the house; there is nobody there. I was beginning to think you had a stomach ache or something, Afanasy Ivanovich—you stayed away for such a long time. How are you? I hear that your honoured father has had a run of good luck!"

"Nothing to speak of, Khavronya Nikiforovna: during the whole fast Father has received nothing but fifteen sacks or so of spring wheat, four sacks of millet, a hundred rolls; and as for chickens they don't run up to fifty, and the eggs were mostly rotten. But the truly sweet offerings, so to say, can only come from you, Khavronya Nikiforovna!" the priest's son continued with a tender glance at her as he edged nearer.

"Here is an offering for you, Afanasy Ivanovich!" she said, setting some bowls on the table and coyly fastening the buttons of her blouse as though they had not been undone on purpose. "Curd doughnuts, wheaten dumplings, buns and cakes!"

"I bet they have been made by the cleverest hands of any daughter of Eve!" said the priest's son, setting to work upon the cakes and with the other hand drawing the doughnuts towards him. "Though indeed, Khavronya Nikiforovna, my heart thirsts for a gift from you sweeter than any buns or dumplings!"

"I don't really know what other dainty you want, Afanasy Ivanovich!" answered the buxom beauty, pretending not to understand.

"Your love, of course, incomparable Khavronya Nikiforovna!" the priest's son whispered, holding a doughnut in one hand and encircling her ample waist with his free arm.

"Goodness knows what you are talking about, Afanasy Ivanovich!" said Khivrya, bashfully casting down her eyes. "Why, you will be trying to kiss me next, I shouldn't wonder!"

"As for that, I must tell you," the young man went on. "When I was still at the seminary, I remember as though it were today—"

At that moment there was a sound of barking and a knock at the gate. Khivrya ran out quickly and came back looking pale.

"Afanasy Ivanovich, we are caught: there are a lot of people knocking, and I fancy I heard Tsibulya's voice."

The doughnut stuck in the young man's gullet. His eyes almost popped out of his head, as though someone had just come from the other world to visit him.

"Climb up there!" cried the frightened Khivrya, pointing to some boards that lay across the rafters just below the ceiling, loaded with all sorts of household odds and ends.

Danger gave our hero courage; he got up on the stove and from there clambered cautiously on to the boards, while Khivrya ran headlong to the gate, as the knocking was getting louder and more insistent.

VII

But here are miracles, my lord!
FROM A UKRAINIAN COMEDY

A strange incident had taken place at the fair: there were rumours all over the place that the Red Jacket had been seen somewhere among the wares. An old bread-woman fancied she saw the devil in the shape of a pig bending over the waggons as though looking for something. The news soon flew to every corner of the now quiet camp, and everyone would have thought it a crime to disbelieve it, in spite of the fact that the old woman, whose stall was next to the drinking-booth, had been helping herself to her neighbour's goods and could not walk straight. To this was added the story, by now greatly exaggerated, of the marvel seen by the district clerk in the tumbledown barn. So, as night was falling people huddled together; their peace of mind was destroyed, and everyone was too terrified to close an eye; while the less hardy ones who had secured a night's lodging in some cottage or other made their way homewards. Among the latter were Cherevik with his daughter and his friend Tsibulya, and they, together with the friends who had offered to keep them company, were responsible for the loud knocking that had so alarmed Khivrya. Tsibulya was already a little tipsy; he had twice driven round the cottage before he could find it. His guests, too, were all rather merry, and they unceremoniously pushed into the cottage before their host. Cherevik's wife sat as though on needles when they began rummaging in every corner of the cottage.

"What's wrong?" asked Tsibulya as he entered. "Are you shaking with fever?"

"Yes, I am not well," answered Khivrya, stealing an uneasy glance upwards.

"Come, wife, get the bottle out of the waggon!" said Tsibulya. "We will empty it with these good folk, for those damned women have given us such a scare that one is ashamed to own it. Yes, mates, there was really no sense in our coming here!" he went on, taking a pull at an earthenware jug. "I bet you a new cap that the women thought they would have a laugh at us. Even if it were Satan—who's Satan? Spit on him! If he stood here before me this very minute, I'd make a long nose at him, damn me if I wouldn't."

"Why did you turn so pale, then?" cried one of the visitors. He was a head taller than any of the rest and he always tried to behave like a courageous man.

"Me? You must have been dreaming!"

The visitors laughed; the boastful hero smiled complacently.

"As if he could turn pale now!" put in another; "his cheeks are as red as a poppy; he is not a Tsibulya* now, but a beetroot—or, rather, the Red Jacket himself that frightened all folks so."

As the bottle went the round of the table the spirits of the visitors rose. Cherevik, still worrying about the Red Jacket who would not let his inquisitive mind rest, appealed to his friend:

"Come, mate, tell me! I keep asking about this cursed Jacket and can't get a straight answer from anyone!"

"It's not a thing to talk about just before nightfall; however, to satisfy you and these good friends here who want, I see, to know about these strange doings as much as you do—I'll tell you. So listen!"

Here Tsibulya scratched his shoulders, mopped his face with the skirt of his coat, leaned both arms on the table, and began:

"Once upon a time a devil was kicked out of hell, what for, God only knows."

"But how?" Cherevik interrupted. "How could it come about that a devil was turned out of hell?"

"I don't know, mate, but turned out he was—just as a man turns a dog out of his house. Perhaps it came over him to do a good deed—and so they showed him the door. And the poor devil was so homesick, so homesick for hell that he was ready to hang himself. Well, there was nothing for it. In his trouble he took to

* Ukrainian for "onion".—*Ed.*

drink. He settled in that tumbledown barn you have seen at the foot of the hill, a place no good man will pass now without making the sign of the cross; and this devil became such a rake you would not find another like him among the lads: he sat all day long in the pot-house!"

At this point the severe Cherevik interrupted again:

"What's this you are saying? How could anyone let a devil into a pot-house? God bless us all, he's got claws and horns, hasn't he?"

"Ah, that was just it—he had a cap and gloves on. Who could recognize him? Well, he kept it up till he drank away all he had with him. They gave him credit for a long time, but at last they would give no more. The devil had to pawn his red jacket for less than a third of its value to the Jew who sold vodka in those days at Sorochintsi fair. He pawned it and said to him: 'Mind now, Jew, I shall come to you for my jacket in a year's time; take care of it!' And he disappeared and no more was seen of him. The Jew examined the coat thoroughly: the cloth was better than anything you could get even in Mirgorod, and the red of it glowed like fire, so that you couldn't take your eyes off it. And it seemed to the Jew a long time to wait till the end of the year. So he scratched his head and at last made up his mind to sell the jacket. He got nearly fifty rubles for it from a gentleman who was passing by.

"The Jew forgot all about the date fixed. But one evening a man turns up. 'Come, Jew, hand me over my jacket!' At first the Jew did not recognize him, but when he had had a good look at him he pretended he had never seen him before. 'What jacket? I have no jacket. I know nothing about your jacket!' The other walked away. Towards nightfall the Jew locked himself up in his room, counted the money in his chests, flung a sheet round his shoulders, and began saying his prayers in Jewish fashion. All at once he heard a rustle and looked up—there were pigs' snouts poking in at every window!"

At that moment an indistinct sound not unlike the grunt of a pig was heard; everyone went pale. Drops of sweat stood out on Tsibulya's face.

"What was it?" cried Cherevik, frightened.

"Nothing," answered Tsibulya, trembling all over.

"Eh?" responded one of the guests.

"Did you say something?"

"No!"

"Who was it grunted?"

"God knows why we are in such a fluster! There's nobody but us here."

They looked about fearfully and began rummaging in the corners. Khivrya was more dead than alive.

"You are a set of women, that's what you are!" she brought out aloud. "Call yourselves Cossacks! Why, you ought to sit spinning and heckling yarn! Maybe someone—someone's bench creaked, and you are all in a fluster like a bunch of madmen!"

This put our heroes to shame and made them pull themselves together. Tsibulya took a pull at the jug and went on with his story:

"The Jew fainted with terror; but the pigs with legs as long as stilts climbed in at the windows and revived him in a trice with plaited thongs, making him skip higher than these rafters. The Jew fell at their feet and confessed everything. Only the jacket could not be restored in a hurry. The gentleman had been robbed of it on the road by a Gypsy who sold it to a woman, and she brought it back again to the fair at Sorochintsi; but no one would buy anything from her after that. The woman wondered and wondered, and at last she saw what was wrong: there was no doubt the red jacket was at the bottom of it. It was not for nothing that she had felt stifled when she put

it on. Without stopping to think she flung it in the fire—but
the devilish thing wouldn't burn! 'That's a gift from the devil!'
she thought. She managed to thrust it into the waggon of a
peasant who had come to the fair to sell his butter. The silly
fellow was delighted; only, no one would ask for his butter.
'An evil hand must have foisted that red jacket on me!' He
took his axe and chopped it into bits; he looked at it—and
each bit joined up to the next till the jacket was whole again!
Crossing himself, he went at it with the axe again; he threw
the pieces about all over the place and went away. Ever since
then, at the time of the fair, the devil walks all over the market-
place with the face of a pig, grunting and collecting the scraps
of his jacket. Now they say there is only the left sleeve missing.
Folks have fought shy of the place ever since, and it is ten
years since the fair has been held on it. But in an evil hour the
assessor—"

The rest of the sentence froze on the speaker's lips: there
was a loud rattle at the window, the panes fell tinkling on the
floor, and a pig's face, terrible to look upon, stared in at the window, rolling its eyes as though asking, "What are you doing
here, good people?"

VIII

His tail between his legs like a dog,
Like Cain, he trembled all over.
The blood dripped from his nose.
KOTLYAREVSKY, "THE AENEID"

Everyone in the room was numb with horror. Tsibulya
sat petrified with his mouth open; his eyes were almost popping
out of his head like bullets; his outspread fingers stayed motionless in the air. In overwhelming terror the valiant giant leapt

up and struck his head against the rafter; the boards shifted, and with a thud and a crash the priest's son fell to the floor.

"Oh! Oh! Oh!" one of the party screamed desperately, flopping on a bench in alarm, his arms and legs waving.

"Help!" yelled another, hiding his head under a sheepskin.

Tsibulya, roused from his stupefaction by this second horror, crept shuddering under his wife's skirts. The valiant giant climbed into the oven, although the opening was narrow, and closed the oven door on himself. And Cherevik clapped a pot on his head instead of a cap, dashed to the door like a scalded cat, and ran through the streets in a frenzy. Only weariness caused him to slacken his pace. His heart was thumping like an oil-press; streams of perspiration rolled down him. He was on the point of sinking to the ground in exhaustion when suddenly he heard someone running after him. His breath failed him.

"The devil! The devil!" he cried frantically, redoubling his efforts, and a minute later he fell unconscious on the ground.

"The devil! The devil!" came a shout behind him, and all he felt was something falling with a thud on top of him. His senses deserted him and he lay dumb and motionless in the middle of the road, like a corpse stretched out in his narrow coffin.

IX

> *In front, like anyone else;*
> *Behind, upon my soul, like a devil!*
> FROM A FOLK TALE

One of the crowd that had settled down for the night in the open air sat up suddenly.

"Did you hear that, Vlas?" he said. "Someone here spoke about the devil!"

"What is that to me ?" a Gypsy near him grumbled, stretching himself. "They may talk of all the devils in hell for all I care!"

"But he bawled as if he was being strangled!"

"A man will cry out anything in his sleep!"

"Maybe, but we must have a look at least. Strike a light!"

The other Gypsy, grumbling to himself, rose to his feet, sent a shower of sparks flying like lightning flashes, blew on the tinder, and with a *kaganets* in his hands—the usual Ukrainian lamp consisting of a broken crock full of mutton fat— set off, lighting the way before him.

"Stop! There is something lying here! Show a light this way!"

They were joined by several others.

"What is it, Vlas ?"

"Looks like two men—one on top of the other. I can't make out yet which of them is the devil!"

"Why, who is on top ?"

"A woman!"

"Well, there'you are—that's the devil!"

A general burst of laughter roused almost the whole street.

"A woman astride of a man! She knows how to ride, I daresay!" one of the bystanders exclaimed.

"Look, lads!" said another, picking up a broken piece of the pot of which only one half still remained on Cherevik's head. "What a cap this fine fellow put on!"

The growing noise and laughter brought our corpses to life; Cherevik and his spouse, full of the panic they had passed through, stared in terror at the swarthy faces of the Gypsies; in the dim and flickering light they looked like a wild horde of gnomes bathed in the heavy fumes of the underworld, in the darkness of perpetual night.

*Fie upon you, out upon you, image
of Satan!*

FROM A UKRAINIAN COMEDY

The freshness of morning breathed over the awakening
folk of Sorochintsi. Clouds of smoke from all the chimneys
floated to meet the rising sun. The fair began to hum with
life. Sheep were bleating, horses neighing; the cackle of geese
and market women sounded all over the encampment again —
and terrible tales of the Red Jacket, which had roused such
alarm in the mysterious hours of darkness, vanished with the
return of morning.

Stretching and yawning drowsily, Cherevik lay in the thatched
barn of his friend Tsibulya, among oxen and sacks of flour
and wheat. Apparently he had no desire to part with his dreams,
but a voice broke in upon him, a voice as familiar as his own
stove, the blessed refuge of his lazy hours, or as the pot-house
kept by his cousin not ten paces from his own door.

"Get up, get up!" his tender spouse squeaked in his ear,
tugging at his arm with all her might.

Cherevik, instead of answering, blew out his cheeks and
began waving his arms, as though beating a drum.

"Crazy fool!" she shouted, dodging his arms, which almost
struck her in the face.

Cherevik sat up, rubbed his eyes and looked about him.

"The devil take me, my dear, if I didn't fancy your face
was a drum and I was forced to beat a tattoo on it like a Muscovite soldier, by those pig-faces that Tsibulya was telling us about."

"Stop talking nonsense! Hurry up and take the mare to
market! We are just a laughing-stock. We've come to the
fair and not sold a handful of hemp."

"That's true," Cherevik assented, "they will laugh at us now, to be sure."

"Get along, get along! They are laughing at you already!"

"But I haven't washed yet," Cherevik went on, yawning and scratching his back as he tried to gain time.

"What a time to be fussy about being clean! When have you cared about that? Here's a towel, wipe your ugly face."

She snatched up something that lay crumpled up—and threw it down aghast: it was the cuff of the Red Jacket!

"Go along and get to work," she repeated, recovering herself, on seeing that her husband was motionless with terror and his teeth were chattering.

"A fine sale there will be now!" he muttered to himself as he untied the mare and led her to the market-place. "It was not for nothing that, while I was getting ready for this cursed fair, my heart was as heavy as if someone had put a dead cow on my back, and twice the oxen tried to turn homewards. And now I come to think of it, I believe it was Monday when we started. And so everything has gone wrong! And the cursed devil is so restless! You'd think he might wear his jacket with one sleeve missing, but no, he can't leave honest folk alone. Now if I were the devil—God forbid—do you suppose I'd go hunting about at night for a lot of damned rags?"

Here Cherevik's meditations were interrupted by a thick harsh voice. Before him stood a tall Gypsy.

"What have you for sale, good man?"

Cherevik was silent for a moment; he looked at the Gypsy from head to foot and said with unruffled composure, neither stopping nor letting go the bridle:

"You can see for yourself what I am selling."

"Harness?" said the Gypsy, looking at the bridle which the other had in his hand.

"Yes, harness, if a mare is like harness."

"One would think you had fed her on straw, neighbour!"

"Straw?"

Here Cherevik would have pulled at the bridle to lead his mare forward and convict the shameless slanderer of his lie; but his hand moved with extraordinary ease and struck his own chin. He looked—in it was a severed bridle, and tied to the bridle—oh horror! his hair stood up on his head—a piece of a red sleeve! Spitting, crossing himself and brandishing his arms, he ran away from the unexpected gift faster than a man half his age, and vanished in the crowd.

XI

For my own wheat I have been beaten.
PROVERB

"Catch him! catch him!" cried several lads at the narrow end of the street, and Cherevik felt himself suddenly seized by stalwart hands.

"Bind him! That's the fellow who stole an honest man's mare."

"God bless you! What are you binding me for?"

"Fancy his asking! What did you want to steal a mare for from the peasant Cherevik?"

"You're out of your wits, lads! Who has ever heard of a man robbing himself?"

"That's an old trick! An old trick! Why were you running your hardest, as though the devil himself were on your heels?"

"Anyone would run when the devil's garment—"

"Try that on others, my good soul! You'll catch it yet from the assessor, to teach you to go scaring people with tales of the devil."

"Catch him! catch him!" came a shout from the other end of the street. "There he is! That's him!"

And Cherevik beheld his friend Tsibulya in the most pitiful plight, with his hands tied behind him, led along by several lads.

"Queer things are happening here!" said one of them. "You should hear what this swindler says! You have only to look at his face to see he is a thief. When we asked him why he was running like a madman, he says he put his hand in his pocket and instead of his snuff-box pulled out a bit of the devil's jacket and it burst into a red flame—and he took to his heels!"

"Ha! Two birds of a feather! We had better tie them together!"

XII

> *"In what am I to blame, good folks?*
> *Why are you torturing me?" said our*
>   *poor wretch.*
> *"Why are you abusing me?*
> *What for, what for?" he said, bursting*
>   *into tears,*
> *Streams of bitter tears, and clutching*
>   *at his sides.*
>
>   ARTEMOVSKY-GULAK,
>   "MASTER AND DOG"

"Maybe you really have pinched something, mate?" Cherevik asked, as he lay bound beside Tsibulya in a thatched shanty.

"You too, mate! May my arms and legs wither if I ever stole anything in my life, except maybe dumplings with cream from my mother, and that only before I was ten years old."

"Why has this trouble come upon us, mate? It's not so bad for you: you are only charged with stealing from somebody else; but what have I, unlucky wretch, done to deserve such a foul slander as stealing my mare from myself? It seems, mate, it was written at our birth that we should have no luck!"

"Woe to us, forlorn and forsaken!"

At this point the two friends burst out sobbing.

"What's the matter with you, Solopy?" said Gritsko, entering. "Who tied you up like that?"

"Ah, Golopupenko!" cried Cherevik, delighted. "This is the lad I was telling you about, mate. God strike me dead on the spot if he did not toss off a whole jug, almost as big as your head, and never turned a hair!"

"What made you put a slight on such a fine lad, then?"

"It seems," Cherevik went on, addressing Gritsko, "God has punished me for having wronged you. Forgive me, good lad! Upon my soul, I'd be glad to do anything for you. But what would you have me do? There's the devil in my old woman!"

"I am not one to remember evil, Solopy. If you like, I'll set you free!"

Here he winked to the other lads, and the very ones who had been guarding them rushed up to untie them. "But you must do your part, too: a wedding! And let us keep it up so that our legs ache with dancing for a year afterwards!"

"Good, good!" said Cherevik, striking his hands together. "I feel as pleased as though the Muscovites had carried off my old woman. Why give it another thought? Whether it's right or wrong, the wedding shall be today—and that's all about it!"

"Mind now, Solopy: in an hour's time I will be with you. Now go home—there you will find people who want to buy your mare and your wheat."

"What! Has the mare been found?"

"Yes."

Cherevik was struck dumb with joy and stood still, gazing after Gritsko.

"Well, Gritsko, you can't say I've bungled the job!" said the tall Gypsy to the hurrying lad. "The oxen are mine now, aren't they?"

"Yes!"

XIII

Fear not, fear not, darling,
Put on your red boots.
Trample your foes
Under foot
So that your ironshod heels
May clang,
So that your foes
May be hushed and still.

A WEDDING SONG

Paraska mused sitting alone in the cottage with her pretty chin propped on her hand. Many dreams hovered about her fair head. At times a faint smile touched her crimson lips and some joyful feeling lifted her dark brows; then a cloud of pensiveness would set them frowning above her clear brown eyes.

"But what if it does not come true as he said?" she whispered with an expression of doubt. "What if they don't let me marry him? What if— No, no; that cannot be! My stepmother does as she likes; why mayn't I do as I like? I've plenty of obstinacy too. How handsome he is! How wonderfully his black eyes glow! How delightfully he says, 'Paraska, darling!' How his white jacket suits him! His belt ought to be a bit brighter, though! I will weave him one when we settle in a new cottage. I can't help being pleased when I think," she went on, taking from her bosom a little red-paper-framed looking-glass bought at the fair and gazing into it with secret pleasure, "how I shall meet her one day somewhere—she may burst before I bow to her! Yes, stepmother, you've beaten your stepdaughter enough. Not until the rock grows flowers and the oak bends down to the water like a willow shall I bow before you. But I was forgetting—I want to try on a married woman's cap, even if it has to be my stepmother's, and see how it suits me."

She got up, holding the looking-glass in her hand and bending her head down to it, walked gingerly about the room, as though in dread of falling, seeing below her, instead of the floor, the ceiling with the boards laid on the rafters, from which the priest's son had so lately dropped, and the shelves set with pots.

"Why, I am like a child," she cried laughing, "afraid to take a step!"

And she began tapping with her feet—growing bolder as she went on; at last she laid her left hand on her hip and went off into a dance, clinking with her metalled heels, holding the looking-glass before her and singing her favourite song:

> *Little green periwinkle,*
> *Twine lower to me!*
> *And you, black-browed dear one,*
> *Come nearer to me!*
> *Little green periwinkle,*
> *Twine still lower to me!*
> *And you, black-browed dear one,*
> *Come nearer still to me!*

At that moment Cherevik peeped in at the door, and seeing his daughter dancing before the looking-glass, he stood still. For a long time he looked on, laughing at this unusual prank of his daughter, who was apparently so absorbed that she noticed nothing; but when he heard the familiar strains of the song, his blood tingled; he stepped forward, his arms jauntily akimbo, and forgetting all he had to do, set to dancing. A loud shout of laughter from his friend Tsibulya startled both of them.

"Here is a pretty thing! The dad and his daughter getting up a wedding on their own account! Make haste and come along: the bridegroom has arrived!"

At the last words, Paraska flushed a deeper crimson than the ribbon which bound her head, and her light-hearted parent remembered his errand.

"Well, daughter, let us hurry up! Khivrya is so pleased that I have sold the mare," he went on, looking timidly about him, "that she has run off to buy herself skirts and all sorts of rags, so we must get it all over before she is back."

Paraska had no sooner stepped over the threshold than she felt herself caught in the arms of the lad in the white jacket, who with a crowd of people was waiting for her outside.

"God bless you!" said Cherevik, joining their hands. "May your lives together cleave as the flowers in the wreaths."

At this point a hubbub was heard in the crowd.

"I'd burst before I'd allow it!" screamed Cherevik's helpmate, who was being shoved back by the laughing crowd.

"Don't get excited, woman!" Cherevik said coolly, seeing that two sturdy Gypsies had caught hold of her hands. "What is done can't be undone; I don't like going back on my word!"

"No, no, that shall never be!" screamed Khivrya, but no one heeded her; several couples surrounded the happy pair and formed an impenetrable dancing wall around them.

A strange, ineffable feeling would have overcome anyone who saw the whole crowd transformed into a scene of unity and harmony at one stroke of the bow of the fiddler, who had long twisted moustaches and wore a homespun jacket. Men whose sullen faces seemed never to have known the gleam of a smile were tapping with their feet and wriggling their shoulders; everyone was whirling and dancing. But an even stranger and more unaccountable feeling would have been stirred in the heart at the sight of old women, whose ancient faces breathed the indifference of the tomb, pushing their way between the young, laughing, living human beings. Nothing but drink, like a mechanic operating a lifeless automaton, made them perform actions that seemed human; caring for nothing, without the joy of youth, without a spark of sympathy, they slowly wagged their drunken heads, dancing after the rejoicing crowd, without so much as glancing at the young couple.

The sounds of laughter and song and uproar grew fainter and fainter. The strains of the fiddle were lost in vague and feeble notes, and died away in the void. In the distance there was still the sound of tapping feet—something like the far-away murmur of the sea—and soon all was silence and emptiness.

Is it not thus that joy, lovely and inconstant guest, flies from us? In vain the last solitary note tries to express gaiety. In its own echo it hears melancholy and emptiness, and listens to it, bewildered. Is it not thus that those who have been sportive friends in free and stormy youth are lost one by one in the wide world, and leave their old comrade lonely and forlorn? Sad is the lot of one left behind! Heavy and sorrowful is his heart, and nothing can help him.

SAINT JOHN'S EVE*

A True Story Told by a Sacristan

It was a peculiarity of Foma Grigoryevich's that he had a mortal aversion for repeating a story. Sometimes one persuaded him to tell a story over again, but then he would throw in something fresh, or would change it so that you hardly knew it for the same. It chanced that one of these people— it is hard for us, simple folk, to know what to call them, for scriveners they are not, but they are more like the dealers at our fairs: they beg, they grab, they filch all sorts of things

* St. John's Day—an old summer holiday. According to popular belief, on St. John's Eve the bracken blooms and he who picks a blossom can find buried treasure.—*Ed.*

49

and then they bring out a little book, no thicker than a child's reader, every month or every week—well, one of these gentry fished this very story out of Foma Grigoryevich, and he quite forgot all about it. And then that young gentleman in the pea-green coat of whom I have told you already and whose story, I believe, you have read, arrived from Poltava, brought with him a little book and, opening it in the middle, showed it to us. Foma Grigoryevich was about to put his spectacles astride his nose, but recollecting that he had forgotten to mend them with thread and wax, he handed the book to me. As I know how to read and do not wear spectacles, I set to reading it aloud. I had hardly turned over two pages when Foma Grigoryevich suddenly grasped my arm.

"Wait a minute; tell me first what you are reading."

I must own I was a little taken aback by the question.

"What do you mean, Foma Grigoryevich? I'm reading your story—your own words."

"Who told you it was my story?"

"What better proof do you want—it is printed here, 'Told by the sacristan of so-and-so.'"

"Hang the fellow who printed that! He's lying, the cur! Is that how I told it? What is one to do when a man has a screw loose in his head? Listen, I'll tell it to you now."

We moved up to the table and he began.

My grandfather (may he rest in peace! May he have nothing but loaves made of fine wheat and poppy-cakes with honey to eat in the other world!) was a great hand at telling stories. Once he started to talk you could sit listening all day without stirring. He was not like the gabblers nowadays who make you feel like picking up your cap and walking out as soon as they begin spinning their yarns in a way which sounds as though they had had nothing to eat for three days. I remember well—the old lady, my mother, was living then—how on a long winter evening, when frost sealed up the narrow window of our cottage, she would sit with her distaff, pulling out a long thread, rocking the cradle with her foot and singing a song which seems to ring in my ears even now. Spluttering and trembling as though it were afraid of something, the lamp lighted up the cottage. The distaff hummed while we children clustered together listening to Grandad, who was so old that he had hardly climbed down from the stove for five years past. But his marvellous accounts of the old days, of the raids of the Zaporozhye Cossacks, of the Poles, of the gallant deeds of Podkova, of Poltora-Kozhukha and Sagaidachny did not interest us so much as stories of uncanny things that had happened long ago; they always made our hair stand on end and our flesh creep. Sometimes we were so terrified by them that when darkness fell everything seemed queer and scary. Sometimes you would step out of the cottage for something at night and fancy that some visitor from the other world had got into your bed. And may I never live to tell this tale again if I did not often take my jacket rolled up by way of pillow for the devil huddling there. But the chief thing about my Grandad's stories was that he never in his life told a lie and everything he told us had really happened.

One of his wonderful stories I am going to tell you now. I know there are lots of smart fellows who scribble in law-courts and even read modern print, though if you put in their hands a simple prayer-book they could not make out a letter of it, and yet they are clever enough at grinning and mocking! They laugh at anything you tell them. Such unbelief is spreading all over the world! Why—may God and the Holy Virgin look ill upon me!—you will hardly believe me: I dropped a word about witches one day, and there was a daredevil who didn't believe in witches! Here I have lived all these long years, thank God, and have met unbelievers who would tell a lie at confession as easily as I'd take a pinch of snuff, but even they made the sign of the cross to keep off witches. But if they dreamed of— I'd rather not say what, where would they be!

Many years ago—over a hundred, my late Grandad told us—no one would have known our village: it was a hamlet, the poorest of hamlets! A dozen of huts or so, without plaster or proper roofs, stood here and there in the fields. No fences, no real barns where cattle or carts could be kept. And it was only the rich lived as well as that—you should have seen the likes of us poor folk: we used to dig a hole in the ground, and that was our hut! You could only tell from the smoke that God's children were living there. You will ask why they lived like that. It was not that they were poor—in those days almost everyone was a Cossack and brought home plenty of good things from other lands—but rather because it was no use having a good hut. All sorts of people were roaming about the country then: Crimeans, Poles, Lithuanians. And sometimes even fellow-countrymen came in gangs and stripped us. All sorts of things used to happen.

In that hamlet there often appeared a man, or rather a devil in human form. Nobody knew why he came or where he came from. He drank and made merry and then vanished as though into thin air, and they heard no news of him. Then all at once he seemed to drop from the sky and prowled about the streets of the village which was hardly more than a hundred paces from Dikanka, though there is no trace of it now. He would pick up with any stray Cossacks, and then there was laughter and singing, the money would fly and vodka would flow like water. Sometimes he'd set upon the girls, heap ribbons, earrings, necklaces on them, till they did not know what to do with them. To be sure, the girls thought twice before they took his presents, because who knew if those things did not come from the devil. My own grandfather's aunt, who used to keep a tavern on what is now Oposhnya Road where Basavryuk—that was the name of this devil of a fellow—often went on the spree, said she wouldn't take a present from him for all the riches in the world. And yet how could they refuse? Everybody was terrified when he scowled with his shaggy eyebrows and gave a look from under them that might make the stoutest take to his heels; and if a girl did accept, the very next night a crony of his from the bog, with horns on his head, was sure to pay her a visit, and would try to strangle her if she wore a necklace, or bite her finger if she had a ring, or pull her hair if she had a ribbon in it. A plague take them then, his fine presents! And the trouble was, there was no getting rid of them: if you threw them into the water, the devilish necklace or ring would float on the top and come back straight into your hands.

In the village there was a church—Saint Pantelei's, if I remember right. The priest there in those days was Father Afanasy of blessed memory. Seeing that Basavryuk did not come to church even on Easter Sunday, he tried to reprimand him and threaten him with a church penance. But no such thing! He had a close shave. "Look here, my good sir," Basavryuk bellowed in reply to him, "you mind your own business and don't meddle with other people's, unless you want your billy-goat's gullet stopped with hot frumenty!" What was to be done with the cursed fellow? Father Afanasy just declared that he would reckon anyone who associated with Basavryuk a Catholic, an enemy of the Church of Christ and of the human race.

In the same village a Cossack called Korzh had a workman who was known as Petro the Kinless—perhaps because no one remembered his parents. The churchwarden used to say that they had died of the plague when he was a year old, but my grandfather's aunt would not hear of it and did her best to provide him with relations, though poor Petro did not care a straw about them. She used to say that his father was still in Zaporozhye, that he had been taken prisoner by the Turks and suffered goodness knows what tortures, and that in some marvellous way he had escaped, disguised as a eunuch. The black-browed girls and young women cared nothing about his relations. All they said was that if he put on a new tunic, a black astrakhan cap with a smart blue top to it, girded himself with a red belt, hung a Turkish sword at his side and carried a whip in one hand and a handsome pipe in the other, he would outshine all the lads of the place. But poor Petro had only one grey jacket with more holes in it than there are gold pieces in a Jew's pocket. Only, that was not what mattered; what did matter was that old Korzh had a daughter, a beauty such as I fancy you have never seen. My grandfather's aunt used to say—and women, you know, would rather kiss the devil, saving your presence, than call any girl a beauty— that the girl's plump cheeks were as fresh and bright as a poppy of the most delicate shade of pink when it glows, washed by God's dew, unfolds its leaves and preens itself in the rising sun; that her eyebrows, like black strings such as our girls buy nowadays from travelling Muscovite pedlars to hang crosses or coins on, were evenly arched and seemed to gaze into her clear eyes; that her little mouth, at which the young men stared greedily, looked as though it had been created to utter the notes of a nightingale; that her hair, black as a raven's wings and soft as young flax, fell in rich curls on her gold-embroidered jacket (in those days our girls did not do their hair in plaits and twine them with bright-coloured ribbons). Ah, may God never grant me to sing "Alleluia" again in the choir, if I could not kiss her on the spot now, in spite of the grey which is spreading all over the old stubble on my head, and of my old woman, always at hand when she is not wanted. Well, if a lad and a girl live near each other you all know what is bound to happen. Before the sun had risen, the footprints of the little red boots could be seen on the spot where Pidorka had been talking to her Petro. But Korzh would never have imagined that anything was wrong if—clearly it was the devil's doing—one day Petro had not been so foolish as to stamp a hearty kiss on the Cossack girl's rosy lips in the ante-room without taking a good look round; and the same devil—may he dream of the Holy Cross, the son of a cur!—prompted the old chap to open the door. Korzh stood flabbergasted, clutching at the door, with his mouth wide open. The accursed kiss seemed to daze him completely. It seemed to him louder than the thud against the wall of the pestle with which in our day the peasants make a bang to frighten off evil spirits for lack of musket and gunpowder.

Recovering himself, he took his grandfather's riding-whip from the wall and was about to lay it on poor Petro's back, when all of a sudden Pidorka's six-year-old brother Ivas ran in and threw his arms round the old man's legs in terror, shouting, "Don't beat Petro, Father!"

There was no help for it: the father's heart was not made of stone; hanging the whip on the wall, he quietly led Petro out of the cottage. "If you ever show yourself again in my cottage, or even under the windows, you can be sure you will lose your black moustaches; and your scalp-lock, too, though it is long enough to go twice round your ear, will take leave of your head, or my name is not Terenty Korzh!"

Saying this he dealt him a light blow on the back of the neck, and Petro flew headlong, seeing nothing. That was what his kisses brought him.

Our cooing doves were overwhelmed with sadness. Then there was a rumour in the village that a new visitor was continually seen at Korzh's—a Pole, all in gold lace, with moustaches, a sabre, spurs, and pockets jingling like the bell on the bag that our sexton Taras carries about the church with him every day. Well, we all know why people visit the father of a black-browed girl. So one day Pidorka, bathed in tears, took her little brother Ivas in her arms. "Ivas my darling, run fast as an arrow from the bow, my golden little one, to Petro, tell him everything: I would love his brown eyes, I would kiss his fair face, but my fate says nay. More than one towel have I soaked with my bitter tears. I am sick and sad at heart. My own father is my enemy: he is forcing me to marry the detested Pole. Tell him that they are making ready the wedding, only there will be no music at our wedding—priests will chant instead of the pipe and the lute. I will not walk out to dance with my bridegroom: they will carry me. Dark will be my dwelling, of maple wood, and instead of a chimney a cross will stand over it!"

Standing stock-still, as though turned to stone, Petro heard Pidorka's words lisped by the innocent child.

"And I, poor luckless lad, was thinking of going to the Crimea or Turkey to win gold in war and then come back to you, my beauty. But it is not to be! An evil eye has looked upon us. I, too, will have a wedding, my darling; but there will be no clergy at that wedding—a black raven will croak over me instead of a priest; the open plain will be my dwelling, the grey storm-clouds will be my roof; an eagle will peck out my brown eyes; the rains will wash my Cossack bones and the whirlwind will dry them. But what am I saying? To whom, of whom am

I complaining? It is God's will, it seems. If I must perish, then perish I will!" And he walked straight away to the tavern.

My grandfather's aunt was rather surprised when she saw Petro at the tavern and at an hour when a good Christian is at matins, and she stared at him open-eyed when he asked for a jug of vodka, almost half a pailful. But in vain the poor fellow tried to drown his sorrow. The vodka stung his tongue like a nettle and seemed to him bitterer than wormwood. He flung the jug upon the ground.

"Give over grieving, Cossack!" something boomed out above him.

He turned—it was Basavryuk! Ugh, what a sight he was! Hair like bristles, eyes like a bullock's.

"I know what it is you lack: it's this!" And then with a fiendish laugh he jingled the leather pouch he carried at his belt.

Petro started.

"Ha! Look how it glitters!" roared the other, pouring the gold pieces into his cupped hand. "How it rings! And you know, only one thing is asked for a whole pile of such baubles."

"The devil!" cried Petro. "Speak up—I will do anything!" They shook hands on it.

"Mind, Petro, you are just in time: tomorrow is St. John the Baptist's Day. This is the only night in the year in which the bracken blossoms. Don't miss your chance! I will wait for you at midnight in the Bear's Ravine."

I don't think the chickens are as eager for the minute when the goodwife brings their grain as Petro was for evening to come. He kept on looking to see whether the shadow from the tree was getting longer, whether the setting sun was flushing red, and as the hours went on he grew more impatient. Oh, how slowly they went! It seemed as though God's day had lost its end somewhere. At last the sun was gone. There was only a streak of red on one side of the sky. And that, too, was fading. It turned colder in the fields. The light grew dimmer and dimmer till it was quite dark. At last! With his heart almost leaping out of his breast, he set off on his way and carefully went down through the thick forest to a deep hollow which was known as the Bear's Ravine. Basavryuk was there already. It was so dark that you could not see your hand before your face. Hand in hand, they made their way over a muddy bog, caught at by the thorns that grew over it and stumbling almost at every step. At last they reached a level place. Petro stopped to look round— he had never chanced to come there before. Basavryuk stopped too.

"You see those three hillocks before you? There will be all sorts of flowers on them, but may the powers from yonder keep you from picking one of them. But as soon as the bracken blossoms, pick it and do not look round, whatever you fancy is behind you."

Petro wanted to ask him a question, but lo! he was gone. He went up to the three hillocks. Where were the flowers? He saw nothing. Rank weeds showed black everywhere and smothered all else with their dense growth. But there came a flash of summer lightning in the sky, and he saw before him a whole bed of flowers, all marvellous, all new to him; and there, too, were the simple plumes of bracken. Petro was puzzled and he stood in perplexity—with his arms akimbo.

"What's unusual about this? One sees the stuff a dozen times a day—there is nothing wonderful in it. Perhaps the devil meant to make fun of me?"

All at once he saw a little flower turning and moving as though it were alive. It really was marvellous! It moved and grew bigger and bigger and turned red like a burning coal. A little star suddenly shone out, something snapped, and the flower opened before his eyes, shedding light on the others about it like a flame.

"Now is the time!" thought Petro, and stretched out his hand. Suddenly he saw hundreds of shaggy hands stretch from behind him towards the flower, and something flitted to and fro behind his back. Shutting his eyes, he pulled at the stalk and the flower was left in his hand. A hush fell. Basavryuk, looking blue like a corpse, appeared sitting on a stump. He did not stir a finger. His eyes were fastened on something which only he could see; his mouth was half open, and no sound came from it. Nothing stirred all round. It was terrible! But at last there was a whistle which turned Petro cold all over, and it seemed to him as though the grass were murmuring, and the flowers were talking among themselves in voices as delicate as silver bells; the trees resounded with angry gusts. Basavryuk's face suddenly came to life, his eyes flashed. "At last you are back, old hag!" he growled through his teeth. "Look, Petro, a beauty is going to appear before you; do whatever she tells you, or you will be lost for ever!"

Then with a gnarled stick he parted a thorn-bush and a little hut—a witch's hut, as they say in fairy-tales—stood before them. Basavryuk struck it with his fist and the wall tottered. A big black dog ran out to meet them, and changing into a cat, with a squeal flew at their eyes.

"Don't be angry, don't be angry, old witch!" said Basavryuk, spicing his words with an oath which would make a good man stop his ears. Where the cat had stood there now was an old woman, wrinkled like a baked apple and bent double, her nose and chin meeting like nutcrackers.

"A fine beauty!" thought Petro, and a shudder ran down his back.

The witch snatched the flower out of his hands and spent

a long time muttering over it and sprinkling it with water of some sort. Sparks flew out of her mouth, there were flecks of foam on her lips. "Throw it!" she said, giving him back the flower. Petro threw it and, marvellous to relate, the flower did not fall at once, but stayed for a long time like a ball of fire in the darkness, and floated in the air like a boat; at last it began to descend slowly, and fell so far away that it looked like a little star no bigger than a poppy-seed. "Here!" the old woman wheezed in a hollow voice, and Basavryuk, giving him a spade, added: "Dig here, Petro; here you will see more gold than you or Korzh ever dreamed of."

Petro, spitting on his hands, grabbed the spade, thrust at it with his foot and threw out the earth... a second spadeful... a third... a fourth... The spade clanked against something hard and would go no further. Then his eyes could clearly distinguish a small iron-bound chest. He tried to get hold of it, but the chest sank deeper and deeper into the earth; and behind him he heard laughter more like the hissing of snakes.

"No, you will never see the gold till you have shed human blood!" said the witch, and brought him a child about six years old covered with a white sheet, signing to him to cut off its head. Petro was dumbfounded. A mere trifle! for no reason to murder a human being, and an innocent child, too! Angrily he pulled the sheet off the child, and what did he see? Before him stood Ivas. The poor child crossed his arms and hung his head. Like one mad, Petro flew at the witch, knife in hand, and lifted his hand to strike.

"And what did you promise for the sake of the girl?" thundered Basavryuk, and his words tore through Petro like a bullet. The witch stamped her foot; a blue flame shot out of the earth and lighted its very bowels, so that they looked as though they were made of crystal; and everything under the surface could be seen clearly. Gold pieces and precious stones in chests and in cauldrons were piled up in heaps under the very spot on which they were standing. His eyes glowed, his brain reeled. Frantic, he seized the knife and the innocent blood spurted into his eyes. Devilish laughter broke out all round him. Hideous monsters jumped in herds before him. Clutching the headless corpse in her hands, the witch drank the blood like a wolf. Petro's head was in a whirl. With a desperate effort he set off running. Everything about him was flooded with a red light. The trees, bathed in blood, seemed to be burning and moaning. The red-hot sky quivered. Gleams of fire like lightning flashed before his eyes. At his last gasp he ran into his hut and slumped down on the ground. He sank into a deathlike sleep.

For two days and two nights he slept without waking. Coming to on the third day, he stared for a long time into the corners of the hut. But he tried in vain to remember what had happened; his memory was like an old miser's pocket out of which you cannot entice a copper. Stretching a little, he heard something clink at his feet. Two sacks of gold were lying there. Only then he remembered as though in a dream that he had been looking for a treasure, that he had been alone and frightened in the forest. But at what price, how he had obtained it—that he could not recall.

Korzh saw the sacks and was softened. Petro was this and Petro was that, and he could not say enough for him. "And wasn't I always fond of him, and wasn't he like my own son to me?" And the old fox carried on so incredibly that Petro was moved to tears. Pidorka began telling him how Ivas had been stolen by some passing Gypsies, but Petro could not even remember the boy's face: that cursed devilry had so confounded him!

There was no reason for delay. They sent the Pole away with

a flea in his ear and began preparing the wedding. They baked wedding-cakes, they hemmed towels and kerchiefs, rolled out a barrel of vodka, set the young people down at the table, cut the wedding-loaf, played the lute, the pipe, the *bandura*, and the cymbals—and the merry-making began.

You can't compare weddings nowadays with what they used to be. My grandfather's aunt used to tell about them—it was a treat! How the girls, in a smart head-dress of yellow, blue, and pink ribbons, with gold braid tied over it, in fine smocks embroidered with red silk on every seam and adorned with little silver flowers, in morocco boots with high heels shod with iron, danced round the room as gracefully as peacocks, swishing like a whirlwind. How the young wives, in a boat-shaped head-dress, the whole top of which was made of gold brocade with a little slit at the back showing a peep of the gold cap below, with two little horns of the very finest black astrakhan, one in front and one behind, in blue coats of the very best silk with red lappets, holding their arms with dignity akimbo, stepped out one by one and rhythmically danced the *hopak*. How the lads, in tall Cossack caps, in fine-cloth jackets girt with silver embroidered belts, with a pipe in their teeth, danced attendance on them and cut all sorts of capers. Korzh himself, looking at the young people, could not help recalling his youth: with a *bandura* in his hands, smoking his pipe and singing, at the same time balancing a goblet on his head, the old man fell to dancing. The things people think of when they are making merry! They would begin, for instance, putting on masks—my goodness, they looked like monsters! Ah, it was a very different thing from dressing up at weddings nowadays. What do they do now? Only rig themselves out like Gypsy women or Muscovites. But in old days one would be a Jew and another a devil; first they would kiss each other and then pull each other's scalp-locks.

Upon my soul! one laughed till one held one's sides. They would put on Turkish and Tatar dresses, all glittering like fire. And as soon as they began fooling and playing tricks, there were no bounds to what they would do! An amusing incident happened to my grandfather's aunt, who was at that wedding herself. Wearing a loose Tatar dress, she was treating the company with a goblet in her hand. The devil prompted someone to splash vodka over her from behind; another one, it seems, was just as clever: at the same moment he struck a light and set fire to her. The flame flared up: poor aunt, terrified, began flinging off all her clothes before everybody. The din, the laughter, the hubbub that arose—it was like a fair! In fact, the old people never remembered a merrier wedding.

Pidorka and Petro began to live like lady and gentleman. They had plenty of everything, it was all spick and span. But good people shook their heads a little as they watched the way they went on. "No good comes from the devil," all said as one man. "Whom did his wealth come from if not from the tempter of good Christians? Where could he have got such a pile of gold? Why did Basavryuk vanish on the very day that Petro grew rich?"

You may say that people invent things! But really, before a month was out, no one would have known Petro. What had happened to him, God only knows. He would sit without stirring and not say a word to anyone; he was always brooding and seemed trying to remember something. When Pidorka succeeded in making him talk, he would seem to forget and keep up a conversation and even be merry, but if by chance his eye fell on the bags, "Wait, wait, I have forgotten!" he would say, and again he would sink into thought and again try to remember something. Sometimes, after he had been sitting still for a long time, it seemed that in another moment he would recall it all...

and then it would pass away again. He fancied he had been sitting in a tavern; they brought him vodka; the vodka burnt him; the vodka was nasty; someone came up, slapped him on the shoulder—but after that everything seemed shrouded in a fog. The sweat rolled down his face and he sat down again, exhausted.

What did not Pidorka do! She sought the advice of quacks, poured wax into water and burnt a bit of hemp*—nothing helped. So the summer passed. Many of the Cossacks had finished their mowing and harvesting; many of the more reckless ones had gone off fighting. Flocks of ducks were still plentiful on our marches, but there was not a wren to be seen. The steppes turned red. Stacks of corn, like Cossacks' caps, were dotted about the field here and there. Waggons laden with faggots and logs were to be met on the roads. The ground became firmer and in places it was touched with frost. Snow began falling and the twigs on the trees were decked in hoarfrost like hare fur. On a frosty day the red-breasted bullfinch, looking for seeds in the heaps of snow, strutted about like a smart Polish squire, and the children were whipping wooden tops on the ice with huge sticks while their fathers lay quietly on the stove-couch, coming out from time to time with a lighted pipe between their teeth to swear roundly at the good Orthodox frost, or to get a breath of air and thresh the corn stored in the outer room.

* When anyone has had a fright and they want to know what has caused it, melted tin or wax is poured into water and it will take the shape of whatever has caused the patient's terror; and after that the terror passes off. Hemp is burnt for sickness or stomach complaint. A piece of hemp is lighted, thrown into a mug which is turned wrong side upwards over a bowl of water stood on the patient's stomach. Then, after repeating a spell, a spoonful of the water is given to the patient to drink.—*Author's note.*

At last the snow began to melt and the pike smashed the ice with its tail, as they say, but Petro was the same, and as time went on he became gloomier still. He would sit in the middle of the hut, as though riveted to the spot, with the sacks of gold at his feet. He shunned company, let his hair grow, began to look dreadful, and thought only about one thing: he kept trying to remember something and was vexed and angry because he could not. Often he would get up from his seat wildly, wave his arms, fix his eyes on something as though he wanted to catch it; his lips would move as though trying to utter some long-forgotten word—and then would remain motionless. He was overcome by fury; he would gnaw and bite his hands as though he were mad, and tear out his hair in handfuls in his vexation, until he would grow quiet again and seem to sink into forgetfulness; and then he would begin to remember again, and again there would be fury and torment. It was a heaven-sent affliction.

Pidorka's life was not worth living. At first she was afraid to remain alone in the hut, but afterwards she grew used to her misfortune, poor thing. But no one would have known her for the Pidorka of earlier days: no colour in her cheeks, no smile on her lips; she was pining and wasting away, she was crying her bright eyes out. Once someone took pity on her and advised her to go to the witch in the Bear's Ravine, who was reputed to cure all the diseases in the world. She made up her mind to try this last resource; little by little, she persuaded the old woman to come home with her. It was after sunset, on St. John's Eve. Petro was lying on the bench lost in forgetfulness and did not notice the visitor come in. But little by little he began to sit up and look at her. All at once he trembled, as though he were on the scaffold; his hair stood on end, and he broke into a laugh that cut Pidorka to the heart with terror.

"I remember, I remember!" he cried with a fearful joy, and snatching up an axe, flung it with all his might at the old woman. The axe made a cut two inches deep in the oak door. The old woman vanished and a child about seven, in a white shirt, with its head covered, was standing in the middle of the hut. The veil flew off. "Ivas!" cried Pidorka and rushed up to him, but the phantom was covered from head to foot with blood and shed a red light all over the hut. She ran into the outer room in terror, but, coming to herself, wanted to help her brother; in vain! the door had slammed behind her so that she could not open it. The neighbours came running up; they began knocking and broke open the door: not a living soul inside! The whole hut was full of smoke, and only in the middle, where Petro had stood, was a heap of ashes from which smoke was still rising. They rushed to the sacks: they were full of broken potsherds instead of gold pieces. This miracle threw them into such a panic that the Cossacks stood as though rooted to the spot, with their mouths open and their eyes starting out of their heads, not daring to move an eyelash.

I don't remember what happened afterwards. Pidorka took a vow to go on a pilgrimage. She gathered together all the property left her by her father, and a few days later she vanished from the village. No one could say where she had gone. Some old gossips were so obliging as to declare that she had followed Petro; but a Cossack who came from Kiev said he had seen in the convent there a nun wasted to a skeleton, who never stopped praying, and in her by every token the villagers recognized Pidorka; he told them that no one had ever heard her say a word; that she had come on foot and brought a setting for the icon of the Mother of God with such bright jewels in it that it dazzled everyone who looked at it.

But let me tell you, this was not the end of it all. The very day that the devil carried off Petro, Basavryuk turned up again; but everyone ran away from him. They knew now the kind of bird he was: no one but Satan himself disguised in human form to unearth buried treasure; and since unclean hands cannot touch treasure he entices reckless young men to help him. The same year everyone deserted their old huts and moved into a big village near by, but even there they had no peace from that cursed Basavryuk. My grandfather's aunt used to say that he was particularly angry with her for having given up her old tavern on Oposhnya Road, and did his utmost to pay her out. One day the elders of the village were gathered at her tavern and were conversing according to their rank, as the saying is, at the table, in the middle of which was a whole roast ram, and it would be a lie to call it a small one. They chatted of one thing and another; of marvels and strange happenings. And all at once they fancied— and of course it would be nothing if it were one of them, but they all saw it at once—that the ram raised its head, its sly black eyes gleamed and came to life; it suddenly sprouted a black bristly moustache and significantly twitched it at the company. They all recognized at once in the ram's head the face of Basavryuk; my grandfather's aunt even thought that in another minute he would ask for vodka. The worthy elders picked up their caps and hurried home. Another day, the churchwarden himself, who liked at times a quiet half-hour with the family goblet, had not drained it twice when he saw the goblet bow to him. "The devil take you!" he cried and set to crossing himself. And at the same time a strange thing happened to his better half: she had only just mixed the dough in a huge tub when suddenly the tub jumped away. "Stop, stop!" Not a bit of it! its arms akimbo, the tub went solemnly dancing about all over the hut. You may laugh; but it was no laughing matter to our forefathers. And though Father Afanasy went all over the village with holy water,

driving the devil out of every street with the sprinkler, my grandfather's aunt complained for a long time that as soon as evening
came someone knocked on the roof and scratched on the wall.

But there! In this place where our village is standing you would
think everything was quiet nowadays; but you know, not so
long ago, within my father's memory—and indeed I remember
it myself—no good man could pass the ruined tavern, which the
unclean race repaired long afterwards at their own expense.
Smoke came out in clouds from the grimy chimney and, rising
so high that one's cap dropped off if one looked at it, scattered
hot embers all over the steppe, and the devil—no need to mention
him, the son of a cur!—used to sob so plaintively in his hole
that the frightened rooks rose up in flocks from the forest near by
and scattered with wild cries over the sky.

A MAY NIGHT OR THE DROWNED MAIDEN

> *The devil only knows what to
> make of it! If Christian folk begin
> any task, they fret and fret them-
> selves like dogs after a hare, and all
> to no purpose; but as soon as the
> devil steps in, it only takes a twitch
> of his tail to get the thing done.*

I

HANNA

A ringing song flowed like a river down the streets of the
village. It was the hour when, weary from the cares and labours
of the day, the lads and girls gather together in the glow of the

clear evening to pour out their gaiety in strains never far removed from melancholy. The brooding evening dreamily embraced the dark blue sky, transforming everything into vagueness and distance. It was already dusk, but the singing did not cease. Levko, a young Cossack, the son of the village Head, slipped away from the singers with a *bandura* in his hands. He was wearing an astrakhan cap. He walked down the street thrumming on the strings and dancing to it. At last he stopped quietly before the door of a cottage surrounded with low-growing cherry-trees. Whose cottage was it? Whose door was it? After a few moments of silence, he began playing and singing:

> *The sun is low, the evening's nigh,*
> *Come out to me, my little heart!*

"No, it seems my bright-eyed beauty is sound asleep," said the Cossack when he had finished the song, and he went nearer to the window. "Hanna! Hanna, are you asleep, or don't you want to come out to me? You are afraid, I suppose, that someone may see us, or perhaps you don't want to put your fair little face out into the cold? Don't be afraid, there is no one about, and the evening is warm. And should anyone appear, I will cover you with my jacket, wrap my sash round you, and shelter you in my arms—and no one will see us. And if there is a breath of cold, I'll press you closer to my heart, I'll warm you with my kisses, I'll put my cap over your little white feet. My heart, my little darling, my pearl! Look out for a minute. Put your little white hand at least out of the window. No, you are not asleep, proud maiden!" he said more loudly, in the voice of one ashamed at having for a moment demeaned himself. "You are pleased to mock at me; farewell!"

He turned away, cocked his cap, and walked haughtily off,

softly thrumming the strings of the *bandura.* At that moment
the wooden handle turned; the door opened with a creak, and a
girl in her seventeenth spring looked about her timidly, shrouded
in the dusk, and, without leaving hold of the handle, stepped over
the threshold. Her bright eyes shone with welcome like stars in
the half-light; her red coral necklace gleamed, and even the
modest blush that suffused her cheeks could not escape the lad's
eagle eye.

"How impatient you are!" she said to him in a low voice.
"You are angry already! Why did you choose this time ? Crowds
of people are walking up and down the street. I am trembling—"

"Oh, don't tremble, my lovely willow! Cling closer to me!"
said the lad, putting his arms round her, and casting aside his
bandura, which hung on a long strap round his neck, he sat down
with her at the door of the cottage. "You know how it hurts me
to pass an hour without seeing you."

"You know what I am thinking ?" the girl broke in, pensively
gazing at him. "Something seems to keep whispering in my ear
that henceforth we shall not meet so often. People here are not
good: the girls all look so jealously, and the lads— I even notice
that of late my mother has taken to watching me more strictly.
I must own I liked it better when I lived away from
home."

A look of sadness passed over her face at the last words.

"Only two months at home and already you are weary of it!
Perhaps you are tired of me, too ?"

"Oh, I am not tired of you," she replied, smiling. "I love you,
my black-browed Cossack! I love you because you have brown
eyes, and when you look at me it seems as though there were
laughter in my heart, and it is gay and happy; because you
twitch your black moustache so delightfully; because you walk

along the streets singing and playing the *bandura*, and it's sweet to listen to you."

"Oh, my Hanna!" cried the lad, kissing her and pressing her to his heart.

"Wait! Enough, Levko! Tell me first, have you told your father?"

"Told him what?" he said, as though waking up from sleep. "That I want to marry and that you will be my wife? Yes, I have told him." But the words "I have told him" sounded sad upon his lips.

"Well?"

"What can I do with him? He pretended to be deaf, the old rogue, as he always does; he wouldn't hear anything, and then began scolding me for strolling God knows where and playing pranks in the streets with the lads. But don't grieve, my Hanna! I give you the word of a Cossack that I will get round him."

"Well, you have only to say the word, Levko, and you will have everything your own way. I know that from myself; sometimes I wouldn't obey you, but you have only to say a word—and I can't help doing what you want. Look, look!" she went on, laying her head on his shoulder and turning her eyes upward to the warm Ukrainian sky, which showed dark blue through the leafy branches of the cherry-trees that stood in front of them. "Look, over there, far away, the stars are twinkling—one, two, three, four, five. It's the angels of God opening the windows of their bright dwellings in the sky and looking out at us, isn't it, Levko? They are looking at our earth, aren't they? If only people had wings like birds, they could fly there, high up. Oh, it's dreadful! Not one oak here reaches to the sky. But they say there is some tree in a distant land the top of which reaches right to heaven and God comes down by it to the earth on the night before Easter."

"No, Hanna, God has a ladder reaching from heaven right down to earth. The holy archangels put it down before Easter Sunday, and as soon as God steps on the first rung, all the evil spirits fall headlong and sink in heaps down to hell. And that is why at Christ's festival there isn't one evil spirit on earth."

"How softly the water murmurs, like a child lying in its cradle!" Hanna went on, pointing to the pond in its gloomy setting of maple-trees and weeping willows, whose drooping boughs dipped into it. Like a feeble old man, it held the dark, distant sky in its cold embrace, covering with its icy kisses the flashing stars, which gleamed in the warm ocean of the night air as though they felt the approach of the brilliant queen of the night. An old wooden house lay slumbering with closed shutters on the hill by the copse; its roof was covered with moss and weeds; apple-trees spread their boughs before the windows; the copse, wrapping the house in its shade, threw an uncanny shadow over it; a thicket of hazel bushes lay at its foot and sloped down to the pond.

"I remember as though it were a dream," said Hanna, not taking her eyes off the house, "long, long ago when I was little and lived with Mother, they used to tell some dreadful story about that house. Levko, you must know it, tell it to me."

"Never mind about it, my beauty! Old women and silly folk tell all sorts of stories. You will only upset yourself, you'll be frightened and won't sleep well."

"Tell me, tell me, my dear black-browed boy!" she said, pressing her face against his cheek and putting her arm round him. "No, I see you don't love me; you have some other girl. I won't be frightened; I will sleep sound at night. Now I shan't

sleep if you don't tell me. I shall be worried and thinking.
Tell me, Levko!"

"It seems folk are right when they say that there is a devil
of curiosity in girls, egging them on. Well, listen then. Long
ago, my little heart, a Cossack officer used to live in that house.
He had a daughter, a fair maiden, white as snow, white as
your little face. His wife had long been dead; he took it into
his head to marry again. 'Will you care for me the same, Father,
when you take another wife?' 'Yes, I shall, my daughter;
I shall press you to my heart more warmly than ever! I shall,
my daughter. I shall give you ear-rings and necklaces brighter
than ever!'

"The father brought his young wife to her new home. The
new wife was fair of face. All ruddy and white was the young
wife; only she gave her stepdaughter such a dreadful look that
the girl uttered a shriek when she saw her, and the harsh stepmother did not say a word to her all day. Night came on. The
father went with his young wife to his sleeping-chamber, and
the fair maiden shut herself up in her little room. She felt sad
at heart and began to weep. She looked up and saw a dreadful
black cat stealing up to her; her fur sparkled and her steely
claws scratched the floor. In terror the maiden jumped on a
bench, the cat followed her; she jumped on the stove-couch,
the cat jumped after her, and suddenly leapt at her neck and
began stifling her. Tearing herself away with a shriek, she
flung the cat on the floor. Again the dreadful cat stole up.
She was overcome with terror. Her father's sword was hanging
on the wall; she snatched it up and brought it down with a
crash on the floor: one paw with its steely claws flew off, and
with a squeal the cat disappeared into a dark corner. For two
days the young wife did not come out of her room; on the
third day she came out with her arm bandaged. The poor

maiden guessed that her stepmother was a witch and that she had cut her arm. On the fourth day the father bade his daughter fetch the water, sweep the house like a humble peasant girl, and not show herself in her father's apartments. It was a hard lot for the poor girl, but there was no help for it; she obeyed her father's will. On the fifth day the father turned his daughter, barefoot, out of the house and did not give her a bit of bread to take with her. Only then did the maiden fall to sobbing, hiding her white face in her hands. 'You have sent your own daughter to perish, Father! The witch has ruined your sinful soul! God forgive you; and it seems it is not His will that I should live in this fair world.' And over there—do you see?" Levko turned to Hanna, pointing towards the house. "Look this way, yonder, on the very highest part of the bank! From that bank the maiden threw herself into the water. And from that hour she was seen no more."

"And the witch?" Hanna asked in a frightened voice, fastening her tearful eyes on him.

"The witch? The old women make out that ever since then all the maidens who have drowned themselves in the pond have come out on moonlight nights into that garden to warm themselves, and the officer's daughter is leader among them. One night she saw her stepmother beside the pond; she pounced upon her, and with a shriek dragged her into the water. But the witch saved herself even then: she changed under water into one of the drowned maidens, and so escaped the scourge of green reeds with which they meant to beat her. Trust these women! They say, too, that the officer's daughter assembles all the drowned maidens every night and looks into the face of each, trying to find out the witch, but so far has not found her. And if she comes across any living man, she makes him guess which it is; or else she threatens to drown him in the water. That's how old people tell the story, Hanna dear. The present master wants to set up a distillery there and has sent a distiller here to see to it. But I hear voices. It's our fellows coming back from singing. Good night, Hanna! Sleep well and don't think about these old women's tales."

Saying this, he embraced her warmly, kissed her, and walked away.

"Good night, Levko," said Hanna, gazing dreamily at the dark copse.

At that moment a huge fiery moon began majestically rising from the earth. Half of it was still below the horizon, yet all the world was already flooded with its solemn light. The pond sparkled and glittered. The shadow of the trees stood out clearly against the dark grass.

"Good night, Hanna!" The words uttered behind her were accompanied by a kiss.

"You have come back!" she said, looking round, but seeing a lad she did not know, she turned away.

"Good night, Hanna!" she heard again, and again she felt a kiss on her cheek.

"The Evil One has brought another!" she said angrily.

"Good night, Hanna darling!"

"That's the third one!"

"Good night, good night, good night, Hanna." And kisses were showered upon her from all sides.

"Why, there is a regular band of them!" cried Hanna, tearing herself away from the crowd of lads, who vied with each other in trying to embrace her. "I wonder they are not sick of this ever-lasting kissing! Soon I won't be able to show myself in the street!"

The door slammed upon these words and nothing more was heard but the iron bolt screeching in its socket.

II

THE HEAD

Do you know the Ukrainian night? Oh, you do not know
the Ukrainian night! Look at it. The moon gazes down from
the middle of the sky; the immense dome of heaven stretches
farther, more immense than ever; it glows and breathes. The
earth is all bathed in silvery light, and the exquisite air is
refreshing and warm and full of voluptuousness, and stirs
an ocean of fragrance. Divine night! Enchanting night! The
woods stand motionless, mysterious, full of gloom, and cast
huge shadows. Calm and still lie the ponds; the cold and gloom
of their waters are walled in by the dark green gardens. The
virginal thickets of wild cherry timidly stretch their roots
into the cold of the water, and from time to time their leaves
murmur, as though angry and indignant when that sweet
rogue—the night wind—steals up suddenly and kisses them.
All the countryside is sleeping. But overhead all is breathing;
all is marvellous, triumphal. And the soul is full of the immensity and the marvel; and silvery visions rise up in harmonious
multitudes from its depths. Divine night! Enchanting night!
And suddenly it all comes alive: the woods, the ponds, the
steppes. The glorious clamour of the Ukrainian nightingale
bursts upon the night and one fancies the moon itself is listening
in mid-heaven. The village on the upland slumbers as though
spellbound. The groups of cottages gleam whiter, fairer than
ever in the moonlight; their low walls stand out more dazzlingly
in the darkness. The singing has ceased. All is still. God-fearing
people are asleep. Only here and there is a light in the narrow
windows. Here and there before the doorway of a cottage
a belated family is still at supper.

"But that's not the way to dance the *hopak*. I knew it was wrong. What was that my crony was saying? Oh, yes: hop, tra-la! hop, tra-la! hop, hop, hop!" So a tipsy middle-aged peasant, who was dancing down the street, talked to himself. "I swear that's not the way to dance the *hopak*. Why should I tell a lie? I swear it's not right. Come: hop, tra-la! hop, tra-la! hop, hop, hop!"

"Look at that drunken fool!" cried an elderly woman who passed by, carrying an armful of straw. "And it isn't a lad, either—it's an old pig dancing in the street at night, as if to make the children laugh! Go home! You ought to have been in bed long ago!"

"I am going," said the man, stopping. "I am going. I don't care about any Head. He thinks—may his father see the Old One—that because he is the Head, because he pours cold water over folks in the frost, he can turn up his nose at everyone. Head indeed! I am my own Head. God strike me dead if I'm not! I am my own Head. That's how it is and nohow else," he went on, and going up to the first cottage he reached and standing before the window, he passed his fingers over the pane and tried to find the door handle. "Wife, open! Look alive, I tell you, open! It's time this Cossack was in bed!"

"Where are you going, Kalenik? It's not your cottage," some girls on their way home from the merry singing shouted from behind him, laughing. "Shall we show you your cottage?"

"Show me the way, kind maidens!"

"Kind maidens! Did you hear," said one of them, "how polite Kalenik is? We must show him the way to his cottage for that—but no, first give us a dance."

"A dance? Ah, you tricky girls!" Kalenik drawled, laughing

and shaking his finger at them, and he lurched forward because his legs were not steady enough to stand still. "And may I kiss you all if I dance? I'll kiss you all, every one of you!" And with staggering steps he ran after them. The girls set up a shriek and huddled together; then, seeing that Kalenik was not very rapid on his feet, they grew bolder and ran over to the other side of the street.

"There is your cottage!" they shouted to him, pointing, as they walked away, to a cottage much larger than the rest, which belonged to the Head of the village. Kalenik obediently turned in that direction, beginning to abuse the Head again.

But who was this Head who aroused such unfavourable opinions and criticisms? Oh, he was an important person in the village. While Kalenik is on his way we shall certainly have time to say something about him. All the villagers took off their caps when they saw him, and the girls, even the youngest, wished him good day. Which of the lads would not have liked to be Head? He was free to help himself to everyone's snuff, and a sturdy peasant would stand respectfully, cap in hand, while the Head fumbled with his fat, coarse fingers in his birch-bark snuff-box. At the village council, although his power was limited to a few votes, he always took the upper hand and almost on his own authority sent whom he pleased to level and repair the road or dig ditches. He was austere, forbidding of aspect, and not fond of wasting words. Long, very long ago when the great Tsarina Catherine, of blessed memory, was going to the Crimea, he had been chosen to act as a guide. For two whole days he had performed this duty, and had even been deemed worthy to sit on the box beside the Tsarina's coachman. It was from that time that he had taken to bowing his head with a dignified and meditative air, to stroking his long, drooping moustaches, and to shooting hawk-like glances from under his brows. And from that time, too, whatever subject was broached, the Head always cleverly turned the conversation to the way in which he had guided the Tsarina, and sat on the box of the Tsarina's carriage. He liked at times to pretend to be deaf, especially when he heard something that he did not want to hear. He could not endure foppishness; he always wore a long jacket of black homespun, always girt with a coloured woollen sash, and no one had ever seen him in any other costume, except on the occasion of the Tsarina's journey to the Crimea, when he wore a dark blue Cossack tunic. But hardly anyone in the village could remember that time; the tunic he still kept locked up in a chest. He was a widower, but he had living in the house with him his sister-in-law, who cooked dinner and supper, scrubbed the benches, whitewashed the cottage, wove him shirts, and looked after the house. They said in the village that she was not his sister-in-law at all, but we have already seen that there were many who bore no goodwill to the Head and were glad to circulate any scandal about him. However, perhaps what gave colour to the story was the fact that the sister-in-law was displeased whenever he went out into a field that was full of girls reaping, or visited a Cossack who had a young daughter. The Head had only one eye, but that eye was a shrewd villain and could see a pretty village girl a long way off. He did not, however, fix it upon a prepossessing face before he had taken a good look round to see whether his sister-in-law was watching him. But we have said almost all that we need about the Head, while tipsy Kalenik was on his way there, still continuing to bestow on the Head the choicest epithets his slow and halting tongue could pitch upon.

III

AN UNEXPECTED RIVAL.

A PLOT

"No, lads, no, I won't! You are up to pranks again! I wonder you are not sick of mischief. Goodness knows, people call us scamps as it is. You had better go to bed!" So said Levko to his rollicking companions who wanted him to join in some fresh pranks. "Farewell, lads! Good night to you!" And with rapid steps he walked away from them down the street.

"Is my bright-eyed Hanna asleep?" he wondered as he approached the cottage with the cherry-trees known to us already. Subdued voices could he heard in the stillness. Levko stopped short. He could see a white shirt through the trees. "What does it mean?" he wondered, and stealing up a little nearer, hid behind a tree. The face of the girl who stood before him gleamed in the moonlight. It was Hanna! But who was the tall man standing with his back towards him? In vain he gazed at him; the shadow covered him from head to foot. Only a little light fell upon him in front, but the slightest step forward would have exposed Levko to the unpleasant risk of being discovered. Quietly leaning against the tree, he resolved to remain where he was. The girl distinctly uttered his name.

"Levko? Levko is a milksop," the tall man said huskily under his breath. "If I ever meet him with you I'll pull out his scalp-lock."

"I should like to know what scoundrel it is, boasting that he will pull out my scalp-lock!" murmured Levko softly, and he craned his neck, trying not to miss one word. But the stranger went on speaking so softly that not a word of what he said could be heard.

"Aren't you ashamed of yourself?" said Hanna, when he had finished speaking. "You are lying; you are deceiving me. You don't love me; I shall never believe that you love me!"

"I know," the tall man went on, "Levko has told you a lot of nonsense and has turned your head." At this point the lad fancied that the voice was not quite unknown to him—it seemed as though he had heard it before. "I'll show Levko what I am made of!" the stranger went on in the same way. "He thinks I don't see all his wanton tricks. He shall find out, the young cur, what my fists are like!"

As he heard that Levko could no longer restrain his rage. Taking three steps towards him, he swung his fist to give him a clout on the ear which might have sent him flying, for all his apparent strength; but at that instant the moonlight fell on his face, and Levko was stupefied to see his father standing before him. An involuntary jerk of the head and a faint whistle were the only expression of his amazement. A rustle was heard: Hanna darted into the cottage, slamming the door after her.

"Good night, Hanna!" one of the lads cried at that moment, stealing up and putting his arm round the Head, and skipped back with horror, meeting his stiff moustache.

"Good night, my beauty!" cried another; but this one was sent flying by a violent push from the Head.

"Good night, good night, Hanna!" called several lads, hanging on his neck.

"Be off, you cursed madcaps!" cried the Head, shaking them off and kicking them. "Hanna indeed! Go and be hanged along with your fathers, you brood of Satan! They come round one like flies after honey! I'll teach you!"

"The Head, it's the Head!" shouted the lads, and scattered in all directions.

"So that's what my father is like!" said Levko, recovering from his amazement and looking after the Head as he walked away swearing. "This is the sort of tricks he's up to! A nice thing! And I have been wondering why he pretended to be deaf each time I began speaking about it. Wait a bit, you old billy-goat, I'll teach you to hang about under young girls' windows! I'll teach you to lure away other men's sweethearts! Hey, lads! Come here, this way!" he shouted, waving his hand to the lads, who had gathered into a group again. "Come here! I tried to send you off to bed, but now I have changed my mind and am ready to make merry with you all night."

"That's the way to talk!" said a stout, broad-shouldered lad who was reckoned the merriest and most mischievous in the village. "It always makes me sick when we can't manage to have a decent bit of fun. I always feel as though I had missed something, as though I had lost my cap or my pipe; not like a Cossack, in fact."

"What do you say to our giving the Head a good stir-up?"

"The Head?"

"Yes. Who does he think he is, after all? He rules us as though he were a Hetman. He is not satisfied with treating us as though we were his serfs, but he must go after our girls, too. I believe there is not a nice-looking girl in the whole village that he has not made up to."

"That's true, that's true!" cried the lads.

"Are we his serfs, lads? Aren't we the same sort as he is? Thank God, we are free Cossacks! Let us show him, lads, that we are free Cossacks!"

"We'll show him!" shouted the lads. "And if we give it to the Head, we won't spare his clerk either!"

"We won't spare the clerk! And I have just made up a splendid song, it's the very thing for the Head. Come along, I will teach you," Levko went on, striking the strings of his *bandura*. "And dress up in anything that comes handy!"

"Go it, brave Cossacks!" said the sturdy scapegrace, striking his feet together and clapping his hands. "How glorious! What fun! When you go in for a frolic you feel as though you were celebrating bygone years. You heart is light and free and your soul might be in paradise. Come on, lads! Come on, let's have some fun!"

The crowd moved noisily down the street, and pious old wo-men, awakened from the sleep by the shouts, pulled up their windows and crossed themselves drowsily, saying: "Well, the lads are making merry now!"

IV

THE LADS MAKE MERRY

Only one cottage at the end of the village was still lighted up. It was the Head's. He had finished his supper long ago, and would no doubt have been asleep by this time, but he had a visitor. The man had been sent to set up a distillery by a landlord, who owned a small plot of land among the holdings of the free Cossacks. The visitor, a short, fat little man with little eyes that were always smiling and seemed to express the pleasure he took in smoking, sat in the place of honour under the icons, continually spitting, and pressing with his thumb the tobacco ash that kept dropping out of his short pipe. Clouds of smoke spread rapidly over him and enveloped him in a dark blue fog. It seemed as though a big chimney of some distillery, weary of staying on its roof, had thought it would like a change, and was sitting decorously in the Head's cottage. Short thick moustaches stuck out below his nose; but they showed so indistinctly in the smoky atmosphere as to seem like a mouse that the distiller, infringing the monopoly of the granary cat, had caught and held in his mouth. The Head, being in his own house, was sitting in his shirt and linen trousers. His eagle eye was closing little by little and growing dim like the setting sun. One of the village constables who made up the Head's staff was smoking a pipe at the end of the table, and out of respect to his host still kept on his tunic.

"Are you thinking of setting up your distillery soon?" the Head asked the distiller, making the sign of the cross over his mouth as he yawned.

"With the Lord's help, perhaps, by the autumn we shall begin distilling. I'll bet that by Intercession our honoured Head will be drawing jigsaw puzzles with his feet on the road."

As he uttered these words, the distiller's eyes disappeared; where they had been were wrinkles stretching to his ears; his whole frame shook with laughter, and for an instant his mirthful lips abandoned the pipe.

"Please God I may," said his host, twisting his face into a semblance of a smile. "Now, thank God, there are a bit more distilleries. But years ago, when I was guiding the Tsarina by Pereyaslav Road, Bezborodko, now dead—"

"Well, old chap, why recall those times! Why, in those days there were only two distilleries between Kremenchug and Romni. But now— Have you heard what the damned Germans are going to do? Instead of burning wood in distilleries like all decent Christians, they are soon going to use some kind of devilish steam, they say." As he said this the distiller looked thoughtfully at the table and at his hands lying on it. "I just cannot imagine how it is done with steam!"

"What fools they are, those Germans, God forgive me!" said the Head. "I'd whip them, the brood of Satan! Did anyone ever hear the like of boiling anything by steam? According to that, you couldn't take a spoonful of soup without boiling your lips like a sucking-pig."

"And you, friend," the sister-in-law, who was sitting on the stove-couch with her feet tucked under her, interposed, "are you going to stay with us all that time without your wife?"

"Why, what do I want with her? It would be different if she were something worth having."

"Isn't she good-looking?" asked the Head, fixing his eye upon him.

"Good-looking, indeed! Old as the devil. Her face all wrinkles like an empty purse." And the stubby frame of the distiller rocked with laughter again.

At that moment something began fumbling at the door; the door opened and a peasant crossed the threshold without taking off his cap, and stood in the middle of the cottage as though in hesitation, gaping and staring at the ceiling. This was our friend Kalenik.

"Here I am home at last," he said, sitting down on the bench near the door, and taking no notice of the company. "How the son of evil, Satan, has lengthened out the road! You go on and on, and there's no end to it! I feel as though someone had broken my legs. Wife, get the sheepskin and put it down for me. I am not joining you on the stove, that I am not, my legs ache! Fetch it, it's lying there under the icons; only mind you don't upset the pot with the snuff. But no—don't touch it, don't touch it! Perhaps you are drunk tonight. Let me get it myself!"

Kalenik tried to get up, but an overwhelming force riveted him to his seat.

"I like that," said the Head. "Walks into another man's house and gives orders as though he were at home! Throw him out neck and crop!"

"Let him take a rest, friend!" said the distiller, holding him back by the arm. "He is a useful man; I wish there were more folk like him, and then our distillery would do finely."

It was not good nature, however, that prompted this remark. The distiller believed in omens of all sorts, and he thought that to turn a man out who had already sat down on the bench would have meant courting misfortune.

"What will become of me when I grow old!" grumbled Kalenik, lying down on the bench. "It would be all right if I were drunk, but I'm not. No, indeed, I am not. Why should I lie about it? I am ready to tell the Head himself so. What do I care for the Head? May he choke, the cur! I spit on him! I wish a waggon would run over him, the one-eyed devil! Why does he drench people in the frost?"

"So the pig has made its way into the cottage, and is now putting its feet on the table!" said the Head, wrathfully rising from his seat; but at that moment a heavy stone, smashing the window to smithereens, fell at his feet. He stopped short. "If I knew," he said, picking up the stone, "if I only knew what gallows-bird did this I'd teach him to throw stones! What tricks!" he went on, looking with his flashing eye at the stone in his hand. "May he choke with this stone!"

"Hold on, friend!" cried the distiller, turning pale. "God preserve you in this world and the next from blessing anyone with such abuse!"

"Here's a champion! Confound him!"

"Throw it out of your head, friend! I suppose you don't know what happened to my late mother-in-law?"

"Your mother-in-law?"

"Yes. One evening—a little earlier perhaps than it is now— they sat down to supper: my mother-in-law and father-in-law and their hired man and their hired girl and their five children. My mother-in-law shook some dumplings out of a big cauldron into a bowl to cool them. They were all hungry after their work and would not wait for the dumplings to get cool. Picking them upon long wooden skewers they began eating them. All at once a man appeared. Where he came from no one could say; who he was, God only knew. He asked them to let him sit down to table. Well, there was no refusing a hungry man food. They gave him a skewer, too. Only the visitor stowed away the dumplings like a cow eating hay. While the others had eaten one each, and were prodding after more with their skewers, the bowl was as clean as a gentleman's floor. My mother-in-law put out some more; she thought the visitor had had enough and would gobble up less. Nothing of the sort: he began gulping them down faster than ever and emptied the second bowl. 'May you choke with the dumplings!' thought my hungry mother-in-law, when all of a sudden the man choked and fell on the floor. They rushed up to him, but he had given up the ghost. He was choked."

"Served him right, the damned glutton!" said the Head.

"Maybe so, but it didn't end with that: from then on my mother-in-law had no rest. As soon as night came, the dead man appeared. He sat astride the chimney, the cursed fellow, holding a dumpling in his teeth. In the day-time all was quiet and they didn't hear a thing about him, but as soon as it began to get dusk, you could see him sitting on the chimney, the son of a cur."

"With a dumpling in his teeth?"

"With a dumpling in his teeth."

"How marvellous, friend! I have heard something of the sort in the day of our late Tsarina—"

The speaker stopped short. Under the window they heard noise and the thump of dancing feet. First there was the soft thrumming of a *bandura*, then a voice chimed in. The strings twanged louder, several voices joined in and the singing rose up like a whirlwind:

A May Night, or the Drowned Maiden

Laddies, have you heard the news now?
Our Head is not sound in his head!
Our one-eyed Head's a barrel-head
Whose staves have come unbound!
Come, cooper, knock upon it hard,
And bind with hoops of steel!
Come, cooper, hammer on the head
And hit with right good will!

Our Head is grey and has one eye;
Old as sin, and what a blockhead!
Full of whims and wanton fancies;
Makes up to the girls, the blockhead!
You must try to ape the young ones!
When you should be in your coffin,
Flung in by the scruff and whiskers!
By the scalp-lock you're so proud of!

"A fine song, friend!" said the distiller, cocking his head a little and turning towards his host, who was struck dumb at such insolence. "A fine one! It's a pity, though, that they refer to the Head in rather disrespectful terms."

And again he put his hands on the table with a sort of gleeful delight in his eyes, preparing to hear more, for from outside came peals of laughter and shouts of "Again! again!" However, a penetrating eye could have seen at once that it was not astonishment that kept the Head rooted to the spot. Sometimes an old experienced tom-cat will in the same way let an inexperienced mouse run round his tail while he is rapidly making a plan to cut off its way back to its hole. The Head's only eye was still fixed on the window, but his hand, after making a sign to the constable, was already on the wooden door-handle, and all at once a shout rose in the street. The distiller, among whose numerous fine qualities curiosity was one, hurriedly filled his pipe and ran out; but the rogues had already scattered.

"No, you won't get away from me!" cried the Head, dragging by the arm a man in a black sheepskin put on inside out. The distiller, seizing the opportunity, ran up to have a look at this disturber of the peace, but he staggered back in fright at seeing a long beard and a horribly painted face. "No, you won't escape me!" shouted the Head, dragging into the house his prisoner, who offered no resistance but followed him quietly, as though going into his own cottage. "Karpo, open the storeroom!" said the Head to the constable. "We'll put him in the dark storeroom. And then we will wake the clerk, get the constables together, catch all these brawlers, and tonight we will pass judgement on them all."

The constable clanked a small padlock and opened the storeroom. At that instant the captive, taking advantage of the darkness, wrenched himself out of his hands with a violent effort.

"Where are you off to?" cried the Head, clutching him more tightly than ever by the collar.

"Let go, it's me!" cried a thin shrill voice.

"That won't help you, my lad. You may squeal like a devil or a woman, you won't take me in." And he shoved him into the dark storeroom, so that the poor prisoner uttered a moan as he fell on the floor. Accompanied by the constable, he went off to the clerk's cottage, and the distiller followed him, puffing like a steamer.

They walked along, all three with their eyes on the ground, lost in meditation, when, at a turning into a dark lane, all of them at once uttered a shriek, from a violent bang on their foreheads, and a similar shriek echoed in response. The Head, screwing up his eye, saw with surprise the clerk and two constables.

"I was coming to see you, worthy clerk!"

"And I was coming to your worship, honoured Head."

"Strange things have been happening, worthy clerk."

"Very strange things, honoured Head!"

"Why, what?"

"The lads have gone crazy. They are going on disgracefully in the street, whole bands of them. They describe your honour in language — I should be ashamed to repeat it. A drunken Muscovite couldn't bring his dirty tongue to utter such words." (All this the lanky clerk, in mottled linen breeches and a waistcoat the colour of wine dregs, accompanied by craning his neck forward and pulling it back again.) "I had just dropped into a doze, when the cursed scamps roused me from my bed with their shameful songs and knocking! I meant to give them a proper dressing down, but while I was putting on my breeches and waistcoat they all ran away. The ringleader did not get away, though. He is singing now in the cottage where we keep prisoners. I was all eagerness to find out what bird it was we'd caught, but his face is all black like the devil's who forges nails for sinners."

"And how is he dressed, worthy clerk?"

"In a black sheepskin put on inside out, honoured Head."

"Aren't you lying, worthy clerk? What if that rascal is sitting now in my storeroom?"

"No, honoured Head. You yourself—no offence meant—are a little in error."

"Give me a light! We will have a look at him."

The light was brought; they unlocked the door, and the Head uttered a cry of amazement when he saw his sister-in-law facing him.

"Tell me, please"—with these words she pounced upon him—"have you lost what little wits you ever had? Was there a grain of sense in your one-eyed pate when you pushed me into the dark storeroom? It was lucky I did not hit my head against the iron hook. Didn't I scream out to you that it was me? You cursed bear, you seized me in your iron paws and shoved me in! May the devils treat you the same in the next world!"

The last words were uttered in the street where she had gone for some purpose of her own.

"Yes, I see that it's you," said the Head, recovering himself. "What do you say, worthy clerk? Isn't that scapegrace a cunning rogue?"

"He is a cunning rogue, honoured Head."

"Isn't it high time we gave all these rascals a good lesson and set them to work?"

"It's high time, honoured Head!"

"They have taken it into their heads, the fools— What the devil is that? I thought I heard my sister-in-law scream in the street— They have taken it into their heads, the fools, that they are as good as I am. They think I am one of them, a simple Cossack! "The little cough that followed this, and the way he looked up from under his brows, indicated that the Head was about to speak of something important. "In the year seventeen— I never can bring out those confounded dates—Ledachy, who was then Commissar, was given orders to pick out from the Cossacks the most intelligent of them all. Oh!"—that "Oh!" he pronounced with his finger in the air—"the most intelligent to act as guide to the Tsarina. At that time I—"

"Yes, honoured Head, we all know that. We all know how you won the royal favour. Own now that I was right: you took a sin upon your soul when you said that you had caught that rogue in the black sheepskin."

"As for that devil in the black sheepskin, we'll put him in chains and punish him severely as an example to others! Let them know what authority means! By whom is the Head appointed if not by the Tsar? Then we'll get hold of the other fellows; I have not forgotten how the confounded scamps drove a herd of pigs into my kitchen garden that ate up all my cabbages and cucumbers; I have not forgotten how the sons of Satan refused to thresh my corn; I have not forgotten—But, damn them all, I must find out who that rascal is, wearing a sheepskin inside out."

"He's a wily bird, it seems!" said the distiller, whose cheeks during the whole of this conversation were continually being charged with smoke like a siege cannon, and his lips, abandoning the short pipe, ejected a veritable fountain of smoke. "It wouldn't be amiss, anyway, to get the fellow to work in the distillery; or, better still, hang him from the top of an oak-tree instead of a censer."

Such a witticism did not seem quite foolish to the distiller, and he at once decided, without waiting for the approval of the others, to reward himself with a husky laugh.

At that moment they drew near a small cottage that almost lay on its side on the earth. Our friends' curiosity grew keener: they all crowded round the door. The clerk took out a key and jingled it about the lock; but it was the key to his chest. The impatience became acute. Thrusting his hand into his pocket he began fumbling for it, and swore because he could not find it.

"Here it is!" he said at last, bending down and fishing it out from the depths of the capacious pocket with which his full mottled trousers were provided.

At that word the hearts of all our heroes seemed melted into one, and that huge heart beat so violently that the sound of its uneven throb was not drowned even by the creaking of the lock. The door was opened, and—The Head turned white as a sheet; the distiller was aware of a cold chill, and the hair of his head seemed rising up heavenwards; horror was depicted on the countenance of the clerk; the constables were rooted to the spot, and were unable to close their mouths, which had fallen open simultaneously; before them stood the Head's sister-in-law!

No less amazed than they, she, however, pulled herself together, and made a movement as though to approach them.

"Stop!" cried the Head wildly, and slammed the door in her face. "Gentlemen, it is Satan!" he went on. "A light! quick, a light! I won't spare the cottage, though it is Crown property. Set fire to it, set fire to it, that even the devil's bones may not be left on earth!"

The sister-in-law screamed in terror, hearing through the door this sinister decision.

"What are you about, friends?" cried the distiller. "Your hair, thank God, is almost white, but you have not gained sense yet: a witch won't burn with ordinary fire! Only a light from a pipe can burn a changeling of the devil's! Wait a bit, I will manage it in a minute!"

Saying this, he shook some hot ash out of his pipe on to a wisp of straw and began blowing on it. The poor sister-in-law was meanwhile overwhelmed with despair; she began loudly imploring and beseeching them.

"Wait, friends! Why take a sin upon us in vain? Perhaps it is not Satan!" said the clerk. "If it—whatever it may be that is sitting there—consents to make the sign of the cross, that's a sure token that it is not a devil."

The proposal was approved.

"Get thee behind me, Satan!" said the clerk, putting his lips to the keyhole. "If you don't stir from your place we will open the door."

The door was opened.

"Cross yourself!" said the Head, looking behind him as though seeking a safe place in case of retreat.

The sister-in-law crossed herself.

"Damn it! It really is my sister-in-law."

"What evil spirit dragged you to this hole, sister?"

The sister-in-law, sobbing, told them that the lads had seized her in the street and, in spite of her resistance, had bundled her in at the wide window of the cottage and had nailed up the shutter. The clerk glanced: the staples of the broad shutter had been pulled out, and it was only fixed on by a board at the top.

"You are a fine one, you one-eyed devil!" she screamed, stepping up to the Head, who staggered back, still scanning her with his only eye. "I know your design—you wanted, you would have been glad to burn me up, so as to be more free to go after the girls, to have no one to see the grey-headed old grandad having fun. You think I don't know what you were saying to Hanna this evening? Oh, I know all about it. It's hard to hoodwink me, let alone for a numskull like you. I am patient, but see that you aren't sorry when I lose my patience!"

Saying this, she shook her fist at him and walked away quickly, leaving him flabbergasted.

"Well, Satan certainly has a hand in this business," he thought, scratching his head vigorously.

"We've got him!" cried the constables, coming in at that instant.

"Got whom?" asked the Head.

"The devil with his sheepskin inside out."

"Give him here!" shouted the Head, seizing the prisoner by the arm. "You are mad! This is the drunken Kalenik."

"What a queer thing! We had the devil in our hands, honoured Head!" answered the constables. "The confounded lads came round us in the lane, began dancing and capering, tugging

at us, sticking out their tongues and snatching him out of
our hands. Damnation take it! And how we hit on this crow
instead of him God only knows!"

"By my authority and in the name of the whole communi-
ty," said the Head, "the command is given to catch that ruffian
this minute, and in the same way all whom you may find in
the street, and to bring them to me to be dealt with!"

"Mercy upon us, honoured Head," cried some of them,
bowing down to his feet. "You should have seen their ugly
faces; strike us dead, we have been born and christened, but
we've never seen such horrid faces. Mischief may come of it,
honoured Head. They may give a simple man such a fright
that no old woman would undertake to cure him of it."

"Fright, indeed! What are you up to? Refusing to obey,
are you? I expect you are hand in glove with them? Are you
mutinying? What's this? What's the meaning of it? You
are getting up a rebellion! You— I'll report you to the Commissar! This minute, do you hear, this minute! Run, run like
the wind! See that I— See that you—"

They all ran off helter-skelter.

V

THE DROWNED MAIDEN

The instigator of all this turmoil, undisturbed by the hue
and cry and untroubled by the search-parties sent in all directions, walked slowly towards the old house and the pond.
There is hardly any need to say that it was Levko. His black
sheepskin was unbuttoned; he held his cap in his hand; the
sweat streamed down his face. The maple wood stood majestic

and gloomily black, barely sprinkled with moonlight. The motionless pond sent a breath of refreshing coolness at the tired wanderer and lured him to rest for a while on the bank. All was still. The only sound was the trilling of the nightingale in the deepest recesses of the wood. An overpowering drowsiness soon closed his eyes; his tired limbs were getting numb; his head drooped. "No, if I go on like this I shall fall asleep here!" he said, getting up and rubbing his eyes.

He looked round and the night seemed even more glorious. A strange, enchanting radiance was mingled with the light of the moon. He had never seen anything like it before. A silvery mist had settled on everything around him. The fragrance of the apple blossom and the night-scented flowers flooded the whole earth. He gazed with amazement at the unruffled water of the pond: the old manor-house, upside down in the water, was distinct and looked serenely dignified. Instead of gloomy shutters there were bright glass windows and doors. There was a glitter of gilt through the clean panes. And then it seemed as though a window opened. Holding his breath, not stirring, nor taking his eyes from the pond, he seemed to pass into its depths and saw—first a white elbow appeared in the window, then a charming little head with bright eyes, shining softly through the dark brown locks, peeped out and rested on the elbow, and he saw the maiden slightly nod her head. She beckoned, she smiled. His heart began throbbing. The water quivered and the window was closed again. He moved slowly away from the pond and looked at the house: the gloomy shutters were open; the window-panes gleamed in the moonlight. "See how little one can trust what people say," he thought to himself; "it's a new house; the paint is as fresh as though it had been put on today. Someone is living there." And in silence he went up closer to it, but all was still in the house. The glorious singing of the nightingales rang out, loud and melodious, and when it seemed to die away in languor and voluptuousness, there was heard the rustle and churr of the grasshoppers, or the deep note of some marsh bird, striking its slippery beak on the broad mirror of the water. There was a sense of sweet stillness and space and freedom in Levko's heart. Tuning his *bandura*, he began playing it and singing:

> *Oh, thou moon, my darling moon!*
> *And thou, my clear-eyed star!*
> *Oh, shine brightly o'er the cottage*
> *Where my lovely maiden lives!*

The window slowly opened and the girl whose reflection he had seen in the pond looked out, listening intently to the singing. Her long eyelashes half-hid her eyes. She was white all over, like a sheet, like the moonlight; but how exquisite, how lovely! She laughed. Levko started.

"Sing me a song, young Cossack!" she said softly, bending her head on one side and veiling her eyes with her thick eyelashes.

"What song shall I sing you, my fair maiden?"

Tears rolled slowly down her pale face.

"Youth," she said, and there was something ineffably touching in her speech. "Youth, find me my stepmother! I will grudge you nothing. I will reward you. I will reward you richly, handsomely. I have sleeves embroidered with silk, corals, necklaces. I will give you a girdle adorned with pearls. I have gold. Youth, find me my stepmother! She is a terrible witch, I had no peace in life because of her. She tormented me, she made me work like a simple peasant girl. Look at my face: by her foul spells she drew the roses from my cheeks. Look at my white neck: they will not wash off, they will not wash off, they never will be washed away, those dark blue marks left by her claws of steel! Look at my white feet, far have they trodden—only not on carpets—but on the hot sand, on the damp earth, on sharp thorns have they trodden! And at my eyes, look at my eyes: they have grown dim with weeping! Find her, youth, find me my stepmother!"

Her voice, which had risen, sank into silence. Tears streamed down her pale face. The young man's heart was oppressed by a painful feeling of grief and compassion.

"I am ready to do anything for you, my fair maiden!" he said with heartfelt emotion, "but how can I, where can I find her ?"

"Look, look!" she said quickly, "she is here, she is on the bank, playing games among my maidens, and warming herself in the moonlight. But she is sly and cunning, she has taken the form of a drowned maiden; but I know, I feel that she is here. I am oppressed, I am stifled by her. I cannot swim lightly and easily like a fish because of her. I drown and sink to the bottom like a key. Find her, youth!"

Levko looked towards the bank: in the delicate silvery mist there were maidens flitting about, light as shadows, in smocks white as a meadow adorned with lilies of the valley; gold necklaces, strings of beads, coins glittered on their necks; but they were pale; their bodies looked as though moulded out of transparent clouds, and it seemed as though the silvery moonlight shone through them. Singing and dancing, the maidens drew nearer to him. He heard their voices.

"Let us play Raven and Chickens," they murmured, like river reeds kissed by the ethereal lips of the wind at the quiet hour of twilight.

"Who will be Raven ?"

They cast lots, and one of the girls stepped out of the group.

Levko scrutinized her. Her face and her dress were exactly like those of the rest. He noticed, however, that she did not like to play her part. The group drew out into a chain and raced away from the rapacious enemy.

"No, I don't want to be Raven," said the maiden, weary and exhausted. "I am sorry to snatch the chickens from their poor mother."

"You are not the witch!" thought Levko.

"Who will be Raven?" The maidens made ready to cast lots again.

"I will be Raven!" one in the middle of the group offered herself.

Levko looked intently at her face. Boldly and swiftly she pursued the chain, and darted from side to side to capture her victim. Suddenly he noticed that her body was not so translucent as the others': something black could be seen inside. Suddenly there was a shriek; the raven had pounced on one of the chain, seized her, and Levko fancied that she put out her claws, and that there was a spiteful gleam in her face.

"The witch!" he said, suddenly pointing his finger at her and turning towards the house.

The maiden at the window laughed, and the girls, shouting, led away the one who had played Raven.

"How am I to reward you, youth? I know you have no need of gold: you love Hanna, but your harsh father will not let you marry her. Now he will not be in your way: here, take this note to him."

Her white hand stretched out, her face filled with a marvellous light and radiance. With his heart beating anxiously, overwhelmed with agitation, he clutched the note, and... woke up.

VI

THE AWAKENING

"Can I have been asleep?" Levko wondered, getting up from the little hillock. "It was all so lifelike, as though it were real. How strange!" he said, looking about him.

The moon standing right over his head showed that it was midnight; it was still everywhere, and a chill air rose from the pond; sadly the old house stood above him with its shutters closed. The moss and tall weeds showed that it had been abandoned long ago. Then he unclenched his fist, which had been tightly closed while he had been asleep, and cried out with astonishment, feeling a note in it. "Oh, if I could only read!" he thought, turning it over and looking at it this way and that. At that moment he heard a noise behind him.

"Don't be afraid, seize him straight away! Why are you afraid? There are a dozen of us. I bet you anything it is a man and not a devil!" So the village Head shouted to his companions and Levko felt himself gripped by several hands, some of which were shaking with fear. "Throw off your dreadful apparel, friend! Leave off making fools of people," said the Head, seizing him by the collar; but he was astounded when he turned his eye upon him. "Levko! son!" he cried, stepping back in amazement and dropping his hands. "It's you, son of a cur! Oh, you devil's brood! I was wondering who could be the rogue, what devil turned inside out was playing those tricks. So it's all your doing—may half-cooked jelly stick in your father's throat! You are pleased to get up rows in the street and compose songs! Ah, ah, Levko! What's the meaning of it? It seems your back is itching for the rod! Bind him!"

"Wait a bit, Father! I was told to give you this note," said Levko.

"This is not the time for notes, my lad. Bind him!"

"Wait, honoured Head," said the clerk, opening the note, "it is in the Commissar's hand."

"The Commissar's?"

"The Commissar's?" the constables repeated mechanically.

"The Commissar's? Strange! It is queerer than ever!" Levko thought to himself.

"Read it, read it!" said the Head. "What does the Commissar write?"

"Let us hear what the Commissar writes," said the distiller, holding his pipe in his teeth and striking a light.

The clerk cleared his throat and began reading:

"Instruction to the Head, Yevtukh Makogonenko. Word has reached us that you, old fool, instead of collecting past arrears and setting the village in order, have gone silly and been behaving disgracefully—"

"Upon my soul," the Head broke in, "I can't hear a word!"

The clerk began over again:

"Instruction to the Head, Yevtukh Makogonenko. Word has reached us that you, old foo—"

"Stop, stop! Don't read that," cried the Head. "Though I didn't hear it, I know that the important thing isn't that. Read what comes later!"

"And therefore I command you to marry your son Levko Makogonenko to Hanna Petrichenko, a Cossack maiden of your village, and also to mend the bridges on the high road, and not to give the villagers' horses to the law-court gentry without my authorization, even if they have come straight from the government office. If on my coming I find these my commands not carried out, I shall hold you alone responsible. Commissar, retired Lieutenant Kozma Derkach-Drishpanovsky."

"Well, upon my word!" said the Head, gaping with wonder." Did you hear that? The Head will be held responsible for it all, and so you must obey me unconditionally, or you will catch it! As for you," he went on, turning to Levko, "since it's the Commissar's orders, though I can't understand how it came to his ears, I'll marry you; only first you shall have a taste of my whip! You know the new one that hangs on the wall near the icons. I'll use it to-morrow. Where did you get that note?"

In spite of his astonishment at this unexpected turn of events, Levko had the wit to get ready an answer in his mind and to conceal the truth about the way he had received the note.

"I was in the town last night," he said, "and met the Commissar getting out of his chaise. Learning that I came from this village, he gave me the note and told me to give you the message, Father, that on his way back he will come and dine with us."

"He told you that?"

"Yes."

"Did you hear?" said the Head with an air of dignity, turning to his companions. "The Commissar is coming in person to the likes of us, that is, to me, to dinner. Oh!" He held up his finger and lifted his head as though he were listening for something. "The Commissar—do you hear, the Commissar!—is coming to dine with me. What do you think, worthy clerk, and you, friend? That's an honour not to be sniffed at, isn't it?"

"As far as I can remember," chimed in the clerk, "no village Head has ever yet entertained the Commissar at dinner."

"There are Heads and Heads," said the Head with a smug

air. His mouth twisted, and something in the nature of a husky laugh, more like the rumbling of distant thunder, came from his lips. "Don't you think, worthy clerk, we ought for this distinguished visitor to give orders that every cottage should contribute at least a chicken, some linen and, well, something else, eh?"

"Yes, we ought to, honoured Head."

"And when is the wedding to be, Father?" asked Levko.

"Wedding? I would have shown you a wedding! Oh, well, for the sake of our distinguished visitor—tomorrow the priest shall marry you. Confound you! Let the Commissar see what punctual discharge of duty means. Well, lads, now it is bedtime! Go home! What has happened today reminds me of the time when I—" At these words the Head glanced from under his brows with his habitual air of importance and dignity.

"Now the Head's going to tell us how he guided the Tsarina," said Levko, and with rapid steps he made his way joyfully towards the familiar cottage surrounded by low-growing cherry-trees. "God give you the kingdom of Heaven, kind and lovely maiden!" he thought to himself. "May you in the other world be smiling for ever among the holy angels. I shall tell no one of the marvel that has happened this night; to you only, Hanna, I will tell it. Only you will believe me, and together we will pray for the peace of the soul of the luckless drowned maiden!"

He drew near the cottage; the window was open, the moonlight shone through it upon Hanna as she lay asleep with her head upon her arm, a soft glow on her cheeks; her lips moved, faintly murmuring his name. "Sleep, my beauty, dream of all that is best in the world, though that will not be better than our awakening."

Making the sign of the cross over her, he closed the window and walked gently away.

And in a few minutes all the village was asleep; only the moon floated, radiant and marvellous, in the infinite expanse of the glorious Ukrainian sky. There was the same triumphal splendour on high, and the night, the divine night glowed with the same solemn grandeur. The earth was as lovely in the marvellous silvery light, but no one was admiring it; all were sunk in sleep. Only from time to time the silence was broken by the bark of dogs, and for a long while the drunken Kalenik was still staggering along the slumbering streets, looking for his cottage.

THE LOST LETTER

A True Story Told by a Sacristan

So you want me to tell you another story about Grandad?
I don't mind—why not amuse you with a tale? Ah, the old
days, the old days! What joy, what gladness it brings to the heart
when one hears of what was done in the world so long ago that
the year and the month are forgotten! And when some kinsman
of one's own is mixed up in it—a grandfather or great-grandfather—then may I be taken with a cough at the Anthem to the
Holy Martyr Varvara if I don't fancy that I'm doing it all myself, as though I had crept into my great-grandfather's soul, or

my great-grandfather's soul were playing tricks in me. I must say that our girls and young women are the worst for plaguing me; the moment they catch a glimpse of me it's "Foma Grigoryevich! Foma Grigoryevich! Come now, some terrible tale! Come now, let's have it!" And they keep on and on. I don't grudge telling them a story, of course, but you should see what happens to them when they are in bed. Why, I know every one of them is trembling under the quilt as though she were in a fever and would be glad to creep under her sheepskin, head and all. If a rat scratches against a pot, or she herself touches the poker with her foot—it's almost enough to scare her out of her wits. But next day she'll pester me over again to tell her a terrible story, as though nothing had happened. Well, what am I to tell you? Nothing comes into my mind at the minute— Oh, yes, I'll tell you how the witches played "Fools" with my grandfather. But I must beg you first, good friends, not to interrupt me or I will make a hash of it not fit to take into one's mouth.

My grandad, I must tell you, was a leading Cossack in his day. He could read and write, and knew how to use the mark of abbreviation. On a saint's day, he would boom out the Acts of the Apostles in a voice that would make any priest's son of today feel small. Well, you know without my telling you that in those days if you collected all who could read and write from the whole of Baturin you'd not need your cap to hold them in—there wouldn't be more than a handful altogether. So it's no wonder that everyone who met my grandad made him a bow, and a low one, too.

One day our noble Hetman took it into his head to send a letter to the Tsarina. The clerk of the regiment in those days—I can't remember his name, it was Viskryak or Motuzochka or Goloputsek, or something like that; all I remember is that it was a queer name that began in an odd way—he sent for my Grandad and told him that the Hetman himself had named him as messenger to the Tsarina. My grandad never liked to waste time getting ready: he sewed the letter up in his cap, led out his horse, kissed his wife and his two sucking-pigs, as he used to call his sons, of whom one was my own father. And he made the dust fly that day as though fifteen lads had been playing a rowdy game in the middle of the street. The cock had not crowed for the fourth time next morning before Grandad had reached Konotop. There was a fair there at that time; there were such crowds in the streets that it made one giddy to watch them. But as it was early the people were all stretched out on the ground, asleep. Beside a cow lay a rakish lad with a nose as red as a bullfinch; a little further a woman-pedlar with flints, packets of blue, small shot, and rolls was snoring where she sat; a Gypsy lay under a cart, a waggoner from the Crimea on a waggon of fish; a bearded Muscovite, with belts and mittens on him, sprawled with his legs stuck out in the middle of the road. In short, there was a rabble of all sorts, as there always is at fairs. My grandad stopped to have a good look round. Meanwhile there began a stir in the booths: the Jewesses made a clatter with their flasks; smoke rolled up in rings here and there, and the smell of hot doughnuts floated all over the encampment. It came into my grandad's mind that he had no tinder or tobacco with him; so he began sauntering about the fair. He had not gone twenty paces when he met a Cossack from Zaporozhye. A gay spark, and you could see it at once from his face! Breeches red as fire, a full-skirted blue coat and bright-flowered girdle, a sabre at his side and a pipe with a fine brass chain right down to his heels—a regular Zaporozhian Cossack if there ever was one! Ah, they were great dancers! One would stand up, stretch himself, stroke his gallant moustaches, clink with his iron heels—and off he would go! And how he would go! His legs would spin round like a distaff

in a woman's hands; his fingers would pluck at all the strings
of the *bandura* like a whirlwind, and then, arms akimbo, he would
set off dancing or burst into a song that thrilled your heart!
Yes, the good old days are over; you don't see such Zaporozhians nowadays!

Well, they met. One word leads to another, and it doesn't
take long to make friends. They fell to chatting and chatting,
so that Grandad quite forgot about his journey. They had a
drinking bout, as at a wedding before Lent. Only at last I suppose
they got tired of smashing pots and flinging money to the crowd,
and, indeed, a fair can't go on for ever! So the new friends agreed
not to part but to travel on together. It was getting on for evening when they rode out into the open country. The sun had
set; here and there streaks of red glowed in the sky where it had
been; the country was gay with different-coloured fields like
the checked petticoats our black-browed young women wear
on holidays.

Our Zaporozhian talked away like mad. Grandad and another
jaunty fellow who had joined them began to think that there
was a devil in him. They wondered where it all came from—
tales and stories of such marvels that Grandad held his sides and
almost split his stomach with laughing. But the further they rode
the darker it grew, and with it the gay talk grew more dis-
connected. At last our story-teller fell altogether silent and
started at the slightest rustle.

"Aha, neighbour!" they said to him, "you have set to nodding
in earnest: you wish now you were at home and on the stove-
couch!"

"I have no reason to hide it from you," he said suddenly,
turning round and fixing his eyes upon them. "Do you know
that I sold my soul to the devil long ago?"

"As though that were something unheard of! Who hasn't

had dealings with the devil in his day ? That's why you must drain the cup of pleasure, as the saying goes."

"Ah, lads! I would, but this night my fatal hour will come. Don't give me up, my friends!" he said, clasping their hands. "Watch over me one night—I will never forget your friendship!"

Why not help a man in such trouble ? Grandad vowed straight off that he would have the scalp-lock cut off his head rather than let the devil sniff with his dog-nose at a Christian soul.

Our Cossacks might have ridden on if the whole sky had not clouded over as though with black homespun and it had not turned as dark as under a sheepskin. There was a light twinkling in the distance, and the horses, feeling that a stall was near, quickened their pace, pricking up their ears and staring into the darkness. It seemed as though the light flew to meet them, and the Cossacks saw before them a tavern, lurching over on one side like a peasant woman on her way home from a merry christening party. In those days taverns were not what they are now. There was no room for a good man to turn round or dance a *hopak*—indeed, he had nowhere to lie down, even if the drink had got into his head and his legs began drawing rings all over the floor. The yard was all blocked up with carters' waggons; under the sheds, in the mangers, in the barns men were snoring like tomcats, one curled up and another sprawling. Only the tavern-keeper before his little pot-lamp was notching a stick to mark the number of quarts and pints the carters had drained.

Grandad, after ordering a third of a pailful for the three of them, went off to the barn. They lay down side by side. But before Grandad had time to turn round his friends were sleeping like the dead. Waking the third Cossack, the one who had joined them, Grandad reminded him of the promise given to their comrade. The man sat up, rubbed his eyes, and fell asleep again. There was nothing for it, Grandad had to watch alone. To keep off sleep in some way, he examined all the waggons, had a look at the horses, lighted his pipe, came back, and sat down again beside his comrades. All was still and it seemed as though not a fly were moving. Then he fancied something grey poked out its horns from behind a waggon close by. But his eyes began to close, so that he had to rub them every minute with his fist and to keep them open with the rest of the vodka. But as soon as they became a little clearer, everything would vanish again. A little later the apparition showed again from under the waggon. Grandad opened his eyes as wide as he could, but the cursed sleepiness made everything misty before them; his hands felt numb, his head rolled to one side, and he fell into such a sound sleep that he lay as though he were dead. Grandad slept for hours, and he sprang up on his feet only when the sun was baking his shaven head. After stretching a couple of times and scratching his back, he noticed that there were no longer so many waggons standing there as in the evening. The carters must have trailed off before dawn. He looked for his companions; the Cossack was still asleep, but the Zaporozhian was gone. No one could tell him anything about the man; only his topcoat was still lying in the same place. Grandad was frightened and didn't know what to think. He went to look for the horses—no sign of his or the Zaporozhian's! What could that mean ? Supposing the Evil One had taken the Zaporozhian; who had taken the horses ? Thinking it over, Grandad concluded that probably the devil had come on foot, and as it's a long way to hell he had carried off his horse. He was terribly upset at not having kept his Cossack word.

"Well," he thought, "there is nothing to be done, I will go on foot. I hope I may come across some horse-dealer on his way from the fair, then I'll have a chance to buy a horse." But when he reached for his cap, his cap was gone too. Grandad wrung his hands when he remembered that the day before he had changed caps for a time with the Zaporozhian. Who else could have carried it off but the devil himself! A fine messenger he was! A nice job he had made of delivering the letter to the Tsarina! My grandad fell to bestowing such names on the devil as, I fancy, must have set him sneezing more than once in hell. But calling one names does not help much, and however often my grandad scratched his head, he could not think of any plan. What was he to do? He turned to take counsel from others: he got together all the good folk who were in the tavern at the time—carters and simple wayfarers—and told them how it all happened and what a misfortune had befallen him. A long time the carters pondered. Leaning their chins on their whips, they shook their heads and said that they had never heard of such a marvel in Christendom as a devil carrying off a Hetman's letter. Others added that when the devil or a Muscovite stole anything, you might whistle for it. Only the tavern-keeper sat silent in the corner. So Grandad went up to him. When a man says nothing, you may be sure he is not a fool. But the tavern-keeper was sparing of words, and if Grandad had not pulled five gold pieces out of his pocket, he might have gone on standing before him to no purpose.

"I will tell you how to find the letter," said the tavern-keeper, leading him aside. His words lifted a weight from Grandad's heart. "I see from your eyes that you are a Cossack and not a ninny. Mind now! Near the tavern you will find a turning on the right into the forest. As soon as it begins to grow dark you must be ready to start. There are Gypsies living in the forest and they come out of their dens to forge iron on nights on which none but witches go abroad on their pokers. What their real trade is you had best not inquire. There will be much knocking in the forest, only you mustn't go where you hear the knocking; there'll be a little path facing you near a burnt tree—go by that little path, go on and on. The thorns may scratch you, the thick hazel bushes may block the path, but you must go on. You may not stop until you come to a little stream. There you will see whom you need. But don't forget to take in your pockets that for which pockets are made. You understand, both devils and men prize that." Saying this, the tavern-keeper went off to his corner and would not say another word.

My grandad was by no means faint-hearted. If he met a wolf, he would take him by the tail straight away; if he used his fists among the Cossacks, they would fall to the ground like so many pears. Nevertheless, he felt creepy when he stepped into the forest on that dark night. There was not a single star in the sky. It was dark and still as a wine-cellar; far, far overhead a cold wind was soughing in the tree-tops, and the trees like the heads of drunken Cossacks wagged recklessly while their leaves whispered a tipsy song. And then there came such a cold blast that Grandad thought of his sheepskin, and all at once it was as though a hundred hammers began striking in the forest with a noise that set his ears ringing. And the whole forest was lit up for a moment as though by summer lightning. Grandad caught sight of a little path winding between the low bushes. And here was the burnt tree and here were the thorn bushes! Everything was as he had been told— the tavern-keeper had not deceived him. It was not altogether pleasant, however, making his way through the prickly bushes; he had never in his life known the damned thorns and twigs to scratch so badly. He felt like crying out almost at every step. Little by little he came out into a glade, and as far as he could see the trees were wider apart, and as he went on he came upon bigger trees than he had ever seen even beyond

Poland. And behold, among the trees gleamed a little stream, dark like tempered steel. For a long time Grandad stood on the bank, looking round. On the other bank a light was twinkling; it seemed every minute about to go out, and then was reflected again in the stream, trembling like a Pole in the hands of Cossacks. And here was the little bridge!

"I suppose none but the devil's cart can cross by it."

Grandad stepped out boldly, however, and before another man would have had time to get out his horn and take a pinch of snuff he was on the other side. Only now did he see that there were people sitting round a fire, and such charming pig-faces that at any other time God knows he would have given anything to escape their acquaintance. But now he could not help making friends with them. So Grandad swung off a low bow, saying: "God help you, good people!"

Not one nodded his head; they all sat in silence and kept dropping something into the fire. Seeing one place empty, Grandad sat down without more ado. The charming pig-faces said nothing; Grandad said nothing either. For a long time they sat in silence. Grandad began to be bored; he fumbled in his pocket, pulled out his pipe, looked round—not one of them glanced at him.

"Well, your worships, will you be so kind; as a matter of fact, in a manner of speaking—" Grandad had knocked about the world a good bit and knew how to turn a phrase, and would hardly have been at a loss even if he had been before the Tsar— "in a manner of speaking, not to forget myself nor to slight you— I have a pipe, but I lack that with which to light it."

To this speech, too, there was not a word. Only one of the pig-faces thrust a hot brand straight in Grandad's face, so that if he had not turned aside a little, he might have parted with one eye for ever. At last, seeing that time was being wasted, he made up his mind to tell his story whether the unholy race would listen or not. They pricked up their ears and stretched out their paws. Grandad guessed what they wanted; he took out all the money he had with him and flung it to them as though to dogs. As soon as he had flung the money, everything was in a turmoil before him, the earth shook, and all at once— he never knew how to explain this part—he found himself almost in hell.

"Merciful heavens!" groaned my grandad when he had taken a good look round. What monsters those were! Each face was uglier than the other. The witches were as many as the snow-flakes that fall sometimes at Christmas. They were all dressed up and painted like fine ladies at a fair. And all the lot of them were dancing some sort of devil's *hopak* as though they were drunk. And the dust they kicked up! Any Christian would have shuddered to see how high the brood of Satan skipped. In spite of his terror, my grandad fell to laughing when he saw the devils, with their dogs' faces and spindly legs, wag their tails, twist and turn about the witches, as our lads do about the pretty girls, while the musicians beat on their cheeks with their fists as though they were tambourines and whistled with their noses as though they were horns. As soon as they saw Grandad, they pressed round him in a crowd. Pig-faces, dog-faces, goat-faces, bustard-faces and horse-faces—all craned for-ward, trying to kiss him. Grandad could not help spitting, he was so disgusted. At last they caught hold of him and seated him at a table as long, maybe, as the road from Konotop to Baturin.

"Well, this is not so bad after all!" thought Grandad, seeing on the table pork, sausages, onion minced with cabbage, and many other dainties. "The hellish rabble don't keep the fasts, it seems."

My grandad, I may as well tell you, never missed his chance when he could have a good bite. He ate with relish, the dear man, and so without wasting words he pulled towards him a bowl of sliced bacon fat and smoked ham, took up a fork not much smaller than those with which a peasant pitches hay, picked out the biggest piece, laid it on a piece of bread—and lo and behold!—put it in another mouth beside his very ear, and, indeed, there was the sound of another fellow's jaws chewing it and clacking with his teeth, so that everyone at the table could hear. Grandad.didn't mind; he took up another piece, and this time it seemed as though he had caught it with his lips, but again he did not get it into his gullet. A third time he tried—again he missed it. Grandad flew into a rage; he forgot his fright and in whose claws he was, and ran up to the witches.

"Are you trying to laugh at me, you brood of Herod? If you don't this very minute give me back my Cossack cap, may I be a Catholic if I don't twist your pig-snouts to the wrong side of your heads!"

Hardly had he finished the last word when the monsters grinned and set up such a roar of laughter that it sent a chill to my grandad's heart.

"Good!" shrieked one of the witches, whom my grandad took to be the leader among them because she was almost the greatest beauty of the lot, "we will give you back your cap, but not until you win it back from us in three games of 'Fools'!"

What was he to do? For a Cossack to sit down and play "Fools" with a lot of women! Grandad kept refusing, but in the end sat down. They brought the cards, a greasy pack such as we only see used by priests' daughters to find out what their husbands will be like.

"Listen!" barked the witch again. "If you win one game, the cap is yours; if you are left 'Fool' in every one of the three games, you'll never see your cap nor, maybe, the world again!"

"Come on, deal, you old hag! What will be, will be."

Well, the cards were dealt. Grandad picked up his, and they were such rubbish that he turned away his eyes in disgust: as though to mock him, there was not a single trump. Of the other suits the highest was a ten and he hadn't even a pair, while the witch kept giving him five at once. It was his fate to be left "Fool." As soon as Grandad was left "Fool," the monsters began neighing, barking, and grunting on all sides: "Fool, fool, fool!"

"Shout till you split, you devils," cried Grandad, stopping his ears with his fingers.

"Well," he thought, "the witch didn't play fair, now I am going to deal myself." He dealt; he turned up the trump and looked at his cards: they were first-rate, and he had trumps. And at first things could not have gone better, till the witch put down five cards with kings among them.

Grandad had nothing in his hand but trumps. Quick as thought he beat all the kings with them.

"Ha! that's not like a Cossack! What are you beating them with, neighbour?"

"What with? With trumps!"

"Perhaps to your thinking they are trumps, but to our thinking they are not!"

Lo and behold! the cards were really of another suit! What devilry was this? A second time he was "Fool" and the devils set off splitting their throats again, "Fool! fool!" so that the table rocked and the cards danced upon it.

Grandad flew into a passion; he dealt for the last time. Again he had a good hand. The witch put down five again; Grandad beat them and took from the pack a handful of trumps.

"Trump!" he shouted, flinging a card on the table so that it crumpled up.

Without saying a word, she covered it with the eight of another suit.

"What are you beating my trump with, old devil?"

The witch lifted her card and under it was the six of a plain suit.

"What devilish trickery!" said Grandad, and in his vexation he struck the table with his fist as hard as he could. Luckily the witch had a poor hand; this time as luck would have it Grandad had pairs. He began drawing cards out of the pack, but they were no good; such rubbish came that Grandad let his hands fall. There was not a single card in the pack. So he just played anything—a six. The witch had to take it, she could not beat it. "Well, well! What is this? There is something wrong, I'll be bound!" Then on the sly, under the table, Grandad made the sign of the cross over the cards, and behold—he had in his hand the ace, king, and knave of trumps, and the card he had just played was not a six, but the queen!

"What a fool I've been! King of trumps! Ha! so you've taken it, eh? You brood of cats! Would you like the ace, too? The ace! the knave!"

A tumult arose in hell; the witch went into convulsions, and all of a sudden the cap flew flop into Grandad's face.

"This isn't enough!" shouted Grandad, plucking up heart and putting on his cap. "If I don't see my gallant horse before me at once, may a thunderbolt strike me dead in this foul place if I do not make the sign of the holy cross over all of you!" And he raised his hand to make good his threat when the horse's bones rattled before him.

"Here is your horse!"

The poor man burst out crying like a child as he looked at them. He was so sorry for his old comrade!

"Give me some sort of a horse," he said, "to get out of your den!" A devil cracked a whip—a horse rose up under him like a flame and Grandad flew upwards like a bird.

Terror came over him, however, when the horse, heeding neither shout nor rein, galloped over ditches and bogs. The places he went through were so dreadful that it made him shudder at the mere telling of it. Once he looked down and was more terrified than ever: an abyss, a fearful precipice! But that was nothing to the satanic beast; he leapt straight over it. Grandad tried to hold on; he could not. Over tree-stumps, over mounds he flew headlong into a hollow, and hit the ground at the bottom so hard that it seemed he had breathed his last. Anyway, he could remember nothing of what happened to him then; and when he recovered a little and looked about him it was broad daylight; he caught glimpses of familiar places and found himself lying on the roof of his own hut.

Grandad crossed himself as he climbed down. What devil's tricks! Damn it all! What marvellous things befall a man! He looked at his hands—they were bathed in blood; he looked into a butt of water—his face was the same. Washing himself thoroughly so as not to scare the children, he went quietly into the hut, and what did he see! The children backed towards him and pointed in alarm, saying: "Look! look, Mother's jumping like mad!" And, indeed, his wife was sitting asleep before her wool-comb, holding her distaff in her hands and in her sleep was bouncing up and down on the bench. Grandad, taking her gently by the hand, woke her. "Good morning, wife! Are you all right?" She stared at him for a long time, but at last she recognized him and told him that she had dreamed that the stove was riding round the hut shovelling out with a spade the pots and tubs, and God knows what else.

"Well," said Grandad, "you have had it asleep, I have had it awake; I see I must have our hut blessed; but I cannot linger now."

Saying this, Grandad rested a little, then got a horse from somebody and did not stop by day or by night till he arrived and gave the letter to the Tsarina herself. There Grandad beheld such wonderful things that for long after he used to tell the tale: how they brought him to the palace, and it was so high that if you were to set ten huts one on top of another they would hardly be high enough; how he glanced into one room and she was not there, into another, a third, and even a fourth, and still she was not there; but in the fifth there she was sitting in her gold crown, in a new grey gown and red boots, eating golden dumplings; how she had bidden them fill a whole cap with blue five-ruble notes for him; how— I can't remember it all! As for all his hob-nobbing with the devils, Grandad forgot even to think about it, and if someone happened to remind him of it, Grandad would say nothing, as though the matter did not concern him, and it was very difficult indeed to persuade him to tell us how it had all happened. And seemingly to punish him for not rushing out at once after that to have the hut blessed, every year just at that same time a strange thing happened to his wife—she would jump up and down and nothing could stop her. Whatever she did, her legs would go their own way and something seemed prompting her to dance.

PART TWO

PREFACE

Here is a second part for you, and I had better say, the last one! I did not want—I did not at all want to bring it out. One ought not to outstay one's welcome. I must tell you they are beginning to laugh at me in the village. "The old fellow has gone silly," they say. "He is amusing himself with children's toys in his old age!" And, indeed, it is high time to rest. I expect you imagine, dear readers, that I am only pretending to be old. Pretend, indeed, when I have not a tooth left in my mouth! Now if anything soft comes my way I manage to chew it, but I can't tackle anything hard. So here is another book for you! Only don't scold me. It is not nice to scold at parting, especially when God only knows whether we will soon meet again. In this book you will find stories told by people you do not know at all, except, perhaps, Foma Grigoryevich. That gentleman in the pea-green coat, who talked in such fine language that many of the wits even from Moscow could not understand him, has not been here for a long time. He never looked in since he quarrelled with us all. I did not tell you about it, did I? It was a regular comedy.

Last year, some time in the summer, I believe it was on my saint's day, I had visitors to see me—I must tell you, dear readers, that my neighbours, God give them good health, do not forget the old man. It is fifty years since I began keeping my name-day; but just how old I am neither I nor my old woman can say. It must be somewhere about seventy. The priest at Dikanka, Father Kharlampy, knew when I was born, but I am sorry to say he has been dead these fifty years. So I had visitors to see me: Zakhar Kirilovich Chukhopupenko, Stepan Ivanovich Kurochka, Taras Ivanovich Smachnenky, the assessor Kharlampy Kirilovich Khlosta; there was another one— I forget his name—Osip—Osip— Upon my soul, everyone in Mirgorod knows him! Whenever he begins speaking he snaps his fingers and puts his arms akimbo. Well, never mind! I shall think of the name presently. The gentleman from Poltava whom you know already came, too. Foma Grigoryevich I do not count, he is one of us. Everybody talked—I must tell you that we never talk about trifles; I always like seemly conversation, so as to combine pleasure and profit, as the saying is—we discussed how to pickle apples. My old woman said that first you had to wash the apples thoroughly, then put them to soak in kvass, and then— "All that is no use whatever!" the gentleman from Poltava interrupted, thrusting his hand into his pea-green coat and pacing gravely about the room, "not the slightest use! First you must sprinkle them with tansy and then—" But, I ask you, dear readers, did you ever hear of apples being sprinkled with tansy? People do use black-currant leaves, swine-herb, trefoil; but to put in tansy—I have never heard of such a thing. And I fancy no one knows more about these things than my old woman. But there you are! I quietly drew him aside, as a good neighbour. "Come now, Makar Nazarovich, don't make people laugh! You are a man of some consequence; you have dined at the same table with the Governor, as you told us yourself. Well, if you were to say anything like this there, you would set them all laughing at you!" And what do you imagine he said to that? Nothing! He spat on the floor, picked up his cap, and walked out. He might have said good-bye to somebody, he might have given us a nod; all we heard was his chaise with a bell on it pull up at the gate; he got in and drove off. And good riddance, too! We don't want guests like that. I tell you what, dear readers, nothing in the world can be worse than those high-class people. Because his uncle was Commissar once, he turns up his nose at everyone. As though there were no rank in the world higher! There certainly are people greater than Commissars. No, I don't like those high-class people. Now take Foma Grigoryevich, for instance—he is not a high-class man, but just look at him; there is a serene dignity in his face. You can't help feeling respect for him, even when he takes a pinch of ordinary snuff. When he sings in the choir in the church, there is no describing how touching it is. You feel as though you were melting! While that other— but never mind him. He thinks we cannot do without his tales. But here is a book of them without him.

I promised you, I remember, that in this book there would be my tale, too. And I meant to put it in, too. But I found that for my tale I should need three books of this size, at least.

I decided to print it separately, but I thought better of it. I know you: you would be laughing at the old man. No, I will not! Good-bye. It will be a long time before we meet again, if ever. But there, it would not matter to you if I never existed at all. One year will pass and then another—and none of you will remember or regret the old bee-keeper,

GINGER PANKO.

CHRISTMAS EVE

The last day before Christmas had passed. A clear winter night had fallen; the stars peeped out; the moon rose majestically in the sky to light good people and all the world so that all might enjoy singing *kolyadki** and praising the Lord. It was freezing harder than in the morning; but it was so still that the crunch of the snow under the boot could be heard

* Among us it is the custom to sing under the windows on Christmas Eve carols that are called *kolyadki*. The mistress or master, or whoever is left in the house, always drops into the singer's bag some sausage or bread or a copper or whatever else he can. It is said that once upon a time there was a blockhead called Kolyada who was taken to be a god and that these *kolyadki* came from that. Who knows? It is not for plain

half a mile away. Not one group of lads had appeared under the cottage windows yet; only the moon peeped in at them stealthily as though calling to the girls, who were dressing up in their best, to make haste and run out on the crunching snow. At that moment the smoke rose in puffs from a cottage chimney and trailed like a cloud over the sky, and a witch, astride a broomstick, rose up in the air together with the smoke.

If the assessor of Sorochintsi, in his cap edged with lambskin and cut like an Uhlan's, in his dark blue greatcoat lined with black astrakhan, had driven by at that minute with his three hired horses and the fiendishly plaited whip, with which it is his habit to urge on his coachman, he would certainly have noticed her, for there is not a witch in the world who could elude the eye of the Sorochintsi assessor. He can count on his fingers how many little ones every peasant woman's sow has farrowed and how much linen she is keeping in her chest, and just which of their clothes or household belongings good people pawn on Sunday at the tavern. But the Sorochintsi assessor did not drive by, and, indeed, what business was it of his? He had his own district to take care of. Meanwhile, the witch rose so high in the air that she was only a little black speck up aloft. But wherever that speck appeared, there the stars vanished one after another. Soon the witch had gathered a whole sleeveful of them. Three or four were still shining. All at once another little speck appeared from elsewhere; it grew larger, began to lengthen out, and was no longer a speck. A

folk like us to give our opinion about it. Last year Father Osip was for forbidding people to sing *kolyadki* about the farms, saying that they honoured Satan by doing so, though to tell the truth there is not a word about Kolyada in the *kolyadki*. They often sing about the birth of Christ, and at the end wish good health to the master, the mistress, the children, and all the household.—*The bee-keeper's note.*

short-sighted man would never have made out what it was, even if he had put the wheels of the Commissar's chaise on his nose by way of spectacles. In front it looked like a regular German;* the narrow little face, continually twisting and turning and sniffing at everything, ended in a little button, like our pigs' snouts; the legs were so thin that if the Head of Yareski had had legs like that, he would certainly have broken them in the first Cossack dance. But behind he was for all the world a district attorney in uniform, for he had a tail as long and pointed as the uniform coat-tails are nowadays. It was only from the goat's beard under his chin, from the little horns sticking up on his forehead, and from his being no whiter than a chimney-sweep, that one could tell that he was not a German or a district attorney, but simply the devil, who had one last night left him to wander about the wide world and teach good folk to sin. On the morrow, when the first bells rang for matins, he would run with his tail between his legs straight off to his lair.

Meanwhile the devil stole silently up to the moon and stretched his hand out to seize it, but drew it back quickly as though he were scorched, sucked his fingers and danced about, then ran up from the other side and again skipped away and drew back his hand. But in spite of all his failures the sly devil did not give up his tricks. Running up, he suddenly seized the moon with both hands; grimacing and blowing, he kept flinging it from one hand to the other, like a peasant who has picked up an ember for his pipe with bare fingers; at last, he hurriedly put it in his pocket and ran on as though nothing had happened.

No one in Dikanka noticed that the devil had stolen the

---

* Among us anyone is called a German who comes from a foreign land; even though he may be a Frenchman, a Hungarian, or a Swede, he is still a German.—*Author's note.*

moon. True, the district clerk, coming out of the tavern on all fours, saw the moon for no reason whatever dancing in the sky, and swore he had to the whole village; but people shook their heads and even made fun of him. But what motive led the devil to this lawless act ? Why, this was how it was; he knew that the rich Cossack, Chub, had been invited by the sacristan to a supper of frumenty at which a kinsman of the sacristan's, who was one of the bishop's choir, wore a dark blue coat and could take the very lowest bass-note; the Head, the Cossack Sverbiguz and some others were to be present, and besides the Christmas frumenty there were to be mulled vodka, saffron vodka, and good food of all sorts. And meanwhile his daughter, the greatest beauty in the village, would be left at home, and there was no doubt that the blacksmith, a very strong and fine young fellow, would pay her a visit, and him the devil hated more than Father Kondrat's sermons. In his spare time the blacksmith gave himself up to painting, and he was reckoned the finest artist in the neighbourhood. Even the Cossack officer L—ko, who was still living in those days, sent for him from Poltava expressly to paint the fence round his house. All the bowls from which the Cossacks of Dikanka supped their soup had been painted by the blacksmith. He was a God-fearing man and often painted icons; even now you may find his Luke the Evangelist in the church of T. But his masterpiece was a picture painted on the church wall in the chapel on the right. In it he depicted St. Peter on the Day of Judgement with the keys in his hand driving the Evil Spirit out of hell; the frightened devil, foreseeing his doom, was darting about, while the freed sinners chased him and struck him with whips, blocks of wood, and anything they could get hold of. While the artist was working at this picture and painting it on a big wooden board, the devil did all he could to hinder him: he gave him a nudge on the arm, unseen, blew some ashes from the forge in the smithy and scattered them on the picture; nevertheless, the work was finished, the picture was brought into the church and set into the wall of the side chapel, and the devil swore he would revenge himself on the blacksmith.

He had only one night left to wander upon earth; he was looking for some means of venting his wrath on the blacksmith that night. And that was why he made up his mind to steal the moon, reckoning that old Chub was lazy and slow to move, and the sacristan's cottage a good long step away; the road ran past the mills and the graveyard outside the village and went round a ravine. On a moonlit night mulled vodka and saffron vodka might have tempted Chub; but in such darkness it was doubtful whether anyone could drag him from the stove-couch and bring him out of the cottage. And the blacksmith, who had for a long time been on bad terms with him, would on no account have ventured, strong as he was, to visit the daughter when the father was at home.

And so, as soon as the devil had hidden the moon in his pocket, it became at once so dark all over the world that not everyone could have found the way to the tavern, let alone to the sacristan's. The witch gave a shriek when she suddenly found herself in darkness. Then the devil ran up, all bows and smiles, took her arm and began whispering in her ear the sort of thing that is usually whispered to all the female sex. Things are queerly arranged in our world. All who live in it are always trying to imitate and ape one another. In old days the judge and the mayor were the only ones in Mirgorod who used to wear cloth overcoats lined with sheepskin in the winter, while all the petty officials wore plain sheepskin; but nowadays the assessor and the land reeve have got themselves new cloth greatcoats lined with astrakhan. The year before last the office clerk and the

district clerk bought dark blue duck at sixty kopeks a yard.
The sexton has got himself nankeen trousers for the summer
and a striped waistcoat of worsted yarn. In short, everyone
tries to be somebody. When will folks give up being vain! I
am ready to bet that many would be surprised to see the devil
carrying on in that way. What is most annoying is that, no
doubt, he fancies himself a handsome fellow, though his figure
is a shameful sight. His face, as Foma Grigoryevich would
say, is the abomination of abominations, and yet even he plays
the gallant! But in the sky and under the sky it had grown so
dark that there was no seeing what followed between them.

"So you have not been to see the sacristan in his new cottage,
mate?" said the Cossack Chub, coming out at his door, to a
tall lean peasant in a short sheepskin, whose stubby beard
showed that for at least a fortnight it had not been touched
by a broken piece of scythe, with which, for lack of a razor,
peasants usually shave their beards. "There will be a fine drinking bout there tonight!" Chub went on, grinning. "I hope we
are not late!"

Hereupon Chub set straight the belt that closely girt his
sheepskin, pulled his cap more firmly on his head and gripped
his whip, the terror of tiresome dogs; but glancing upwards,
he stopped.

"What the devil! Look! Look, Panas!"

"What is it?" asked his friend, looking skywards in his turn.

"What, indeed! There is no moon!"

"What a nuisance! There really is no moon."

"That's just it—there isn't!" Chub brought out with some
annoyance at his friend's imperturbable indifference. "You don't
care, I'll be bound."

"Well, what can I do about it ?"

"Some devil," Chub went on, wiping his moustaches on his sleeve, "must needs go and meddle—may he never have a glass of vodka to drink in the morning, the dog! Upon my word, it's as though to mock us. As I sat indoors I looked out of the window and the night was so lovely! It was light, the snow was sparkling in the moonlight; you could see everything as though it were day. And here before I'm out of the door, you can't see your hand before your face!"

Chub went on grumbling and scolding for a long while, and at the same time he was thinking what to do. He longed to chat about all sorts of nonsense at the sacristan's, where no doubt the Head was already sitting, as well as the bass choir-singer, and Mikita, the tar-dealer, who used to go once a fort-night to the market in Poltava, and who cracked such jokes that all the villagers held their sides with laughing. Already in his mind's eye Chub saw the mulled vodka on the table. All this was alluring, sure enough; but the darkness of the night reminded him of the charms of laziness, so dear to every Cossack. How nice it would be now to lie on the stove-couch with his legs tucked under him, quietly smoking his pipe and listening through a luxurious drowsiness to the songs and *kolyadki* of the light-hearted lads and lasses who gathered in groups under the windows! He would undoubtedly have decided on the latter course had he been alone; but for the two together, it was not so dreary and terrible to go through the dark night; besides, he did not care to seem sluggish or cowardly to others. When he had finished scolding he turned again to his friend.

"So there is no moon, mate ?"

"No."

"It's strange, really! Let me have a pinch of snuff. You have splendid snuff, mate. Where do you get it ?"

"Splendid, is it?" replied his friend, shutting the birch-bark snuff-box with patterns pricked out upon it. "Why, it wouldn't make an old hen sneeze!"

"I remember," said Chub, "the tavern-keeper Zuzulya once brought me some snuff from Nezhin. Ah, that was snuff! It was good snuff! So how is it to be, mate? It's dark, you know."

"Well, I think we'd better stay home," his friend answered, taking hold of the door-handle.

If his friend had not said that, Chub would certainly have made up his mind to stay at home; but now something seemed egging him on to oppose it. "No, mate, let us go! It won't do—we must go."

Even as he was saying it, he was vexed with himself for doing so. He very much disliked turning out on such a night, but it was a comfort to him that he was acting on his own decision and not following advice.

His friend looked round and scratched his shoulders with the handle of his whip, without the slightest sign of vexation on his face, like a man to whom it makes no difference whatsoever whether he sits at home or turns out—and the two friends set out.

Now let us see what Chub's beautiful daughter was doing all by herself. Before Oksana was seventeen, people were talking about nothing but her in almost the whole world, both on this side of Dikanka and beyond it. The lads were all at one in declaring that there never had been, and never would be, a finer girl in the village. Oksana heard and knew all that was said about her and, like a beauty, was full of caprices. If, instead of a checked skirt and an apron, she had been dressed as a lady, she could never have kept a servant. The lads ran after her in crowds, but, losing patience, one by one gave up the wilful beauty, and turned to others who were not so spoilt. Only the blacksmith persisted in his courtship, although he was treated not a whit better than the rest.

When her father went out, Oksana spent a long time dressing herself in her best and prinking before a little looking-glass in a pewter frame; she could not admire herself enough.

"What put it into folks' heads to spread it abroad that I am pretty?" she said, as it were absent-mindedly, simply to talk to herself about something. "They lie, I am not pretty at all!"

But the fresh face reflected in the looking-glass, with its childish youthfulness, its sparkling black eyes, and its inexpressibly charming smile that thrilled the soul, at once proved the contrary.

"Can my black eyebrows and my eyes," the beauty went on, still holding the mirror, "be so beautiful that there are none like them in the world? What is there pretty in that turned-up nose, and in the cheeks and the lips? Are my black plaits pretty? Ugh, they might frighten one in the evening, they twist and twine round my head like long snakes. I see now that I am not pretty at all!" And, moving the looking-glass a little further away, she cried out: "Oh, yes, I am pretty. Ah, how pretty! It is marvellous. What a joy I shall be to the man who marries me! How my husband will admire me! He'll be wild with joy. He will kiss me to death."

"Wonderful girl!" whispered the blacksmith, coming in softly. "And hasn't she a little conceit! She's been standing looking in the mirror for an hour and she just can't tear herself away, and praising herself aloud, too!"

"Am I a match for you, lads? Look at me!" the pretty coquette went on: "See how gracefully I step; my blouse is embroidered with red silk. And the ribbons on my head! You will never see richer braid. My father bought me all this for the finest young man in the world to marry me." And, chuckling, she turned round and saw the blacksmith.

She uttered a cry and stood coldly facing him.

The blacksmith's hands dropped helplessly to his sides.

It is hard to describe what the darkish face of the lovely girl expressed. There was sternness in it, and through the sternness there showed a sort of mockery at the embarrassed blacksmith, and at the same time a hardly perceptible flush of vexation delicately suffused her face; and all this was so mingled and so indescribably pretty that to give her a million kisses was the best thing that could have been done at the moment.

"Why have you come?" was how Oksana began. "Do you want me to shove you out of the door with a spade? You are all very clever at calling on us. You sniff out in a minute when there are no fathers in. Oh, I know you! Well, is my chest ready?"

"It will be ready, my little heart—after Christmas. If only you knew how I have worked at it; for two nights I didn't leave the smithy. But then no priest's daughter will have a chest like it. The iron I bound it with is better than what I put on the officer's carriage, when I worked in Poltava. And how it will be painted! You wouldn't find one like it if you wandered over the whole neighbourhood with your little white feet. Red and blue flowers will be scattered all over it. It will glow like fire. So don't be angry with me. Allow me at least to speak to you, to look at you!"

"You may speak and look as much as you like—nobody's stopping you."

She sat down on the bench, glanced again at the looking glass, and began arranging her hair. She looked at her neck at her new blouse embroidered with red silk, and a subtle feeling of complacency could be read on her lips and fresh cheeks, and was reflected in her eyes.

"Allow me to sit beside you," said the blacksmith.

"Sit down," said Oksana, with the same emotion still perceptible on her lips and in her gratified eyes.

"Wonderful, lovely Oksana, allow me to kiss you!" said the blacksmith, growing bolder, and he drew her towards him with the intention of snatching a kiss. But Oksana turned away her cheek, which had been very close to the blacksmith's lips, and pushed him away.

"Anything else you want? When there's honey he must have a spoonful! Go away, your hands are harder than iron. And you smell of smoke. I believe you have smeared me all over with your soot."

Then she picked up the looking-glass and began preening herself again.

"She does not love me!" the blacksmith thought to himself, hanging his head. "It's all play to her while I stand before her like a fool and cannot take my eyes off her. And I should like to stand before her always and never to take my eyes off her. Strange girl! What would I not give to know what is in her heart, and whom she loves. But she cares for nobody. She is admiring herself; she is tormenting poor me, while I am so sad that everything is darkness to me. I love her as no man in the world ever has loved, or ever will."

"Is it true that your mother's a witch?" said Oksana, and laughed. And the blacksmith felt that everything within him was laughing. That laugh seemed to echo at once in his heart and in his softly thrilling veins, but for all that his soul was vexed because he had not the right to kiss that sweetly laughing face.

"What do I care for Mother? You are father and mother

to me, and all that is precious in the world. If the Tsar summoned me and said: 'Smith Vakula, ask me for all that is best in my kingdom, and I will give it to you. I will bid them make you a gold forge and you shall work with silver hammers.' 'I don't care,' I should say to the Tsar, 'for precious stones or a gold forge or for your kingdom; give me rather my Oksana.'"

"See what a fellow you are! Only my father's no fool either. You'll see that, when he doesn't marry your mother!" Oksana said, smiling slyly. "But the girls are not here. What's the meaning of it? We ought to have started singing *kolyadki* long ago. I am getting tired of waiting."

"Let them stay away, my beauty!"

"Oh, no! I expect the lads will come with them. And then there will be fun. I can fancy what stories they will tell!"

"So you'll be merry with them?"

"Yes, merrier than with you. Ah! someone knocked; it must be the girls and the lads."

"What's the use of my staying longer?" the blacksmith said to himself. "She is jeering at me. I am no more to her than an old rusty horseshoe. But if that's so, I won't let another man laugh at me. If only I see for certain that she likes someone better than me, I'll teach him to keep off."

A knock at the door and a cry of "Open!" rang out sharply in the frost, interrupting his reflections.

"Wait, I'll open the door," said the blacksmith, and he went out, intending in his vexation to break the ribs of anyone who might be there.

The frost grew sharper, and up aloft it turned so cold that the devil kept hopping from one hoof to the other and blowing into his fists, trying to warm his frozen hands. And indeed it is small wonder that he should be cold, being used day after day to knocking about in hell, where, as we all know, it is not as cold as it is with us in winter, and where, putting on his cap and standing before the hearth, like a real cook, he fries sinners with as much satisfaction as a peasant woman fries sausage at Christmas.

The witch, too, felt that it was cold, although she was warmly clad; and so, throwing her arms upwards, she stood with one foot out, and putting herself into the attitude of a man racing along on skates, without moving a single muscle, she slid through the air, as though down an ice-slope, and straight into her chimney.

The devil followed her in the same way. But as the creature is nimbler than any dandy in stockings, there is no wonder that at the top of the chimney he almost landed on the neck of his mistress, and both found themselves in a roomy oven among the pots.

The witch stealthily moved back the oven door to see whether her son, Vakula, had invited visitors to the cottage; but seeing that there was no one, except the sacks that lay on the floor, she crept out of the oven, flung off her warm coat, set herself to rights, and no one could have told that she had been riding on a broom the minute before.

Vakula's mother was not more than forty years old. She was neither handsome nor ugly. Indeed, it is hard to be handsome at such an age. However, she was so clever at alluring even the steadiest Cossacks (who, it may not be amiss to observe, do not care much about beauty) that the Head and the sacristan, Osip Nikiforovich (when his wife was not at home, of course), and the Cossack Korny Chub, and the Cossack Kasyan Sverbiguz, used all to call on her. And it must be said to her credit that she was very skilful in managing them: not one of them dreamed that he had a rival. If a God-fearing peasant or a gentleman (as the Cossacks call themselves) wearing a cape with a hood went to church on Sunday or, if the weather was bad, to the tavern, he never failed to look in on Solokha, eat curd dumplings with sour cream, and gossip in the warm cottage with its chatty and agreeable mistress. And the Cossack would purposely go a long way round before reaching the tavern, and would call that "looking in on his way." And when Solokha went to church on a holiday, dressed in bright-checked skirts with a cotton apron, and above it a dark blue overskirt on the back of which gold flourishes were embroidered, and took up her stand close to the right side of the choir, the sacristan would be sure to cough and unwittingly screw up his eyes in her direction; the Head would smooth his moustaches, twist his scalp-lock behind his ear, and say to the man standing next to him: "Ah, there's a real woman—a devil of a woman!" Solokha would bow to each one of them, and each one would think that she was bowing to him alone.

But anyone fond of meddling in other people's business would have noticed at once that Solokha was most gracious to the Cossack Chub. Chub was a widower. Eight stacks of corn always stood before his cottage. Two pairs of stalwart oxen poked their heads out of the wattled barn by the roadside and lowed every time they saw their crony, the cow, or their uncle, the stout bull, passing. A bearded billy-goat used to clamber on to the roof, from which he would bleat in a harsh voice like the mayor's, taunting the turkeys stalking about the yard, and turn his back when he saw his enemies, the boys, who used to jeer at his beard. In Chub's trunks there was plenty of linen and many coats and old-fashioned overdresses with gold lace on them; his wife had been fond of fine clothes. In his kitchen garden, besides poppies, cabbages, and sunflowers, two patches were sown every year with tobacco. Solokha thought that it would not be amiss to join all that to her own farm, and, already reckoning in what good order it would be when it passed into her hands, she doubled the favours she showered upon old Chub. And to prevent her son Vakula from courting Chub's daughter and getting possession of it all himself (then he would very likely not let her interfere in anything), she had recourse to the common manoeuvre of all dames of forty—that is, setting Chub at loggerheads with the blacksmith as often as she could. Possibly these sly tricks and subtlety were the reason why the old women said here and there, particularly when they had drunk a drop too much at some merry gathering, that Solokha was certainly a witch; that the lad Kizyakolupenko had seen a tail on her back no longer than a peasant woman's distaff; that as recently as the Thursday before last she had run across the road in the shape of a black cat; that once a sow had run up to the priest's wife, had crowed like a cock, put Father Kondrat's cap on her head, and run away again.

It so happened that just when the old women were talking about this, Timish Korostyavy, a cowherd, came up. He did not fail to tell them how in the summer, just before St. Peter's Fast, when he had lain down to sleep in the cowshed, putting some straw under his head, he saw with his own eyes a witch, with her hair down, in nothing but her shift, begin milking the cows, and he could not stir, he was so spellbound, and she had smeared his lips with something so nasty that he was spitting the whole day afterwards. But all that was somewhat doubtful, for the only one who could see a witch was the assessor of Sorochintsi. And so all the notable Cossacks waved their hands impatiently when they heard such tales. "They are lying, the bitches!" was their usual answer.

After she had crept out of the stove and set herself to rights, Solokha, like a good housewife, began tidying up and putting everything in its place; but she did not touch the sacks. "Vakula brought those in, let him take them out himself!" she thought. Meanwhile the devil, who had chanced to turn round just as he was flying into the chimney, had caught sight of Chub arm-in-arm with his neighbour, already a long way from home. Instantly he flew out of the chimney, cut across their road and began flinging up heaps of frozen snow. A blizzard rose. All was whiteness in the air. The snow whirled behind and in front, and threatened to plaster up the eyes, the mouth, and the ears of the two friends. And the devil flew back to the chimney again in the firm conviction that Chub would go back home with his neighbour, would find the blacksmith there and probably give him such a dressing down that it would be a long time before he would be able to handle a brush and paint offensive caricatures.

As a matter of fact, as soon as the blizzard began and the wind blew straight in their faces, Chub wished they had never set out, and pulling his fur cap further down on his head showered abuse on himself, the devil, and his friend. His annoyance was feigned, however. Chub was really glad of the snow-storm: they had still eight times as far to go as they had gone already before they would reach the sacristan's. They turned back. The wind blew on the back of their heads, but they could see nothing through the whirling snow.

"Stop, mate! I think we are going wrong," said Chub, after walking on a little. "I cannot see a single cottage. What a snow-storm! You go a little that way, mate, and see whether you can find the road, and meanwhile I'll look this way. It was the foul fiend put it into my head to go trudging out in such a storm. Don't forget to call when you find the road. Oh, what a heap of snow Satan has driven into my eyes!"

The road was not to be seen, however. Chub's friend, turning off, wandered up and down in his high boots, and at last came straight upon the tavern. This lucky find so cheered him that he forgot everything else and, shaking the snow off, walked straight in, not worrying himself in the least about the friend he had left outside. Meanwhile Chub fancied that he had found the road. He stopped and shouted at the top of his voice, but as his friend did not appear he made up his mind to go on alone. After walking on a little he saw his own cottage. Snow-drifts lay all about it and on the roof. Clapping his frozen hands together, he knocked at the door and shouted peremptorily to his daughter to open it.

"What do you want here?" the blacksmith called grimly, as he came out.

Chub, recognizing the blacksmith's voice, stepped back a little. "Oh, so this isn't my cottage," he said to himself. "The blacksmith wouldn't have dropped into my cottage. Though, as I come to look well, it is not the blacksmith's either. Whose cottage may it be? I know! I didn't recognize it! It's where lame Levchenko lives, who has lately married a young woman. His is the only cottage that is like mine. I did think it was a little queer that I had reached home so soon. But Levchenko is at the sacristan's now, I know that. Then why is the blacksmith here? Ha! he comes to see his young wife. So that's it! Good! Now I understand."

"Who are you and what are you hanging about at people's doors for?" said the blacksmith more grimly than before, coming closer up to him.

"I won't tell him who I am," thought Chub. "He might

give me a good drubbing, the bastard." And, disguising his voice, he answered: "It's me, good man! I have come for your diversion to sing *kolyadki* under your windows."

"Go to the devil with your *kolyadki!*" Vakula shouted angrily. "Why are you standing there? Do you hear? Be off with you."

Chub already had that prudent intention; but it annoyed him to have to obey the blacksmith's orders. It seemed as though some evil spirit nudged his arm and compelled him to gainsay. "Why are you bawling like that?" he said in the same voice. "I want to sing *kolyadki*, and that's that!"

"Oh! I see words aren't enough for you!" And upon that Chub felt a very painful blow on his shoulder.

"I see you are beginning to fight!" he said, stepping back a little.

"Be off, be off!" shouted the blacksmith, giving Chub another shove.

"What are you doing?!" said Chub in a voice that betrayed pain, annoyance and timidity. "You are fighting in earnest, I see, and hitting pretty hard, too."

"Be off, be off!" shouted the blacksmith, and slammed the door.

"Look how he swaggers!" said Chub when he was left alone outside. "Just try going near him! What a fellow! Thinks he's a somebody! Do you suppose I won't have the law on you? No, my dear lad, I am going straight to the Commissar. I'll teach you! I don't care if you are a blacksmith and a painter. But I must look at my back and shoulders; I believe they are black and blue. The devil's son must have hit hard. It's a pity that it is cold, and I don't want to take off my coat. You wait, you fiend of a blacksmith; may the devil give you a drubbing and your smithy, too; I'll make you dance! Ah, the damned rascal! But, I say, he is not at home now. I expect Solokha is all alone. H'm, it's not far off, I might go! It's such weather now that no one will come in on us. Perhaps we'll have a chance— Oh, dear, how hard that damned blacksmith did whack!"

Rubbing his back, Chub set off in a different direction. The agreeable possibilities awaiting him in a tryst with Solokha took off the pain a little and made him insensible even to the frost, the crackling of which could be heard on all the roads above the howling of the storm. At moments a look of mawkish sweetness came into his face, though the blizzard had soaped his beard and moustaches with snow more briskly than any barber who tyrannically holds his victim by the nose. But if everything had not been hidden by the criss-cross of the snow, Chub might have been seen long afterwards stopping and rubbing his back as he muttered: "The damned blacksmith did whack hard!" and then going on his way again.

While the nimble dandy with the tail and goat's beard flew out of the chimney and back again, the pouch which hung on a shoulder-belt at his side and in which he had put the stolen moon chanced to catch on something in the stove and came open—and the moon took advantage of it to fly up through the chimney of Solokha's cottage and to float smoothly through the sky. Everything was flooded with light. It was as though there had been no snow-storm. The snow sparkled—a broad silvery plain studded with crystal stars. The frost seemed less cold. Groups of lads and girls appeared with sacks. Songs rang out, and under almost every cottage window were groups of *kolyadki*-singers.

How wonderful is the light of the moon! It is hard to put

into words how pleasant it is on such a night to mingle in a group of singing, laughing girls and among lads ready for every jest and sport which the gaily smiling night can suggest. It is warm under the thick pelisse; the cheeks glow brighter than ever from the frost and the Old Sly himself prompts to mischief.

Groups of girls with sacks burst into Chub's cottage and gathered round Oksana. The blacksmith was deafened by the shouts, the laughter, the stories. They vied with one another in telling the beauty some bit of news, in emptying their sacks and boasting of the little loaves, the sausages, and curd dumplings of which they had already gathered a fair harvest by their singing. Oksana seemed to be delighted, she chatted first with one and then with another, and laughed without ceasing.

The blacksmith looked with envy and vexation at the gaiety, and cursed the *kolyadki*-singing, though he was passionately fond of it himself.

"Oh, Odarka!" cried the light-hearted beauty, turning to one of the girls, "you have new slippers. Ah, how pretty! And with gold on them! You are a lucky girl, Odarka; you have a man who will buy you anything, but I have no one to get me such splendid slippers."

"Don't grieve, my precious Oksana!" put in the blacksmith. "I will get you slippers such as not many a lady wears."

"You!" said Oksana, with a rapid and haughty glance at him. "I should like to know where you'll get hold of slippers such as I could put on my feet. Perhaps you will bring me the very ones the Tsarina wears?"

"See the sort she wants!" cried the girls, laughing.

"Yes!" the beauty went on proudly, "all of you be my witnesses: if the blacksmith Vakula brings me the very slippers the Tsarina wears, here's my word on it, I'll marry him that very day."

The girls walked off with the capricious beauty.

"You may laugh if you like!" thought the blacksmith as he followed them out. "I laugh at myself! I can't understand what's become of my senses! She does not love me—well, what of it! As though there were no one in the world but Oksana. Thank God, there are lots of fine girls besides her in the village. And what is Oksana? She'll never make a good housewife; the only thing she is good at is dressing up. I must end this, really. It's time I gave up making a fool of myself!"

But at the very time when the blacksmith was making up his mind to be firm, some evil spirit set floating before him the laughing image of Oksana as she said mockingly, "Get me the Tsarina's slippers, blacksmith, and I will marry you!" Everything within him was stirred, and he could think of nothing but Oksana.

The crowds of *kolyadki*-singers, the lads in one party and the girls in another, hurried from one street to another. But the blacksmith went on and saw nothing, and took no part in the merry-making which he had once loved more than anyone else had.

Meanwhile the devil was ardently making love to Solokha: he kissed her hand with the same airs and graces as the assessor does the priest's daughter's, put his hand to his heart, sighed, and said bluntly that unless she consented to gratify his passion and duly reward his devotion, he was ready for anything—that he would fling himself in the water and let his soul go straight to hell. Solokha was not so cruel; besides, the devil, as we know, acted hand in glove with her. She was fond of seeing a crowd hanging about her, and was rarely without company. That evening, however, she expected to spend alone, because all the noteworthy inhabitants of the village had been invited to keep Christmas Eve at the sacristan's. But it turned out otherwise: the devil had only just urged his suit, when suddenly they heard a knock and the voice of the stalwart Head. Solokha ran to open the door, while the nimble devil crept into a sack that was lying on the floor.

The Head, after shaking the snow off his cap and drinking a glass of vodka from Solokha's hand, told her that he had not gone to the sacristan's because of the blizzard; and, seeing a light in her cottage, had dropped in, meaning to spend the evening with her.

The Head had hardly finished saying that when they heard a knock at the door and the voice of the sacristan.

"Hide me somewhere," whispered the Head. "I don't want to meet the sacristan now."

Solokha thought for some time where to hide so bulky a visitor; at last she selected the biggest coal sack. She shook the coal out into a barrel, and the stalwart Head—moustaches, cap, pelisse, and all—crept into the sack.

The sacristan walked in, clearing his throat and rubbing his hands, and told her that no one had come to his party and that he was heartily glad of this opportunity to enjoy a visit to her and was not afraid of the snow-storm. Then he went closer to her and, with a cough and smirk, touched her plump bare arm with his long fingers and said with an air expressive both of slyness and satisfaction:

"And what have you here, magnificent Solokha?" And saying this he started back a little.

"How do you mean? My arm, Osip Nikiforovich!" answered Solokha.

"H'm! Your arm, eh? He—he—he!" cried the sacristan, highly delighted with his opening. And he paced up and down the room.

"And what have you here, most precious Solokha?" he said with the same air, going up to her again, lightly touching her neck and skipping back again in the same way.

"As though you don't see, Osip Nikiforovich!" answered Solokha. "My neck and my necklace."

"H'm! A necklace! He—he—he!" And the sacristan walked again up and down the room, rubbing his hands.

"And what have you here, incomparable Solokha?" There is no telling what the sacristan might have touched next with his long fingers unless they had suddenly heard a knock at the door and the voice of the Cossack Chub.

"Good Lord, an intruder!" cried the sacristan in alarm. "What now if I am caught here, a person of my position! It will come to Father Kondrat's ears!"

But the sacristan's apprehensions were really of a different nature; he was more afraid that his doings might come to the knowledge of his better half, whose terrible hand had already turned his thick mane into a very scanty one.

"For God's sake, virtuous Solokha!" he said, trembling all over, "your loving kindness, as it says in the Gospel of St. Luke, chapter thirt— thirt— There's a knock, oh dear, there's a knock! Hide me somewhere!"

Solokha turned the coal out of another sack, and the sacristan, whose proportions were not too ample, crept into it and settled at the very bottom, so that a good half-sack of coal might have been put in on top of him.

"Good evening, Solokha!" said Chub as he came into the cottage. "You didn't expect me, eh? You didn't, did you? Perhaps I am in the way?" Chub went on with a good-humoured and significant expression on his face, which suggested that his slow-moving mind was at work preparing to utter some sarcastic and amusing jest. "Perhaps you had some

entertaining companion here? Perhaps you have someone
in hiding already? Eh?" And enchanted by this observation
of his, Chub laughed, inwardly triumphant at being the only
man to enjoy Solokha's favour. "Well, Solokha, let me have
a drink of vodka now. I believe my throat's frozen stiff
with this damned frost. What weather God has sent us for
Christmas Eve! What a snow-storm, Solokha— Ah, my hands
are stiff, I can't unbutton my sheepskin! What a snow-
storm!"

"Open the door!" a voice rang out in the street, accompanied
by a thump on the door.

"Someone is knocking," said Chub, standing still.

"Open!" the shout rang out even louder.

"It's the blacksmith!" cried Chub, catching up his cap.
"I say, Solokha, put me where you like; for nothing in the
world will I show myself to that damned bastard! May he
have a pimple as big as a haycock under each of his eyes, the
devil's son!"

Solokha, herself alarmed, rushed about like one distraught
and, forgetting what she was doing, motioned to Chub to
creep into the same sack in which the sacristan was already
sitting. The poor sacristan dared not betray his pain by a
cough or a groan when the heavy Cossack sat down almost
on his head and put a frozen boot on each side of his face.

The blacksmith walked in, not saying a word nor removing
his cap, and almost fell down on the bench. It could be seen
that he was in a very bad humour.

At the very moment when Solokha was shutting the door
after him, someone knocked again. This was the Cossack Sverbiguz. This one could not be hidden in a sack, because no sack
big enough could be found anywhere. He was more corpulent
than the Head and taller than Chub's neighbour, Panas. Solokha

therefore led him into the kitchen garden to hear from him all that he had to tell her.

The blacksmith looked absent-mindedly at the corners of his cottage, listening from time to time to the voices of the singers floating far away through the village. At last his eyes rested on the sacks. "Why are those sacks lying there? They ought to have been cleared away long ago. This foolish love has turned me quite silly. Tomorrow's Christmas and rubbish of all sorts is still lying about the cottage. I'll carry them to the smithy!"

Thereupon the blacksmith stooped down to the huge sacks, tied them up tightly, and made ready to hoist them on his shoulders. But it was evident that his thoughts were straying God knows where; or he would have heard how Chub gasped when the hair of his head was twisted in the string that tied the sack and the stalwart Head began hiccuping quite distinctly.

"Can nothing get that wretched Oksana out of my head?" the blacksmith was saying. "I don't want to think about her; but I keep thinking and thinking and, as luck will have it, of nobody but her. Why is it that thoughts creep into my mind against my will? Damn it! the sacks seem to have grown heavier than they were. Something besides coal must have been put into them. I am a fool! I forget that now everything seems heavier to me. In old days I could bend or unbend a copper coin or a horseshoe with one hand, and now I can't lift a few sacks of coal. I shall be blown over by the wind next. No!" he cried, pulling himself together after a pause, "I am not a weakling! I won't let anyone make a mock of me! If there were ten such sacks, I would lift them all." And he briskly hoisted on his shoulders the sacks which two stalwart men could not have carried. "I'll take this one too," he went on, picking up the little one at the bottom of which the devil lay curled up. "I believe I put my tools in this one." Saying this he went out of the hut, whistling the song: "I can't be bothered with a wife."

The singing, laughter, and shouts sounded louder and louder in the streets. The crowds of jostling people were reinforced by new-comers from neighbouring villages. The lads were full of mischief and mad pranks. Often among the *kolyadki* some gay song was heard, made up on the spot by one of the young Cossacks. All at once one of the crowd would let out a New Year's song instead of a carol and bawl at the top of his voice:

> *Christmas faring!*
> *Be not sparing!*
> *A tart or pie, please!*
> *Bowl of porridge!*
> *String of sausage!*

A roar of laughter rewarded the wag. Little windows were thrown up and the withered hand of an old woman (the old women, together with the sedate fathers, were the only people left indoors) was thrust out with a sausage or a piece of pie.

The lads and the girls vied with one another in holding out their sacks and catching their booty. In one place the lads, coming together from all sides, would surround a group of girls. There was loud noise and clamour; one flung a snowball, another pulled away a sack full of all sorts of good things. In another place, the girls would catch a lad, trip him up, and send him flying headlong with his sack into the snow. It seemed as though they were ready to make merry the whole night through. And the night was so splendid! And the light of the moon seemed brighter still from the glitter of the snow.

The blacksmith stood still with his sacks. He fancied he heard among the crowd of girls the voice and ringing laugh of Oksana. Every vein in his body throbbed; flinging the sacks on the ground so that the sacristan at the bottom groaned over the bruise he received, and the Head gave a loud hiccup, he strolled with the little sack on his shoulders together with a group of lads after a crowd of girls, among whom he heard the voice of Oksana.

"Yes, it is she! She stands like a queen, her black eyes sparkling. A handsome lad is telling her something. It must be amusing, for she is laughing. But she is always laughing." As it were unwittingly, he could not say how, the blacksmith squeezed his way through the crowd and stood beside her.

"Oh, you are here, Vakula! Good evening!" said the beauty, with the smile which almost drove Vakula mad. "Well, did you get a lot for your carols? Oh, but what a little sack! And have you got the slippers that the Tsarina wears? Get me the slippers and I will marry you!" And laughing she ran off with the other girls.

The blacksmith stood as though rooted to the spot. "No, I cannot bear it; it's too much for me," he muttered at last. "But, my God, why is she so fiendishly beautiful? Her eyes, her words and everything—they scorch me, they fairly scorch me. No, I cannot master myself. It's time to put an end to it all. Damn my soul, I'll go and drown myself in an ice-hole, and it will all be over!"

Then with a resolute step he walked on, caught up the group of girls, came alongside Oksana, and said in a firm voice, "Farewell, Oksana! Find any lover you like, make a fool of whom you like; but me you will not see again in this world."

The beauty seemed amazed, and would have said something, but with a wave of his hand the blacksmith ran away.

"Where are you off to, Vakula?" cried the lads, seeing the blacksmith running.

"Good-bye, lads!" the blacksmith shouted in answer. "Please God we shall meet again in the next world, but we shall not make merry together again in this. Farewell! Do not think unkindly of me! Tell Father Kondrat to sing a requiem service for my sinful soul. Sinner that I am, for the sake of worldly things I did not finish painting the candles for the icons of the Saint and the Holy Mother. All the goods which will be found in my chest are for the church. Farewell!"

Saying this, the blacksmith ran on with the sack.

"He is gone crazy!" said the lads.

"A lost soul!" an old woman, who was passing, murmured piously. "I must go and tell them that the blacksmith has hanged himself!"

Meanwhile, after running through several streets, Vakula stopped to take breath. "Where am I running as though everything were over already?" he thought. "I'll try one way more: I'll go to the Zaporozhian, Paunchy Patsyuk; they say he knows all the devils and can do anything he likes. I'll go to him, for my soul is lost anyway!"

At that the devil, who had lain for a long while without moving, skipped with joy in the sack; but the blacksmith, thinking that he had somehow twitched the sack with his hand and caused the movement himself, gave the sack a punch with his heavy fist and, shaking it on his shoulders, set off to Paunchy Patsyuk.

Patsyuk at one time *had* been a Zaporozhian Cossack; but

no one knew whether he had been turned out of the camp
or had run away from Zaporozhye of his own accord.

For a long time, ten years or perhaps fifteen, he had been
living in Dikanka. At first he had lived like a true Zaporozhian;
he had done no work, slept three-quarters of the day, ate as
much as six mowers, and drank almost a whole pailful of vodka
at a time. He had somewhere to put it all, however, for though
Patsyuk was not very tall he was fairly bulky in width. Moreover,
the trousers he used to wear were so full that, however long
a step he took, no trace of his leg was visible, and it seemed as
though a wine distiller's butt were moving down the street.
Perhaps that was why he had been nicknamed Paunchy. Before many days had passed after his coming to the village,
everyone knew that he was a sorcerer. If anyone was ill, he
called in Patsyuk at once; Patsyuk had only to whisper a
few words for the ailment to vanish. If a hungry gentleman
happened to be choked by a fish-bone, Patsyuk could clap
him so skilfully on the back that the bone went the proper
way without causing any harm to the gentleman's throat.
Of late years he was rarely seen anywhere. The reason might
be sloth, or the fact that it was every year becoming increasingly
difficult for him to squeeze through a doorway. People
had of late been obliged to go to him if they wanted his
help.

Not without some timidity, the blacksmith opened the
door and saw Patsyuk sitting cross-legged on the floor before
a little tub, on which stood a bowl of dumplings. This bowl
stood on a level with his mouth, as though placed there purposely. Without moving a finger, he bent his head a little
towards the bowl and sipped the soup, from time to time catching
the dumplings with his teeth.

"Well," thought Vakula to himself, "this fellow's even

lazier than Chub: Chub eats with a spoon, but this fellow won't even lift his hand!"

Patsyuk must have been entirely engrossed in the dumplings, for he seemed to be quite unaware of the entrance of the blacksmith, who made him a very low bow as soon as he stepped on the threshold.

"I have come to ask you a favour, Patsyuk," said Vakula, bowing again.

Fat Patsyuk lifted his head and again began swallowing dumplings.

"They say that you—no offence meant—" the blacksmith said, taking heart, "I speak of this not by way of any insult to you—that you are a little akin to the devil."

When he had uttered these words, Vakula was alarmed, thinking that he had expressed himself too bluntly after all and had not sufficiently softened his language, and, expecting that Patsyuk would pick up the tub together with the bowl and throw them straight at his head, he turned aside a little and covered his face with his sleeve so that the hot dumpling soup might not spatter it. But Patsyuk looked up and again began swallowing the dumplings.

The blacksmith, thus encouraged, made up his mind to go on.

"I have come to you, Patsyuk. God give you everything —goods of all sorts in abundance and bread in proportion!" (The blacksmith could sometimes put in a fashionable word: he had got into the way of it during his stay in Poltava when he was painting the fence for the officer.) "There is nothing but ruin before me, a sinner! Nothing in the world will help! What will be, will be. I have to ask help from the devil himself. Well, Patsyuk," the blacksmith said, seeing his unchanged silence, "what am I to do?"

"If you need the devil, then go to the devil," answered Patsyuk, without looking up, as he went on stowing away the dumplings.

"That's just why I've come to you," answered the blacksmith, dropping another bow to him. "I think nobody in the world but you knows the way to him."

Patsyuk answered not a word, but ate up the remaining dumplings.

"Do me a kindness, good man, don't refuse me!" persisted the blacksmith. "Whether it is pork or sausage or buckwheat flour or linen or millet or anything else, in case of need—as is usual between good people—I will not grudge it. Tell me at least how to get on the road to him."

"He need not go far who has the devil on his shoulders!" Patsyuk said indifferently, without changing his position.

Vakula fastened his eyes upon him as though the interpretation of those words were written on the sorcerer's brow. "What does he mean?" his face asked dumbly, while his mouth stood half-open, ready to swallow the first word like a dumpling.

But Patsyuk was silent.

Then Vakula noticed that there were neither dumplings nor a tub before him; but two wooden bowls were standing on the floor instead—one was filled with curd turnovers, the other with cream. His thoughts and his eyes involuntarily fastened on those dainties. "Let us see," he said to himself, "how Patsyuk will eat the turnovers. He certainly won't want to bend down to lap them up like the dumplings; besides he couldn't—he must first dip the turnovers in the cream."

No sooner had he thought this than Patsyuk opened his mouth, looked at the turnovers, and opened his mouth wider still. At that moment a turnover popped out of the bowl, splashed into the cream, turned over on the other side, leapt upwards, and flew straight into his mouth. Patsyuk ate it up and opened his mouth again, and another turnover went through the same performance. The only trouble he took was to munch it up and swallow it.

"My word, what a miracle!" thought the blacksmith, his mouth dropping open with surprise, and at the same moment he was aware that a turnover was on its way into his mouth and had already smeared his lips with cream. Pushing away the turnover and wiping his lips, the blacksmith began to reflect what marvels there are in the world and to what subtle devices the evil spirit may lead a man, saying to himself that no one but Patsyuk could help him.

"I'll bow to him once more, maybe he will explain properly. What the devil, though! Today is a fast day and he is eating turnovers! What a fool I am really, standing here and making ready to sin! Back!" And the pious blacksmith ran headlong out of the cottage.

But the devil sitting in the sack and already gloating over his prey could not bear to let such a glorious catch slip through his fingers. As soon as the blacksmith put down the sack the devil skipped out of it and straddled his neck.

A cold shudder ran over the blacksmith's flesh; pale and scared, he did not know what to do; he was on the point of crossing himself. But the devil, putting his dog's nose down to Vakula's right ear, said: "It's me, your friend; I'll do anything for a friend and comrade! I'll give you as much money as you like," he squeaked into his left ear. "Oksana shall be yours this very day," he whispered, turning his nose again to the blacksmith's right ear.

The blacksmith stood still, thinking.

"Very well," he said at last; "for such a price I am ready to be yours!"

The devil waved his hands in delight and began galloping up and down on the blacksmith's neck. "Now the blacksmith is done for!" he thought to himself: "Now I'll pay you out for all your paintings and slanderous tales thrown up at the devils! What will my comrades say now when they learn that the most pious man of the whole village is in my hands!"

The devil laughed with joy, thinking how he would taunt all the long-tailed crew in hell, how furious the lame devil, who was reckoned the most resourceful among them, would be.

"Well, Vakula," piped the devil, not dismounting from his neck, as though afraid he might escape, "you know nothing is done without a contract."

"I am ready!" said the blacksmith. "I have heard that among you contracts are signed with blood. Wait, I'll get a nail out of my pocket."

Here he put his hand behind him and caught the devil by the tail.

"You are a great one for a joke!" cried the devil, laughing. "Come, let go, that's enough mischief!"

"Wait a bit, friend!" cried the blacksmith. "What do you think of this?" As he said that he made the sign of the cross and the devil became as meek as a lamb. "Wait a bit," said the blacksmith, pulling him by the tail to the ground, "I'll teach you to entice good men and honest Christians into sin."

Here the blacksmith leaped astride on the devil and lifted his hand to make the sign of the cross.

"Have mercy, Vakula!" the devil moaned piteously; "I will do anything you want, anything; only let me off with my life, do not lay the terrible cross upon me!"

"Ah, so that's your note now, you damned German! Now I know what to do. Carry me at once on your back! Do you hear? And fly like a bird!"

"Where?" asked the melancholy devil.

"To Petersburg, straight to the Tsarina!" And the black smith almost swooned with terror, as he felt himself mounting into the air.

Oksana stood for a long time pondering on the strange words of the blacksmith. An inner voice was telling her that she had treated him too cruelly. "What if he does make up his mind to do something dreadful! I shouldn't wonder! Perhaps his sorrow will make him fall in love with another girl, and in his vexation he will begin calling her the greatest beauty in the village. But no, he loves me. I am so beautiful! He will not give me up for anything; he is playing, he is pretending. In ten minutes he will come back to look at me, for certain. I really am too severe. I must, as though it were against my will, let him kiss me. Won't he be delighted!" And the frivolous beauty went back to jesting with her companions.

"Wait," said one of them, "the blacksmith has forgotten his sacks; look what terrible great sacks they are! He has made more by his carol-singing than we have. I fancy they must have been putting here a quarter of a sheep each, and I am sure that there are no end of sausages and loaves in them. Glorious! We shall have enough to feast on for all Christmas week."

"Are they the blacksmith's sacks?" asked Oksana. "Let us drag them to my cottage, quick, and have a good look at what he has put in them."

All the girls laughingly approved of the proposal.

"But we can't lift them!" the whole group cried, trying to move the sacks.

"Wait a minute," said Oksana; "let's run for a sledge and take them away on it!"

And the girls ran out to get a sledge.

The captives were dreadfully bored with staying in the
ᴋcks, although the sacristan had poked a fair-sized hole to
ᴇep through. If there had been no one about, he might have
ᴏund a way to creep out; but to creep out of a sack before
ᴠerybody, to be a laughing-stock—that thought restrained
ɪm, and he made up his mind to wait, only uttering a slight
ᴦoan under Chub's ill-mannered boots.

Chub himself was no less desirous of freedom, feeling that
ᴜere was something under him that was terribly uncomfortable
ᴏ sit upon. But as soon as he heard his daughter's plan he
ᴇlt relieved, and decided not to creep out, reflecting that
ᴛ must be at least a hundred paces, or perhaps two hundred,
ᴏ his hut; if he crept out, he would have to set himself to
ᴦghts, button up his sheepskin, fasten his belt—such a lot
ᴏf trouble! Besides, he had left his cap at Solokha's. Let the
ᴦirls drag him in the sledge.

But things turned out not at all as Chub was expecting.
ᴜst when the girls were running to fetch the sledge, his lean
ᴇighbour, Panas, came out of the tavern, upset and ill-humoured.
ᴛhe woman who kept the tavern could not be persuaded
ᴏ serve him on credit. He thought of sitting on in the tavern
ᴎ the hope that some godly gentleman would come along
ᴎd stand him a drink; but as ill luck would have it, all the
ᴇentlefolk were staying at home and like good Christians were
ᴀting rice and honey in the bosom of their families. Meditating
ᴎ the degeneration of manners and the hard heart of the
ᴇwess who kept the tavern, Panas came upon the sacks and
ᴛopped in amazement.

"What sacks somebody has flung down in the road!" he
ᴀid, looking about him. "I'll be bound there is pork in them.
ᴏme carol-singer is in luck to get so many gifts of all sorts.

What sacks! Suppose they are only stuffed full of buckwheat cakes and biscuits, they are worth having just the same; if there should be nothing but loaves in them, that would be welcome, too; the Jewess would give me a dram of vodka for each loaf. I must make haste and get them away before anyone sees them."

He shouldered the sack with Chub and the sacristan in it, but felt it was too heavy. "No, it'll be too heavy for one to carry," he said; "and here by good luck comes the weaver Shapuvalenko. Good evening, Ostap!"

"Good evening!" said the weaver, stopping.

"Where are you going?"

"Oh, just following my nose."

"Help me carry these sacks, good man! Someone has been singing carols, and has dropped them on the road. We'll go halves over the things."

"Sacks? sacks of what? White loaves or what?"

"All sorts of things, I expect."

They hurriedly pulled some sticks out of the fence, laid a sack on them and carried it on their shoulders.

"Where shall we take it? To the tavern?" the weaver asked on the way.

"That's what I was thinking. But the damned Jewess won't trust us, she'll think we have stolen it somewhere; besides I have only just come from the tavern. We'll take it to my hut. No one will hinder us there, my wife's not at home."

"Are you sure she is not at home?" the prudent weaver inquired.

"I am not quite a fool yet, thank God," said Panas; "the devil only could send me where she is. I think she will be trailing round with the other women till daybreak."

"Who is there?" shouted Panas's wife, opening the door

of the hut as she heard the noise in the outer room made by the two friends with the sack. Panas was dumbfounded.

"Here's a go!" said the weaver helplessly.

Panas's wife was a treasure of the kind that is not uncommon in this world. Like her husband, she hardly ever stayed at home, but almost every day visited various cronies and well-to-do old women, flattered them and ate with good appetite at their expense; she only fought with her husband in the mornings, as it was only then that she sometimes saw him. Their hut was twice as old as the district clerk's trousers; there was no straw in places on their thatched roof. Only the remnants of a fence could be seen, for everyone, as he went out of his house, thought it unnecessary to take a stick for the dogs, relying on passing by Panas's kitchen garden and pulling one out of his fence. The stove was not heated for three days at a time. Whatever the tender wife managed to beg from good Christians she hid as far as possible out of her husband's reach, and often wantonly robbed him of his own gains if he had not had time to spend them on drink. In spite of his habitual imperturbability Panas did not like to give way to her, and consequently left his house nearly every day with both eyes blackened, while his better half, sighing and groaning, waddled off to tell the old women of her husband's unmannerliness and the blows she had to put up with from him.

Now you can imagine how disconcerted the weaver and Panas were by this unexpected apparition. Dropping the sack, they stood before it, and concealed it with the skirts of their coats, but it was too late; Panas's wife, though she did not see well with her old eyes, had observed the sack.

"That's good!" she said, with a face which betrayed the joy of a hawk. "That's good, that you have gained so much by singing carols! That's how it always is with good Christians;

but no, I expect you have filched it somewhere. Show me your sack at once, do you hear, show me this very minute!"

"The bald devil may show you, but not we," said Panas, assuming a dignified air.

"What's it to do with you?" said the weaver. "We sang the *kolyadki*, not you."

"Yes, you will show me, you wretched drunkard!" screamed the wife, striking her tall husband on the chin with her fist and forcing her way towards the sack. But the weaver and Panas manfully defended the sack and compelled her to beat a retreat. Before they recovered themselves the wife ran out again, with a poker in her hands. She nimbly caught her husband a whack on the arms and the weaver one on the back, and reached the sack.

"Why did we let her get at it?" said the weaver, coming to himself.

"Why we let her get at it? Why did you?" said Panas coolly.

"Your poker must be made of iron!" said the weaver after a brief silence, rubbing his back. "My wife bought one last year at the fair—gave twenty-five kopeks for it; but that one's all right—it doesn't hurt."

Meanwhile the triumphant wife, setting the pot-lamp on the floor, untied the sack and peeped into it. But her old eyes, which had so well descried the sack, this time certainly deceived her.

"Oh, but there is a whole pig lying here!" she cried, clapping her hands in glee.

"A pig! Do you hear, a whole pig!" The weaver nudged Panas. "And it's all your fault."

"It can't be helped!" replied Panas, shrugging his shoulders.

"Can't be helped! What are we waiting for? Let us take away the sack! Here, come on! Go away, it's our pig!" shouted the weaver, stepping forward.

"Go along, go along, you devilish woman! It's not your property!" said Panas, approaching.

His spouse picked up the poker again, but at that moment Chub crawled out of the sack and stood in the middle of the room, stretching like a man who had just woken up from a long sleep. Panas's wife shrieked, and they all stood with open mouths.

"Why did she say it was a pig, the silly! It's not a pig!" said Panas, gazing open-eyed.

"My word! What a man has been dropped into a sack!" said the weaver, staggering back in alarm. "You may say what you please, you may burst if you like, but the foul fiend has had a hand in it. Why, he would not go through a window!"

"It's Chub!" cried Panas, looking more closely.

"Who else did you think it was?" said Chub, laughing. "Well, haven't I played you a fine trick? I'll be bound you meant to eat me by way of pork! Wait a bit, I'll console you: there is something else in the sack, if not a whole pig, it's certainly a little porker or some other live beast. Something kept moving under me."

The weaver and Panas rushed to the sack, the lady of the house clutched at the other side of it, and the battle would have been renewed, had not the sacristan, seeing that he had no more chance of concealment, scrambled out of the sack of his own accord.

The woman, astounded, let go of the leg by which she had begun to drag the sacristan out of the sack.

"Here's another of them!" cried the weaver in horror, "The devil knows what has happened to the world! My head's going round. Men are put into sacks instead of loaves or sausages!"

"It's the sacristan!" said Chub, more surprised than any of them. "Well, now! You're a nice one, Solokha! To put one in a sack— I thought at the time her hut was very full of sacks. Now I understand: she had a couple of men hidden in each sack! While I thought it was only me she—What a woman!"

The girls were a little surprised on finding that one sack was missing.

"Well, there is nothing for it, this one will be enough," murmured Oksana.

They took up the sack and dumped it on the sledge.

The Head made up his mind to keep quiet, saying to himself that if he called out to them to untie the sack and let him out, the silly girls would run away, thinking that the devil was in the sack—and he would be left in the street till next day. Meanwhile the girls, linking arms together, flew like a whirlwind with the sledge over the crunching snow. Many of them sat on the sledge for fun; others even clambered on to the top of the Head. The Head made up his mind to endure everything.

At last they arrived, threw open the door into the outer room of the hut, and dragged in the sack amid laughter.

"Let us see what is in it," they all cried, hastening to untie it.

At this point the hiccup which had tormented the Head became so much worse that he began hiccuping and coughing loudly.

"Oh, there is someone in it!" they shrieked, and rushed out in horror.

"What the devil is it? Where are you running off to as though you were all possessed?" said Chub, walking in.

"Oh, Dad!" cried Oksana. "There is someone in the sack!"

"In the sack? Where did you get this sack?"

"The blacksmith left it on the road," they all said at once.

"So that's it; didn't I say so?" Chub thought to himself.

"What are you afraid of? Let us look. Come now, my man—I beg you won't be offended at our not addressing you by your proper name—crawl out of the sack!"

The Head did so.

"Oh!" shrieked the girls.

"So the Head got into one, too," Chub said to himself in bewilderment, scanning him from head to foot. "Well, well!" He could say nothing more.

The Head himself was no less confused and did not know how to begin.

"I expect it is a cold night," he said, addressing Chub.

"There is a bit of a frost," answered Chub. "Allow me to ask you what you rub your boots with, goose fat or tar?" He had not meant to say that; he had meant to ask: "How did you get into that sack, Head?" But somehow he had come to ask something utterly different.

"Tar is better," said the Head. "Well, good night, Chub!" He pulled his cap down over his head and walked out of the hut.

"Why was I such a fool as to ask him what he rubbed his boots with?" said Chub, looking towards the door by which the Head had gone out. "Well, Solokha is a fine one! To put a man like that in a sack! My word, she is a devil of a woman! And I, fool that I am— But where is that damned sack?"

"I threw it into the corner—there is nothing more in it," said Oksana.

"I know all about that; nothing in it, indeed! Bring it here; there is another one in it. Shake it well. What, nothing? The cursed woman! And to look at her she is like a saint, as though she had never tasted anything but lenten fare."

But we will leave Chub to pour out his vexation at leisure, and will go back to the blacksmith, for it must be well past eight.

At first it seemed dreadful to Vakula, particularly when he rose up from the earth to such a height that he could see nothing below, and flew like a fly so close under the moon that if he had not bent down he would have caught his cap on it. But in a little while he gained confidence and even began mocking at the devil. He was extremely amused by the way the devil sneezed and coughed when he took the little cyprus-wood cross off his neck and held it down to him. He purposely raised his hand to scratch his head, and the devil, thinking he was going to make the sign of the cross over him, flew along more swiftly than ever. It was quite light at the height. The air was transparent, bathed in a light silvery mist. Everything was visible, and he could even see a wizard whisk by them, like a hurricane, sitting in a pot, and the stars gathering together to play hide-and-seek, a whole swarm of spirits whirling away in a cloud, a devil dancing in the light of the moon and taking off his cap at the sight of the blacksmith galloping by, a broom flying back home, from which evidently a witch had just alighted at her destination. And many nasty things besides they met. They all stopped at the sight of the blacksmith to stare at him for a moment, and then raced on. The blacksmith flew on till all at once Petersburg flashed before him, glittering with lights. (There happened to be an illumination that day.) The devil, flying over the city gate, turned into a horse and the blacksmith found himself mounted on a fiery steed in the middle of the street.

My goodness! the rattle, the uproar, the brilliant light;

the walls rose up, four storeys on each side; the clatter of horses'
hoofs and the rumble of wheels echoed and resounded from
every quarter; houses seemed to start up out of the ground
at every step; the bridges trembled; carriages raced along;
sledge-drivers and postilions shouted; the snow crunched
under the thousand sledges flying from all parts; people passing
along on foot huddled together, crowded under the houses
which were studded with little lamps, and their immense
shadows flitted over the walls with their heads reaching the
roofs and the chimneys.

The blacksmith looked about him in amazement. It seemed
to him as though all the houses had fixed their innumerable
fiery eyes upon him, watching. He saw so many gentlemen
in cloth overcoats that he did not know whom to take off his
cap to. "Good gracious, what a lot of gentry here!" thought
the blacksmith. "I fancy everyone who comes along the street
in a fur coat is an assessor and again an assessor! And those
who are driving about in such wonderful chaises with glass
windows, if they are not mayors they certainly must be commissars, or perhaps something grander still." His thoughts
were cut short by a question from the devil:

"Am I to go straight to the Tsarina?"

"No, I'm frightened," thought the blacksmith. "The Zaporozhian Cossacks who rode in the autumn through Dikanka are
stationed somewhere here. They came from the camp with
papers for the Tsarina; anyway I might ask their advice."

"Hey, Satan! Get into my pocket and take me to the
Zaporozhians!"

And in one minute the devil became so thin and small that
he had no difficulty in creeping into the blacksmith's pocket.
And before Vakula had time to look round he found himself
in front of a big house, went up a staircase, hardly knowing

what he was doing, opened a door and drew back a little from
the brilliant light on seeing the smartly furnished room; but
he regained confidence a little when he recognized the Zaporozhians who had ridden through Dikanka and now, sitting
on silk-covered sofas, their tar-smeared boots tucked under
them, were smoking the strongest tobacco.

"Good day to you, gentlemen! God be with you, this is
where we meet again," said the blacksmith, going up to them
and swinging off a low bow.

"Who is that man?" the one who was sitting just in front
of the blacksmith asked another who was further away.

"You don't know me?" said the blacksmith. "It's me, Vakula,
the blacksmith! When you rode through Dikanka in the autumn
you stayed nearly two days there. God give you all health
and long years! And I put a new iron hoop on the front wheel
of your chaise!"

"Oh!" said the same Zaporozhian, "it's that blacksmith
who paints so well. Good day to you, neighbour! What business
brings you here?"

"I just wanted to have a look round. I was told—"

"Well, neighbour," said the Zaporozhian, drawing himself
up with dignity and, wishing to show he could speak Russian,
added with a strong Ukrainian accent: "Well, it's a big city,
isn't it?"

The blacksmith, too, wanted to keep up his credit and not
to seem like a novice. Moreover, as we have had occasion to
see before, he, too, could speak like a book.

"A considerable town!" he answered carelessly, likewise
in Russian. "There is no denying the houses are very large,
the pictures that are hanging up are uncommonly good. Many
of the houses are painted with letters in gold leaf to exuberance.
The proportion is superb, sure enough!"

The Zaporozhians, hearing the blacksmith express himself so freely, drew the most flattering conclusions in regard to him.

"We will have more talk with you later, neighbour; but now we are going to the Tsarina."

"To the Tsarina? Oh, be so kind, gentlemen, as to take me with you!"

"You?" a Zaporozhian pronounced in the tone in which a grown-up speaks to his four-year-old charge when the latter asks to be mounted on a real big horse. "What would you do there? No, we can't do that. We are going to talk about our own affairs to the Tsarina." And his face assumed an expression of great significance.

"Do take me!" the blacksmith persisted. "Ask them to!" he whispered softly to the devil, banging on the pocket with his fist.

He had hardly said this when another Zaporozhian brought out, "Let us take him, mates!"

"Yes, let us!" others joined in.

"Put on the same dress as we are wearing, then."

The blacksmith was hastily putting on a green tunic when all at once the door opened and a man covered with gold lace said it was time to go.

Again the blacksmith was moved to wonder, as he was whisked along in an immense coach swaying on springs, as four-storeyed houses raced by him on both sides and the rumbling pavement seemed to be moving under the horses' hoofs.

"My goodness, how light it is!" thought the blacksmith to himself. "At home it is not so light as this even in the day-time."

The coaches stopped in front of the palace. The Zaporozhians got out, went into a magnificent vestibule, and began ascending a brilliantly lighted staircase.

"What stairs!" the blacksmith murmured to himself. "It's a pity to trample it with one's feet. What decorations! They say the stories tell lies. The devil a bit they do! My goodness! What banisters, what workmanship! Quite fifty rubles must have gone on the iron alone."

When they had mounted the staircase, the Zaporozhians walked through the first drawing-room. The blacksmith followed them timidly, afraid of slipping on the parquet at every footstep. They walked through three drawing-rooms, the blacksmith still overwhelmed with admiration. On entering the fourth, he could not help going up to a picture hanging on the wall. It was the Holy Virgin with the Child in her arms.

"What a picture! What a wonderful painting!" he thought. "It seems to be speaking! It seems to be alive! And the Holy Child! It's pressing its little hands together and smiling, poor thing! And the colours! My, what colours! I fancy there is not a kopek's worth of ochre on it—it's all emerald green and crimson lake. And the blue simply glows. A fine piece of work! I expect the priming was put in with the most expensive white lead. Wonderful as that painting is, though, this copper handle," he went on, going up to the door and fingering the lock, "is even more wonderful. Ah, what a fine finish! That's all done, I suppose, by German blacksmiths, and most expensive."

Perhaps the blacksmith would have gone on in the same manner for a long time, if a flunkey in livery had not nudged his arm and reminded him not to lag behind the others. The Zaporozhians passed through two more rooms and then stopped. They were told to wait in the third, in which there were several generals in gold-laced uniforms. The Zaporozhians bowed right and left and stood all together.

A minute later, a rather thickset man of majestic stature, wearing the uniform of Hetman and yellow boots, walked in, accompanied by a regular suite. His hair was tousled, and he squinted a little; his face wore an expression of haughty dignity, and his every movement bespoke the habit of command. All the generals, who had been walking up and down rather superciliously in their gold uniforms, bustled about and seemed with low bows to be hanging on every word he uttered, and even on his slightest gesture, so as to rush at once to carry out his wishes. But the Hetman took no notice af all that; he barely nodded to them and went up to the Zaporozhians.

The Zaporozhians all bowed down to the ground.

"Are you all here?" he drawled, speaking a little through his nose.

"All, *Batko*!*" answered the Zaporozhians, bowing again.

"Don't forget to speak as I have told you."

"We will not forget, *Batko.*"

"Is that the Tsar?" asked the blacksmith of one of the Zaporozhians.

"Tsar, indeed! It's Potemkin himself," answered the other.

Voices were heard in the other room, and the blacksmith did not know which way to look for the number of ladies who walked in, wearing satin gowns with long trains, and courtiers in gold-laced coats with their hair tied in a tail at the back. He could see a blur of brilliance and nothing more.

The Zaporozhians all fell down on their hands and knees and cried out with one voice: "Have mercy, *Mamo***, mercy!"

The blacksmith, too, stretched himself very zealously on the floor, though he saw nothing.

"Get up!" an imperious and at the same time pleasant voice sounded above them. Some of the courtiers bustled about and nudged the Zaporozhians.

* Ukrainian for Father.—*Ed.*
** Ukrainian for Mother.—*Ed.*

"We will not get up, *Mamo!* We will not get up! We will die, but we will not get up!" shouted the Zaporozhians.

Potemkin bit his lips. At last he went up himself and whispered peremptorily to one of the Zaporozhians. They rose to their feet.

Then the blacksmith, too, ventured to raise his head, and saw standing before him a short and, indeed, rather stout woman with blue eyes, and at the same time with that majestic radiant air which was so well able to subdue everyone and could only belong to a queen.

"His Excellency has promised to make me acquainted today with my people whom I have not hitherto seen," said the lady with the blue eyes, scrutinizing the Zaporozhians with curiosity. "Are you well cared for here?" she went on, going nearer to them.

"Yes, thank you, *Mamo!* The provisions they give us are excellent, though the mutton here is not all like what we have in Zaporozhye. But we are getting along."

Potemkin frowned, seeing that the Zaporozhians were saying something quite different from what he had taught them.

One of the Zaporozhians, drawing himself up with dignity, stepped forward:

"Be gracious, *Mamo!* Why do you punish your faithful people? How have we angered you? Have we taken the hand of the vile Tatar? Have we come to agreement with the Turk? Have we been false to you in deed or in thought? Why have we lost your favour? First we heard that you were commanding fortresses to be built everywhere against us; then we heard you meant to make us into regular soldiers; now we hear of new misfortunes coming. Wherein are the Zaporozhian troops in fault? In having brought your army across the Perekop and helped your generals to beat the Crimeans?"

Potemkin carelessly rubbed with a little brush the diamonds with which his hands were studded, and said nothing.

"What is it you want?" Catherine asked solicitously.

The Zaporozhians looked meaningly at one another.

"Now is the time! The Tsarina asks what we want!" the blacksmith said to himself, and he suddenly flopped down on the floor.

"Your Royal Majesty, do not command me to be punished! Show me mercy! Of what, be it said without offence to your Royal Grace, are the little slippers made that are on your feet? I fancy there is no shoemaker in any kingdom in the world can make them like that. Merciful heavens, if only my wife could wear slippers like that!"

The Empress laughed. The courtiers laughed too. Potemkin frowned and smiled all at once. The Zaporozhians nudged the blacksmith under the arm, wondering whether he had not gone mad.

"Rise!" the Empress said graciously. "If you wish so much to have slippers like these, it is very easy to arrange it. Bring him at once the very best slippers with gold on them! Indeed, this simple-heartedness greatly pleases me. Here you have a subject worthy of your witty pen!" the Empress went on, turning to a middle-aged gentleman with a full but rather pallid face, who stood a little apart from the others and whose modest coat with big mother-of-peal buttons on it showed that he was not one of the courtiers.

"You are too gracious, your Imperial Majesty. It needs a La Fontaine at least to do justice to it!" answered the man with the mother-of-pearl buttons, bowing.

"I tell you sincerely, I have not yet got over my delight at your *Brigadier*.* You read so wonderfully well! I have heard,

* The comedy *Brigadier* was written by the Russian satirist D. I. Fonvizin (1745-1792).—*Ed.*

though," the Empress went on, turning again to the Zaporozhians, "that none of you are married in the Sech."

"How can that be, *Mamo!* You know yourself that a man cannot live without a wife," answered the Zaporozhian who had talked to the blacksmith, and the blacksmith wondered, hearing him address the Tsarina as though purposely in coarse language, speaking like a peasant, though he could speak like a book.

"They are sly fellows!" he thought to himself. "I suppose he does not do that for nothing."

"We are not monks," the Zaporozhian went on, "but sinful folk. Ready like all honest Christians to fall into sin. There are among us many who have wives, but do not live with them in the Sech. There are some who have wives in Poland; there are some who have wives in the Ukraine; there are some who have wives even in Turkey."

At that moment they brought the blacksmith the slippers.

"My goodness, what fine embroidery!" he cried joyfully, taking the slippers. "Your Royal Majesty! Since the slippers on your feet are like these—and in them Your Honour, I expect, goes skating on the ice—what must the feet themselves be like! They must be made of pure sugar at least, I should think!"

The Empress, who had in fact very well-shaped and charming feet, could not help smiling at hearing such a compliment from the lips of a simple-hearted blacksmith, who in his Zaporozhian dress might be reckoned a handsome fellow in spite of his swarthy face.

Delighted with such gracious attention, the blacksmith would have liked to question the pretty Tsarina thoroughly about everything: whether it was true that tsars eat nothing but honey, fat bacon, and the like; but feeling that the Zaporozhians were digging him in the ribs, he made up his mind to keep quiet. And when the Empress, turning to the older men, began questioning them about their manner of life and customs in the Sech, he stepped back, stooped down to his pocket, and said softly: "Take me away from here and make haste!" And at once he found himself outside the city gates.

"He is drowned! On my word he is drowned! May I never leave this spot if he is not drowned!" lisped the weaver's fat wife, standing with a group of Dikanka women in the middle of the street.

"Why, am I a liar then? Have I stolen anyone's cow? Have I put the evil eye on someone, that I am not to be believed?" shouted a purple-nosed woman in a Cossack jacket, waving her arms. "May I never want to drink water again if old Pereperchikha didn't see with her own eyes the blacksmith hanging himself!"

"Has the blacksmith hanged himself? Well, I never!" said the Head, coming out of Chub's hut, and he joined the group.

"You had better say, may you never want to drink vodka, you old drunkard!" answered the weaver's wife. "He had need to be as mad as you to hang himself! He drowned himself! He drowned himself in the ice-hole! I know that as well as I know that you were in the tavern just now."

"You hussy! See what she throws up against me!" the woman with the purple nose retorted wrathfully. "You had better hold your tongue, you wretch! Do you think I don't know that the sacristan comes to see you every evening?"

The weaver's wife flared up.

"What about the sacristan? Whom does the sacristan go to? What lies are you telling?"

"The sacristan?" squeezing her way up to the combatants,

piped the sacristan's wife in a blue cotton coat lined with hare-skin. "I'll show you the sacristan! Who was it said the sacristan?"

"This is the hussy the sacristan visits!" said the woman with the purple nose, pointing to the weaver's wife.

"So it's you, you bitch!" said the sacristan's wife, stepping up to the weaver's wife. "So it's you, is it, witch, who cast a spell over him and give him a foul potion to make him come to you!"

"Get thee behind me, Satan!" said the weaver's wife, stagger-ing back.

"Oh, you cursed witch, may you never live to see your child-ren! Wretched creature!"

Here the sacristan's wife spat straight into the other woman's face.

The weaver's wife endeavoured to do the same, but spat instead on the unshaven chin of the Head, who had come close up to the combatants that he might hear the quarrel better.

"Ah, nasty woman!" cried the Head, wiping his face with the skirt of his coat and lifting his whip.

This gesture sent them all flying in different directions, scolding loudly.

"How disgusting!" repeated the Head, still wiping his face. "So the blacksmith is drowned! My goodness! What a fine painter he was! What good knives and reaping-hooks and ploughs he could forge! What a strong man he was! Yes," he went on musing, "there are not many fellows like him in our village. To be sure, I did notice while I was in that damned sack that the poor fellow was very much depressed. So that is the end of the blacksmith! He was, and now he is no more. And I was going to have my dapple mare shod!"

And filled with such Christian reflections, the Head quietly made his way to his own cottage.

Oksana was much troubled when the news reached her. She put little faith in Pereperchikha's having seen it and in the women's talk; she knew that the blacksmith was too pious to send his soul to perdition. But what if he really had gone away, intending never to return to the village? And, indeed, in any place it would be hard to find as fine a fellow as the blacksmith. How he loved her! He had borne with her caprices longer than anyone of them. All night long the beauty turned over from her right side to her left and from her left to her right, and could not go to sleep. Now tossing in bewitching nakedness, which the darkness concealed even from herself, she reviled herself almost aloud; now growing quieter, she made up her mind to think of nothing—and kept thinking all the time. She was in a perfect fever, and by the morning she was head over ears in love with the blacksmith.

Chub expressed neither pleasure nor sorrow at Vakula's fate. His thoughts were absorbed by one subject: he could not forget the treachery of Solokha and never left off abusing her even in his sleep.

Morning came. Even before daybreak the church was full of people. Elderly women in white linen wimples, in white cloth jackets, crossed themselves piously at the church porch. Ladies in green and yellow blouses, some even in dark blue overdresses with gold flourishes behind, stood in front of them. Girls who had a whole shopful of ribbons twined on their heads, and necklaces, crosses, and coins round their necks, tried to make their way closer to the icon-stand. But in front of all stood the gentlemen and humble peasants with moustaches, with scalp-locks, with thick necks and newly-shaven chins, for the most part wearing hooded cloaks, below which peeped a white or sometimes a dark blue jacket. Wherever one looked every face had a festive air. The Head was licking his lips in anticipation of

the sausage with which he would break his fast; the girls were
thinking how they would skate with the lads on the ice; the
old women murmured prayers more zealously than ever. All
over the church one could hear the Cossack Sverbiguz bowing
to the ground. Only Oksana stood feeling unlike herself: she
prayed without praying. So many different feelings, each more
vexing, each more distressing than the other, crowded upon her
heart that her face expressed nothing but overwhelming confusion; tears quivered in her eyes. The girls could not think
why it was and did not suspect that the blacksmith was responsible. However, not only Oksana was concerned about the
blacksmith. All the villagers observed that the holiday did not
seem like a holiday, that something was lacking. To make
things worse, the sacristan was hoarse after his travels in the
sack and he wheezed scarcely audibly; it is true that the chorister
who was on a visit to the village sang the bass splendidly,
but how much better it would have been if they had had the
blacksmith, too, who used always when they were singing *Our
Father* or the *Holy Cherubim* to step up into the choir and from
there sing it with the same chant with which it was sung in
Poltava. Moreover, he alone performed the duty of a churchwarden. Matins were already over; after matins mass was
over... Where indeed could the blacksmith have vanished to ?

In the early hours the devil flew even more swiftly back
with the blacksmith, and in a trice Vakula found himself by
his own cottage. At that moment the cock crowed.

"Where are you off to ?" cried the blacksmith, catching the
devil by his tail as he was about to run away. "Wait a bit,
friend, that's not all: I haven't thanked you yet." Then, seizing
a switch, he gave him three lashes and the poor devil set to

running like a peasant who has just had a hiding from the assessor. And so, instead of tricking, tempting, and fooling others, the enemy of mankind was fooled himself. After that Vakula walked into the outer room, made himself a hole in the hay, and slept till dinner-time. When he woke up he was frightened at seeing that the sun was already high. "I've overslept myself and missed matins and mass!"

Then the pious blacksmith was overwhelmed with distress, thinking that no doubt God, as a punishment for his sinful intention of damning his soul, had sent this heavy sleep, which had prevented him from even being in church on this solemn holiday. However, comforting himself with the thought that next week he would confess all this to the priest and that from that day on he would make fifty bows a day for a whole year, he glanced into the cottage; but there was no one there. Apparently Solokha had not yet returned.

Carefully he drew out from the breast of his coat the slippers and again marvelled at the costly workmanship and the wonderful adventure of the previous night. He washed and dressed himself in his best, put on the very clothes which he had got from the Zaporozhians, took out of a chest a new cap of good astrakhan with a dark blue top not once worn since he had bought it while staying in Poltava; he also took out a new girdle of rainbow colours; he put all this together with a whip in a kerchief and set off straight to see Chub.

Chub opened his eyes wide when the blacksmith walked into his cottage, and did not know what to wonder at most—the blacksmith's having risen from the dead, his having dared to come to see him, or his being dressed up such a dandy, like a Zaporozhian. But he was even more astonished when Vakula untied the kerchief and laid before him a new cap and a girdle such as had never been seen in the village, and then plumped down on his knees before him, and said in a tone of entreaty: "Have mercy, *Batko!* Beat me if you like but don't be angry! Here is a whip; beat me as much as your heart may desire. I give myself up, I repent of everything! Beat, only be not wroth. You were once a comrade of my father's, you ate bread and salt together and drank the cup of goodwill."

It was not without secret satisfaction that Chub saw the blacksmith, who had never knocked under to anyone in the village and who could twist five-kopek pieces and horseshoes in his hands like pancakes, lying now at his feet. In order to keep up his dignity still more, Chub took the whip and gave him three strokes on the back.

"Well, that's enough; get up! Always obey your elders! Let us forget everything that has passed between us. Now tell me what it is that you want."

"Give me Oksana to wife, *Batko!*"

Chub thought a little, looked at the cap and the girdle. The cap was delightful and the girdle was not inferior to it; he thought of the treacherous Solokha and said resolutely: "Good! Send the matchmakers!"

"Ah!" cried Oksana as she crossed the threshold and saw the blacksmith, and she gazed at him with astonishment and delight.

"Look, what slippers I have brought you!" said Vakula. "They are the same as the Tsarina wears!"

"No, no! I don't want slippers!" she said, waving her arms and keeping her eyes fixed upon him. "I am willing without slippers—" She blushed and could say no more.

The blacksmith went up to her and took her by the hand; the beauty looked down. Never before had she looked so exquisitely lovely. The enchanted blacksmith gently kissed her; her face flushed crimson and she was lovelier still.

The bishop of blessed memory was driving through Dikanka. He admired the site on which the village stands, and as he drove down the street he stopped before a new cottage.

"And whose is this cottage so gaily painted?" asked his reverence of a beautiful woman, who was standing near the door with a baby in her arms.

"The blacksmith Vakula's," Oksana, for it was she, told him, bowing.

"Splendid! splendid work!" said his reverence, examining the doors and windows. The windows were all outlined with red paint; everywhere on the doors there were Cossacks on horseback with pipes in their teeth.

But his reverence was even warmer in his praise of Vakula when he learned that by way of church penance he had painted free of charge the whole of the left choir green with red flowers.

Nor was that all. On the wall, to one side as you go in at the church, Vakula had painted the devil in hell—such a loathsome figure that everyone spat as he passed. And the women would take a child up to the picture, if it went on crying in their arms, and would say: "There, look! What a fright!" And the child, restraining its tears, would steal a glance at the picture and nestle closer to its mother.

A TERRIBLE REVENGE

I

There was a bustle and an uproar in a quarter of Kiev: Captain Gorobets of the Cossacks was celebrating his son's wedding. A great many people had come as guests. In old days they liked good fare, better still liked drinking, and best of all they liked merry-making. Among others the Zaporozhian Mikitka came on his sorrel horse straight from a riotous feast at the Pereshlai Plain where for seven days and seven nights he had been plying the Polish king's soldiers with red wine. The captain's adopted brother, Danilo Burulbash, came too, with his young wife Katerina and his twelve-month-old son, from

beyond the Dnieper, where his homestead lay between two
hills. The guests marvelled at the fair face of young Katerina,
her eyebrows black as German velvet, her smart cloth dress
and petticoats of blue silk, and her boots with silver heels;
but they marvelled still more that her old father had not come
with her. He had been living in that region for scarcely a year,
and for twenty-one years before nothing had been heard of
him and he had only come back to his daughter when she was
married and had borne a son. No doubt he would have many
strange stories to tell. How could he fail to have them, after
being so long in foreign parts! Everything there is different:
the people are not the same and there are no Christian churches.
But he had not come.

They brought the guests mulled vodka with raisins and
plums in it and a wedding-loaf on a big dish. The musicians
fell to upon the bottom crust in which coins had been baked
and put their fiddles, cymbals, and tambourines down for a
brief rest. Meanwhile the girls and young women, after wiping
their mouths with embroidered handkerchiefs, stepped out
again; and the lads, putting their arms akimbo and looking
haughtily about them, were on the point of going to meet
them, when the old captain brought out two icons to bless the
young couple. These icons had come to him from the venerable
hermit, Father Varfolomey. They had no rich setting, there
was no gleam of gold or silver on them, but no evil power dared
approach the man in whose house they stood. Raising the icons
high the captain was about to deliver a brief prayer when all
at once the children playing on the ground cried out in terror,
and the people drew back, and everyone pointed in alarm at
a Cossack who was standing in their midst. Who he was nobody
knew. But he had already danced splendidly and had diverted
the people standing round him. But when the captain lifted

up the icons, at once the Cossack's face completely changed: his nose grew bigger and twisted to one side, his eyes turned from brown to green, his lips became blue, his chin quivered and grew pointed like a spear, a tusk peeped out of his mouth, a hump appeared behind his head, and the Cossack turned into an old man.

"It is he! It is he!" shouted the crowd, huddling close together.

"The wizard has appeared again!" cried the mothers, snatching up their children.

Majestically and with dignity the captain stepped forward and, turning the icons towards him, said in a loud voice: "Avaunt, image of Satan! This is no place for you!" And hissing and clacking his teeth like a wolf, the strange old man vanished.

Talk and conjecture arose among the people and the hubbub was like the roar of the sea in a storm.

"What is this wizard?" asked young people who knew nothing about him.

"There will be trouble!" muttered their elders, shaking their heads. And everywhere about the spacious courtyard folks gathered in groups listening to the story of the dreadful wizard. But almost everyone told it differently and no one could tell anything certain about him.

A barrel of mead was rolled out and many gallons of Greek wine were brought into the yard. The guests regained their light-heartedness. The orchestra struck up—the girls, the young women, the gallant Cossacks in their gay-coloured coats whirled round in the dance. After a glass or two, old folks of ninety, or a hundred, fell to dancing too, remembering the years that had not passed in vain. They feasted till late into the night and feasted as none feasts nowadays. The guests began to disperse, but only a few made their way home: many of them stayed to spend the night in the captain's wide courtyard; and even

more Cossacks dropped to sleep uninvited under the benches,
on the floor, by their horses, by the cowshed; wherever the
tipplers stumbled there they lay, snoring for the whole town
to hear.

II

There was a soft light all over the earth: the moon had come
up from behind the hill. It covered the steep bank of the Dnieper
as with a costly damask muslin, white as snow, and the shadows
drew back further into the pine forest.

A boat, hollowed out of an oak tree, was floating down the
Dnieper. Two lads were sitting in the bow; their black Cossack
caps were cocked on one side, and the spray flew from their
oars like sparks from a flint.

Why were the Cossacks not singing? They were not telling
of the Polish priests who went about the Ukraine, forcing
the Cossacks to turn Catholic, nor of the two days' battle
with the Tatars at the Salt Lake. But how could they sing,
how could they tell of gallant deeds when their lord, Danilo,
was plunged in thought, and the sleeve of his crimson tunic
hung out of the boat and trailed in the water; their mistress,
Katerina, was softly rocking her child, her eyes fixed upon
it, while her elegant cloth gown, unguarded by its linen cover,
was splashed by the fine grey dust of the spray.

It is a pleasure to look from mid-Dnieper at the high hills
and broad meadows and green forests. Those hills are not
hills: they end in peaks below, as above, and both under and
above them lie the high heavens. Those forests on the slopes
are not forests: they are the hair that covers the shaggy head
of the wood-demon. Down below he washes his beard in the
water, and under his beard and over his head lie the high heavens.

Those meadows are not meadows: they are a green girdle encircling the round sky; and the moon hangs above and below it.

Lord Danilo did not look about him; he looked at his young wife. "Why are you plunged in sadness, my young wife, my golden Katerina?"

"I am not plunged in sadness, my lord Danilo! I am full of dread at the strange tales about the wizard. They say he was born so terrible to look at, and not one of the children would play with him. Listen, my lord Danilo, what dreadful things they say: he fancied all were mocking at him. If he met a man in the dark he thought that he opened his mouth and grinned at him; and next day they found that man dead. I marvelled and was frightened hearing those tales," said Katerina, taking out a handkerchief and wiping the face of the sleeping child. The handkerchief had been embroidered by her with leaves and berries in red silk.

Lord Danilo said not a word, but looked into the darkness where, far away beyond the forest, there was the dark ridge of an earthen wall and beyond the wall rose an old castle. Three lines furrowed his brow; his left hand stroked his gallant moustaches.

"It is not that he is a wizard that is terrible," he said, "but that he is an evil guest. What whim has brought him hither? I have been told that the Poles mean to build a fort to cut us off from the Zaporozhians. That may be true. I will scatter that devil's nest if any rumour reaches me that he harbours our foes there. I will burn the old wizard so that even the ravens will find nothing to peck at. I fancy he has gold and wealth of all kinds. It is there the devil lives! If he has gold—We shall soon pass by the crosses—that's the graveyard! There his evil forefathers lie rotting. I am told they were all ready to sell themselves to Satan for money—soul and threadbare coat and all. If truly he has gold, there is no need to tarry: there is not always booty to be won in war!"

"I know what you are planning: my heart bodes no good from your meeting him. But you are breathing so hard, you are looking so fierce, your brows are knitted so angrily above your eyes—"

"Hold your peace, woman!" said Danilo angrily. "If one has dealings with you, one will turn woman oneself. Lad, give me a light for my pipe!" Here he turned to one of the rowers who, knocking some hot ash from his pipe, began putting it into his master's. "She would scare me with the wizard!" Danilo went on. "A Cossack, thank God, fears neither devil nor Polish priest. What should we come to if we listened to women, my lads, eh? The best wife for us is a pipe and a sharp sabre!"

Katerina sat silent, looking down into the slumbering river; and the wind ruffled the water and the Dnieper shimmered with silver like a wolf's skin in the night.

The boat turned and hugged the wooded bank. A graveyard came in sight; tumbledown crosses stood huddled together. No guelder rose grew among them and no grass; only the moon warmed them from the heavenly heights.

"Do you hear the shouts, lads? Someone is calling for our help!" said Danilo, turning to his oarsmen.

"We hear shouts, and seemingly from that bank," the two lads cried together, pointing to the graveyard.

But all was still again. The boat turned, following the curve of the projecting bank. All at once the rowers dropped their oars and stared before them without moving. Danilo stared too; a chill of horror ran through the Cossack's veins.

A cross on one of the graves tottered and a withered corpse rose up out of the earth. Its beard reached to the waist; the claws on its fingers were longer than the fingers themselves. It slowly raised its hands upwards. Its face was all twisted and distorted. One could see it was suffering terrible torments. "I am stifling, stifling!" it moaned in a dreadful, inhuman voice. Its voice seemed to scrape on the heart like a knife, and suddenly the corpse disappeared under the earth. Another cross tottered and again a dead body came forth, more terrible and taller than the one before; it was all hairy, with a beard to its knees and even longer claws. Still more terribly it shouted, "I am stifling," and vanished into the earth. A third cross tottered and a third corpse rose. It seemed like a skeleton rising from the earth; its beard reached to its heels; the claws on its fingers pierced the ground. Terribly it raised its hands towards the sky as though it would seize the moon, and shrieked as though someone were sawing its yellow bones.

The child asleep on Katerina's lap screamed and woke up; the lady screamed too; the oarsmen let their caps fall in the river; even their master shuddered.

Suddenly it all vanished as though it had never been; but it was a long time before the rowers took up their oars again. Burulbash looked anxiously at his young wife who, terrified, was rocking the screaming child in her arms; he pressed her to his heart and kissed her on the forehead.

"Don't be afraid, Katerina! Look, there is nothing!" he said, pointing around. "It's the wizard who would frighten folk, that none may dare break into his foul nest. He will scare but women by that! Let me hold my son!"

With those words Danilo lifted up his son and kissed him. "Well, Ivan, you are not afraid of wizards, are you? Say: 'No, Daddy, I'm a Cossack!' Stop, give over crying! Soon we shall be home. Then Mother will give you your porridge, put you to bed in your cradle, and sing:

> *Lullaby, my little son,*
> *Lullaby to sleep!*
> *Play about and grow a man!*
> *To the glory of the Cossacks*
> *And confusion of our foes.*

Listen, Katerina. I fancy that your father will not live at
peace with us. He was sullen, gloomy, as though angry when
he came. If he doesn't like it, why come? He would not drink
to Cossack freedom. He has never dandled the child. At first
I would have trusted him with all that lay in my heart, but
I could not do it, the words stuck in my throat. No, he has
not a Cossack heart! When Cossack hearts meet, they almost
leap out to greet each other. Well, my dear lads, is the bank
near? I will give you new caps. You, Stetsko, I will give one
made of velvet and gold. I took it from a Tatar with his head;
all his trappings came to me; I let nothing go but his soul.
Well, land here! Here, we are home, Ivan, but still you cry!
Take him, Katerina."

They all got out. A thatched roof came into view behind
the hill: it was Danilo's ancestral home. Beyond it was another
hill, and then the open plain, and there you might travel a
hundred miles and not see a single Cossack.

III

Danilo's house lay between two hills in a narrow valley
that ran down to the Dnieper. It was a low-pitched house
like a humble Cossack's cottage and there was only one large
room in it; but he and his wife and their old serving-woman
and a dozen picked lads all had their place in it. There were

oak shelves running round the walls at the top. Bowls and cooking-pots were piled upon them. Among them were silver goblets and drinking-cups mounted in gold, gifts or booty brought from wars. Lower down hung costly sabres, muskets, arquebuses, spears; willingly or unwillingly, they had come from the Tatars, the Turks, and the Poles, and many a dent there was in them. Looking at them, Danilo was reminded as by tokens of his encounters. At the bottom of the wall were smooth-planed oak benches; beside them, in front of the stove-couch, the cradle hung on cords from a ring fixed in the ceiling. The whole floor of the room was beaten hard and plastered with clay. On the benches slept Danilo and his wife; on the stove-couch the old serving-woman; the child played and was lulled to sleep in the cradle; and on the floor the serving-men slept in a row. But a Cossack likes best to sleep on the flat earth in the open air; he needs no feather bed nor pillow; he piles fresh hay under his head and stretches at his ease upon the grass. It rejoices his heart to wake up in the night and look at the lofty sky spangled with stars and to shiver at the chill of night which refreshes his Cossack bones; stretching and muttering in his sleep, he lights his pipe and wraps himself more closely in his sheepskin.

Burulbash did not wake early after the merry-making of the day before; when he woke he sat on a bench in a corner and began sharpening a new Turkish sabre, for which he had just bartered something; and Katerina set to work embroidering a silken towel with gold thread.

All at once Katerina's father came in, angry and frowning, with a foreign pipe in his teeth; he went up to his daughter and began questioning her sternly why she had come home so late the night before.

"It is not her, but me, you should question about that,

father-in-law! Not the wife but the husband is responsible. That's our way here, if you don't mind my saying so," said Danilo, going on with his work. "Perhaps in infidel lands it is not so—I don't know."

The father-in-law's face flushed and there was a wild gleam in his eye.

"Who but a father should watch over his daughter!" he muttered to himself. "All right, I ask *you:* where were you gadding till late at night?"

"Ah, that's the way to talk, dear father-in-law! To that I will answer that I grew out of swaddling clothes long ago. I can ride a horse, I can wield a sharp sword, and there are other things I can do. I can refuse to answer to anyone for what I do."

"I know, Danilo, you seek a quarrel! A man who is not open has some evil in his mind."

"You may think as you please," said Danilo, "and I will think as I please. Thank God, I've had no part in any dishonourable deed so far; I have always stood for the Orthodox faith and my country, not like some vagrants who go tramping God knows where while good Christians are fighting to the death, and afterwards come back to reap a harvest they have not sown. They are worse than the Uniats: they never look into the church of God. It is such men that should be strictly questioned where they have been gadding."

"Hey, Cossack! Do you know—I am no great shot: my bullet pierces the heart at seven hundred feet; I am nought to boast of at sword-play either: my man is left in bits smaller than the grains you use for porridge."

"I am ready," said Danilo, jauntily making the sign of the cross in the air with the sabre, as though he knew what he had sharpened it for.

"Danilo!" Katerina cried aloud, seizing him by the arm and hanging on it, "think what you are doing, madman, see against whom you are lifting your hand! Father, your hair is white as snow, but you have flown into a rage like a senseless lad!"

"Wife!" Danilo cried menacingly, "you know I don't like that; you mind your woman's business!"

There was a terrible clatter of swords; steel hacked steel and the Cossacks sent sparks flying like dust. Katerina went out weeping into a room apart, flung herself on the bed, and covered her ears that she might not hear the clash of the swords. But the Cossacks did not fight so faint-heartedly that she could smother the sound of their blows. Her heart was ready to break; she seemed to hear all over her the clank of the swords. "No, I cannot bear it, I cannot bear it! Perhaps the crimson blood is already flowing out of the white body; maybe by now my dear one is helpless and I am lying here!" Palefaced and scarcely breathing, she went back.

A terrible and even fight it was; neither of the Cossacks was winning the day. At one moment Katerina's father attacked and Danilo seemed to give way; then Danilo attacked and the sullen father seemed to yield, and again they were equal. They boiled with rage, they swung their swords. The swords clashed—and with a clatter the blades flew out of the handles.

"Thank God!" said Katerina, but she screamed again when she saw that the Cossacks had picked up their muskets. They put in the flints and cocked the hammers.

Danilo fired and missed. Her father took aim. He was old, he did not see so well as the younger man, but his hand did not tremble. A shot rang out. Danilo staggered; the crimson blood stained the left sleeve of his Cossack tunic.

"No!" he cried, "I will not yield so easily. Not the left but the right hand is ataman. I have a Turkish pistol hanging on the wall: never yet has it failed me. Come down from the wall, old comrade! Do your friend a service!" Danilo stretched out his hand.

"Danilo!" cried Katerina in despair, clutching his hands and falling at his feet. "Not for myself I beseech you. There is but one end for me; unworthy is the wife who will outlive her husband; the Dnieper, the cold Dnieper will be my grave. But look at your son, Danilo, look at your son! Who will cherish the poor child? Who will be kind to him? Who will teach him to race on the black steed, to fight for faith and freedom, to drink and carouse like a Cossack? You must perish, my son, you must perish! Your father will not think of you! See how he turns away his head. Oh, I know you now! You are a wild beast and not a man! You have the heart of a wolf and the mind of a crafty reptile! I thought there was a drop of pity in you, that there was human feeling in your breast of stone. Terribly have I been deceived! This will be a delight to you. Your bones will dance in the grave with joy when they hear the foul brutes of Poles throwing your son into the flames, when your son shrieks under the knife or the scalding water. Oh, I know you! You would be glad to rise up from the grave and fan the flames under him with your cap!"

"Stay, Katerina! Come, my precious Ivan, let me kiss you! No, my child, no one shall touch a hair on your head. You shall grow up to the glory of your country; like a whirlwind you shall fly at the head of the Cossacks with a velvet cap on your head and a sharp sabre in your hand. Give me your hand, Father! Let us forget what has been between us! For what wrong I have done you I ask pardon. Why do you not give me your hand?" said Danilo to Katerina's father, who stood without moving, with no sign of anger nor of reconciliation on his face.

"Father!" cried Katerina, embracing and kissing him, "don't be merciless, forgive Danilo; he will never offend you again!"

"For your sake only, my daughter, I forgive him!" he answered, kissing her with a strange glitter in his eyes.

Katerina shuddered faintly: the kiss and the strange glitter seemed uncanny to her. She leaned her elbows on the table, at which Danilo was bandaging his wounded arm, while he mused that he had acted ill and unlike a Cossack in asking pardon when he had done no wrong.

IV

The day broke, but without sunshine: the sky was overcast and a fine rain was falling on the plains, the forest, and the broad Dnieper. Katerina woke up with a heavy heart: her eyes were tear-stained, and she was restless and uneasy.

"My dear husband, my precious husband! I have had a strange dream!"

"What dream, my sweet Katerina?"

"I had a strange dream, and as vivid as though it were real, that my father was that very monster whom we saw at the captain's. But I entreat you, do not put faith in the dream: one dreams all manner of foolishness. I dreamed that I stood before him, trembling and frightened, and all my veins moaned at every word he said. If only you had heard what he said!"

"What did he say, my golden Katerina?"

"He said: 'Look at me, Katerina—look how handsome I am! People are wrong in saying I am ugly. I should make you a splendid husband. See what a look there is in my eyes!' Then he turned his eyes full of fire upon me; I cried out and woke up."

"Yes, dreams tell many a true thing. But do you know that all is not quiet beyond the hills? I fancy the Poles have begun to show themselves again. Gorobets sent me a message to keep awake; but he need not have troubled—I am not asleep as it is. My lads have piled up a dozen barricades of felled trees during the night. The common soldiers we will regale with leaden plums and the gentry shall dance to the whips."

"And Father, does he know of this?"

"You father is a burden on my back! I cannot make him out. He must have committed many sins in foreign parts. What other reason can there be? Here he has lived with us more than a month, and not once has he made merry like a true Cossack! He would not drink mead! Do you hear, Katerina, he would not drink the mead which I wrung out of the Jews at Brest. Hey, lad!" cried Danilo, "run to the cellar, boy, and bring me the Jews' mead! He won't even drink vodka! What do you make of that? I verily believe, my lady Katerina, that he does not believe in Christ. Eh, what do you think?"

"God knows what you are saying, my lord Danilo!"

"It is strange, wife!" Danilo went on, taking the earthenware mug from the Cossack, "even the unclean Catholics have a weakness for vodka; it is only the Turks who do not drink. Well, Stetsko, have you had a good sip of mead in the cellar?"

"I just tried it, master."

"You are lying, you son of a dog! See how the flies have settled on your moustache! I can see from your eyes that you have gulped down half a pailful. Oh, you Cossacks! What reckless fellows! Ready to give all else to a comrade, but he keeps his drink to himself. It is a long time, my lady Katerina, since I have been drunk. Eh?"

"A long time indeed! Why, last—"

"Don't be afraid, don't be afraid, I won't drink more than a mugful! And here is the Turkish abbot at the door!" he muttered through his teeth, seeing his father-in-law stooping to come in.

"What's this, my daughter?" said the father, taking off his cap and setting straight his girdle where hung a sabre studded with precious stones. "The sun is already high and your dinner is not ready."

"Dinner is ready, my lord, we will serve it at once. Bring out the pot of dumplings!" said the young mistress to the old serving-woman, who was wiping the wooden bowls. "Wait, I had better get it out myself, while you call the men."

They all sat down on the floor in a ring; facing the icons sat the father, on his left Danilo, on his right Katerina, and ten of the trustiest lads in blue and yellow tunics.

"I don't like dumplings!" said the father, laying down his spoon after eating a little. "There is no flavour in them."

"I know you like Jewish noodles better," thought Danilo.

"Why do you say there is no flavour in the dumplings, father-in-law?" he continued aloud. "Are they not properly made or what? My Katerina makes dumplings such as the Hetman does not often taste. And there is no need to despise them: it is a Christian food. All holy people and Godly saints have eaten dumplings."

Not a word came from the father; nor did Danilo say any more.

They served roast pork with cabbage and plums.

"I don't like pork," said Katerina's father, picking out a spoonful of cabbage.

"Why don't you like pork?" said Danilo. "It is only Turks and Jews who won't eat pork."

The father frowned more angrily than ever.

He ate nothing but some buckwheat porridge with milk, and instead of vodka drank some black liquid from a bottle he took out of his bosom.

After dinner Danilo slept soundly and only woke towards evening. He sat down to write to the Cossack camp, while his young wife sat on the stove-couch, rocking the cradle with her foot. Danilo sat there, his left eye on his writing, while his right eye looked out of the window. From the window far away he could see the shining hills and the Dnieper; beyond the Dnieper lay the dark blue forest; overhead glimmered the clear night sky. But Danilo was not gazing at the far-away sky or the blue forest; he was watching the spit on which stood the old castle. He fancied that a light gleamed in a narrow little window in the castle. But everything was still; it must have been his imagination. All he could hear was the hollow murmur of the Dnieper down below and the resounding splash of the waves that followed one another. It was not in a turmoil; like an old man, it muttered and grumbled and found nothing to its taste. Everything had changed about it; it kept up a feud with the hills, woods, and meadows on its banks, and carried its complaints against them to the Black Sea.

Now, on the wide expanse of the Dnieper, he saw the black speck of a boat, and again there was a gleam of light in the castle. Danilo gave a low whistle and the faithful serving-man came running.

"Make haste, Stetsko, bring with you a sharp sabre and a musket, and follow me!"

"Are you going out?" asked Katerina.

"Yes, wife. I must look everywhere and see that all is in order."

"But I am afraid to be left alone. I am weighed down

with sleep: what if I should have the same dream again? And, indeed, I am not sure it was a dream—it looked all so real."

"The old woman will stay with you, and there are Cossacks sleeping in the outer room and in the courtyard."

"The old woman is asleep already, and somehow I put no trust in the Cossacks. Listen, my lord Danilo: lock me in the room and take the key with you. Then I shall not be so fearful; and let the Cossacks lie before the door."

"So be it!" said Danilo, wiping the dust off his musket and loading it with powder.

The faithful Stetsko stood already equipped with all the Cossack's accoutrements. Danilo put on his astrakhan cap, closed the window, bolted and locked the door, and, softly stepping between his sleeping Cossacks, went out across the courtyard towards the hills.

The sky was almost completely clear now. A light breeze blew from the Dnieper. Save for the wail of a gull in the distance all would have seemed dumb. But suddenly there was a faint rustle. Burulbash and his faithful servant hid behind the brambles that screened a barricade of felled trunks. Someone in a red coat, with two pistols, and with a sword at his side, was coming down the hill-side.

"It's my father-in-law," said Danilo, scanning him from behind the bushes. "Where is he going at this hour, and with what design? Mind, Stetsko, keep a sharp watch to see which road he takes."

The man in the red coat went down to the river-bank and turned towards the spit.

"Ah, so that is where he is going!" said Danilo. "Why, Stetsko, he has gone to the wizard's den!"

"Nowhere else, for certain, my lord Danilo! Or we should

have seen him on the other side; but he disappeared near the castle."

"Let us get out and follow his track. There is some secret in this. Well, Katerina, I told you your father was an evil man; he did nothing like a good Christian."

Danilo and his faithful servant darted across the spit. Soon they were out of sight; the dense forest around the castle hid them. A gleam of light came into an upper window; the Cossacks stood below wondering how to climb to it; neither gate nor door was to be seen; doubtless there was a door in the courtyard, but how could they climb in? They could hear in the distance the clanking of chains and the stirring of dogs.

"Why am I wasting time?" said Danilo, seeing a big oak-tree by the window. "Stay here, lad! I will climb up the oak; from it I can look straight in at the window."

He took off his girdle, put down his sabre that it might not jingle, and gripping the branches lifted himself up. The light was still there. Sitting on a branch close to the window, he held on to the tree and looked in: it was light in the room though there was no candle; on the walls were mysterious symbols; weapons were hanging there, but all were strange— not such as are worn by Turks, or Crimeans, or Poles, or Christians, or the noble Swedish people. Bats flitted to and fro under the ceiling and their shadows flitted to and fro over the floor, the doors and the walls. Then the door swung noiselessly open. Someone in a red coat walked in and went straight up to the table, which was covered with a white cloth. "It is he, it is my father-in-law!" Danilo crept a little lower down and huddled closer to the tree.

But his father-in-law had no time to look whether anyone was peeping in at the window. He had come in morose and ill-humoured; he drew the cloth off the table, and at once the room was filled with transparent blue light; but the waves of pale golden light, with which the room had been filled, eddied and dived, as in a blue sea, without mingling with it, and ran through it in streaks like the lines in marble. Then he set a pot upon the table and began throwing some herbs into it.

Danilo looked more closely and saw that he was no longer wearing the red coat; and that now he had on loose trousers, such as Turks wear, with pistols in his girdle and on his head a queer cap embroidered all over with letters that were neither Russian nor Polish. As he looked at his face it began to change; his nose grew longer and hung right down over his lips; in one instant his mouth stretched to his ears; a crooked tooth stood out beyond his lips; and he saw before him the same wizard who had appeared at the captain's wedding-feast. "Your dream told truth, Katerina!" thought Burulbash.

The wizard began pacing round the table; the symbols on the walls began changing more rapidly, the bats flitted more swiftly up and down and to and fro. The blue light grew dimmer and dimmer, and at last seemed to fade away. And now there was a lovely rosy light in the room. With a faint ringing sound this marvellous light seemed to flood every corner, and suddenly it vanished and all was darkness. Nothing was heard but a murmur like the wind in the quiet evening hour when, hovering over the mirror-like water, it bows the silvery willows lower into its depths. And it seemed to Danilo as though the moon were shining in the room, the stars were moving, there were vague glimpses of the dark blue sky within it, and he even felt the chill of night coming from it. And Danilo fancied—he began pulling his moustaches to make sure he was not dreaming—that it was no longer the sky but his own home he was seeing through the window; his Tatar and Turkish sabres were hanging on the walls; round the walls were the shelves with pots and pans; on the table stood bread and salt; the cradle hung from the ceiling—but terrible faces looked out where the icons should have been; on the stove-couch—but a thick mist hid all, and it was dark again. And with a wonderful sound the rosy light flooded the room again, and again the wizard stood motionless in his strange turban. The sounds grew louder and deeper, the delicate rosy light shone more brilliant, and something white like a cloud hovered in the middle of the room; and it seemed to Danilo that the cloud was not a cloud, that a woman was standing there. But what was she made of? Of air, surely? Why did she stand without touching the floor, not leaning on anything? Why did the rosy light and the magic symbols on the wall show through her? And now she moved her transparent head; a soft light shone in her pale blue eyes; her hair curled and fell over her shoulders like a pale grey mist; a faint flush coloured her lips like the scarcely perceptible crimson glimmer of dawn glowing through the white transparent sky of morning; the dark brows showed dimly. Ah, it was Katerina! Danilo felt his limbs turned to stone; he tried to speak, but his lips moved without uttering a sound.

The wizard stood without moving.

"Where have you been?" he asked, and the figure standing before him trembled.

"Oh, why did you call me up?" she moaned softly. "I was so happy. I was in the place where I was born and lived for fifteen years. Ah, how good it was there! How green and fragrant was the meadow where I used to play in childhood! The darling wild flowers were the same as ever, and our hut and the garden! Oh, how my dear mother embraced me! How much love there was in her eyes! She caressed me, she kissed my lips and my

cheeks, and combed out my fair hair with a fine comb. Father!"
Then she fixed her pale eyes on the wizard. "Why did you
slay my mother?"

The wizard shook his finger at her menacingly. "Did I ask
you to speak of that?" And the ethereal beauty trembled.
"Where is your mistress now?"

"My mistress Katerina has fallen asleep and I was glad
of it: I flew up and darted off. For many years I have longed
to see my mother. I am suddenly fifteen again, I feel light as
a bird. Why have you sent for me?"

"You remember all I said to you yesterday?" the wizard
said, so softly that it was hard to catch the words.

"I remember, I remember! But what would I not give to
forget it. Poor Katerina, she does not know much of what
her soul knows."

"So it is Katerina's soul," thought Danilo, but still he dared
not stir.

"Repent, father! Is it not dreadful that after every murder
you commit the dead rise up from their graves?"

"You are at your old tune again!" said the wizard
menacingly. "I will have my way, I will make you do as
I will: Katerina shall love me."

"Oh, you are a monster and not my father!" she moaned.
"No, your will shall not be done! It is true that by your foul
spells you have power to call up and torture her soul; but
only God can make her do what He wills. No, never shall
Katerina, so long as I am living in her body, bring herself
to so ungodly a deed. Father, a terrible judgement is at hand!
Even if you were not my father, you would never make me
false to my faithful and beloved husband. Even if my husband
were not true and dear to me, I would not betray him, for
God loves not souls that are faithless and false to their vows."

Then she fixed her pale eyes on the window under which Danilo was sitting, and stood stock-still.

"What are you looking at? Whom do you see there?" cried the wizard.

The wraith of Katerina trembled. But already Danilo was on the ground and with his faithful Stetsko making his way to his home in the valley. "Terrible, terrible!" he murmured to himself, feeling a thrill of fear in his Cossack heart, and he rapidly crossed his courtyard, in which the Cossacks slept as soundly as ever, all but one who sat on guard smoking a pipe.

The sky was spangled with stars.

V

"How glad I am you have awakened me!" said Katerina, wiping her eyes with the embroidered sleeve of her smock and looking her husband up and down as he stood facing her. "What a terrible dream I have had! I could hardly breathe! Oh! I thought I was dying!"

"What was your dream? Was it like this?" And Burulbash told his wife all that he had seen.

"How did you know it, husband?" asked Katerina in amazement. "But no, many things you tell me I do not know. No, I did not dream that my father had murdered my mother; I did not dream of the dead. No, Danilo, you have not told the dream right. Oh, what a fearful man my father is!"

"It is no wonder that you have not dreamed of that. You do not know a tenth part of what your soul knows. Do you know your father is an antichrist? Last year when I was getting ready to go with the Poles against the Crimeans— I was still allied with those faithless people then—the Father Superior of the Brotherhood Monastery (he is a holy man, wife) told me that an antichrist has the power to call up every man's soul; for the soul wanders at its own will when the body is asleep and flies with the archangels about the dwelling of God. I disliked your father's face from the first. I would not have married you had I known you had such a father; I would have given you up instead of taking upon myself the sin of being allied to the brood of an antichrist."

"Danilo!" cried Katerina, hiding her face in her hands and bursting into tears. "In what have I been to blame? Have I been false to you, my beloved husband? How have I roused your wrath? Have I not served you truly? Do I say a word to cross you when you come back merry from a drinking bout? Have I not borne you a black-browed son?"

"Do not weep, Katerina; now I know you and nothing would make me abandon you. The sin lies at your father's door."

"Don't call him my father! He is not my father. God is my witness—I disown him, I disown my father! He is an anti-christ, a rebel against God! If he were perishing, if he were drowning, I would not hold out a hand to save him; if his throat were parched by some magic herb I would not give him a drop of water. You are my father!"

VI

In a deep underground cellar at Danilo's, the wizard lay bound in iron chains and locked in with three locks, while his devilish castle above the Dnieper was blazing and the waves, glowing red as blood, splashed and surged round the ancient walls. It was not for sorcery, not for ungodly deeds, that the wizard lay in the underground cellar—for his wickedness God was his judge; it was for secret treachery that he was imprisoned, for plotting with the foes of Orthodox Russia to sell the Ukrainian people to the Catholics and burn Christian churches. The wizard was gloomy; thoughts black as night strayed through his mind; he had but one day left to live, and on the morrow he would have to take leave of the world; his execution was awaiting him on the morrow. It was not to be a light one; it would be an act of mercy if he were boiled alive in a cauldron, or if his sinful skin were flayed from him. The wizard was melancholy, his head was bowed. Perhaps he was already repenting on the eve of death; but his sins were not such as God would forgive. Above him was a little window set with an iron grating. Clanking his chains, he looked out of the window to see whether his daughter was passing. She was gentle and forgiving as a dove; she might have mercy on her father. But there was no one. The road ran below the window, no one passed along it. Beneath it rippled the Dnieper, it cared for no one; it murmured, and its monotonous splash sounded dreary to the captive.

Then someone appeared upon the road—it was a Cossack. The prisoner heaved a deep sigh. Again it was empty. Yonder someone was coming downhill; a green coat flapped in the wind; a golden head-dress glittered on her head. It was she! He pressed still closer to the window. Now she was coming nearer.

"Katerina, my daughter! Have pity on me, be merciful!"

She was dumb, she would not listen, she did not turn to look at the prison, and had already passed by and vanished. The whole world was empty; dismally the Dnieper murmured; it laid a load of sadness on the heart. But did the wizard know aught of such sadness?

The day was drawing to a close. The sun was setting; now

it had vanished. It was evening, it was cool; an ox was lowing somewhere; sounds of voices floated from afar: doubtless people going home from their work and making merry; a boat flashed into view on the Dnieper—no one thought of the chained prisoner. A silver crescent gleamed in the sky. Someone came along the road in the opposite direction; it was hard to tell the figure in the darkness; it was Katerina coming back.

"Daughter, for Christ's sake! Even the savage wolf-cubs will not tear their mother to pieces—daughter, give one look at least to your guilty father!"

She did not heed him but walked on.

"Daughter, for the sake of your unhappy mother!"

She stopped.

"Come close and hear my last words!"

"Why do you call me, enemy of God? Do not call me daughter! There is no kinship between us. What do you want of me for the sake of my unhappy mother?"

"Katerina, my end is near; I know that your husband means to tie me to the tail of a wild mare and send it racing in the open country, and maybe he will invent an end more dreadful yet!"

"But is there in the world a punishment severe enough for your sins? Look forward to receiving it. No one will plead for you."

"Katerina! It is not punishment in this world that I fear but tortures in the next. You are innocent, Katerina; your soul will fly about God in paradise; but your ungodly father's soul will burn in a fire everlasting and never will that fire be quenched; it will burn more and more hotly; no drop of dew will fall upon it, nor will the wind breathe on it."

"I can do nothing to ease that punishment," said Katerina, turning away.

"Katerina, stay for one word! You can save my soul! You

don't know yet how good and merciful God is. Have you heard
of the Apostle Paul? What a sinful man he was—but afterwards he repented and became a saint."

"What can I do to save your soul?" said Katerina. "It
is not for a weak woman like me to think of that."

"If I could but get out, I would abandon everything. I would
repent, I would go into a cave, I would wear a hair shirt next to
my skin and will spend day and night in prayer. I would give
up not only meat, but even fish! I would put nothing under
me when I lay down to sleep! And I would pray without ceasing!
And if God's mercy did not release me from at least a hundredth
part of my sins, I would bury myself up to the neck in the
earth or lock myself up in a wall of stone; I would take neither
food nor drink and perish; and I would give all my goods to
the monks that they might sing a requiem for me for forty
days and forty nights".

Katerina pondered. "If I were to unlock you I could not
undo your fetters."

"I do not fear chains," he said. "You say that they have
fettered my hands and feet? No, I threw a mist over their
eyes and held out dry wood instead of hands. Here, see: I
have not a chain upon me now!" he said, walking into the
middle of the cellar. "I should not fear these walls either and
should pass them; but your husband does not know what
walls these are: they were built by a holy hermit, and no evil
power can deliver a prisoner from them without the very key
with which the hermit used to lock his cell. Just such a cell
will I build for myself, incredible sinner that I have been, when
I am free again."

"Listen, I will let you out; but what if you deceive me,"
said Katerina, standing still at the door, "and instead of repenting, again become the devil's associate?"

"No, Katerina, I have not much longer to live; my end is near even if I am not put to death. Can you believe that I will give myself up to eternal punishment?"

The key grated in the lock.

"Farewell! May God in His mercy keep you, my child!" said the wizard, kissing her.

"Do not touch me, you fearful sinner; make haste and go!" said Katerina.

He was gone.

"I let him out!" she said to herself, terror-stricken, looking wildly at the walls. "What answer shall I give my husband now? I am undone. There is nothing left for me but to bury myself alive!" And sobbing she almost fell upon the block on which the prisoner had sat. "But I have saved a soul," she said softly, "I have done a godly deed; but my husband —I have deceived him for the first time. Oh, how terrible, how hard it will be for me to lie to him! Someone is coming! It is he—my husband!" She uttered a cry of despair and fell senseless on the ground.

VII

"It is I, my daughter! It is I, my darling!" Katerina heard, as she came to and saw the old serving-woman before her. The woman bent down and seemed to whisper to her, and stretching out her withered old hand sprinkled her with water.

"Where am I?" said Katerina, sitting up and looking round her. "The Dnieper is splashing before me, behind me are the hills. Where have you taken me?"

"I have taken you out; I have carried you in my arms from the stifling cellar; I locked up the cellar again that you might not be in trouble with my lord Danilo."

"Where is the key?" asked Katerina, looking at her girdle. "I don't see it."

"Your husband has taken it, to have a look at the wizard, my child."

"To look! I am lost!" cried Katerina.

"God mercifully preserve us from that, my child! Only hold your peace, my little lady, no one will know anything."

"He has escaped, the cursed antichrist! Do you hear, Katerina, he has escaped!" said Danilo, coming up to his wife. His eyes flashed fire; his sabre clanked at his side. His wife was like one dead.

"Has someone let him out, dear husband?" she muttered, trembling.

"Yes, you are right—the devil has. Look, where he was is a log in chains. It is God's pleasure, it seems, that the devil should not fear a Cossack's hands! If anyone of my Cossacks had dreamed of such a thing and I knew of it, I could find no punishment bad enough for him!"

"And if it had been I?" Katerina could not resist saying, and she stopped, frightened.

"If you had done it you would be no wife to me. I would sew you up in a sack and drown you in mid-Dnieper!"

Katerina gasped for air and felt the hair stand up on her head.

VIII

On the frontier road the Poles had gathered at a tavern, where they had been feasting for two days. There were not a few of the rabble. They had doubtless met for some raid: some had muskets; spurs jingled and swords clanked. The nobles made merry and boasted, they talked of their marvellous deeds, they mocked at the Orthodox Christians, calling the Ukrainian people their serfs, and insolently twirled their moustaches and sprawled on the benches. There was a priest among them, too; but he was like themselves and had not even the semblance of a Christian priest: he drank and caroused with them and uttered shameful words with his sinful tongue. The servants were no better than their masters: tucking up the sleeves of their tattered tunics, they walked about with a swagger as though they were of consequence. They played cards and struck each other on the nose with cards. They had brought with them other men's wives; there was shouting and quarrelling. Their masters were at the height of their revelry, playing all sorts of tricks, pulling the Jewish tavernkeeper by the beard, painting a cross on his impious brow, shooting blank charges at the women, and dancing the cracovienne with their impious priest. Such sinfulness had never been seen on Russian soil even among the Tatars; it was God's chastisement, seemingly, for the sins of Russia that she should be put to so great a shame. In the midst of the bedlam, talk could be heard of Danilo's homestead above the Dnieper and of his lovely wife.

The band was obviously plotting foul deeds.

IX

Danilo sat at the table in his house leaning on his elbow, thinking. Katerina sat on the stove-couch, singing.

"I am sad, my wife!" said Danilo. "My head aches and my heart aches. I feel weighed down. It seems my death is not far off."

"Oh, my precious husband! Lean your head upon me! Why

lo you cherish such black thoughts?" Katerina wanted to say, but dared not utter the words. It was bitter to her, feeling her guilt, to receive her husband's caresses.

"Listen, my wife!" said Danilo. "Do not desert our son when I am no more. God will give you no happiness either in this world or the next if you forsake him. It will be sad for my bones to rot in the damp earth, and sadder still it will be for my soul!"

"What are you saying, my husband? Was it not you who mocked at us weak women? And now you are talking like a weak woman yourself. You must live long years yet."

"No, Katerina, my heart feels death near at hand. The world grows a sad place; cruel days are coming. Ah, I remember, I remember the years—they will not return for sure! He was living then, the honour and glory of our army, old Konashevich! The Cossack regiments pass before my eyes as though it were today. Those were golden days, Katerina! The old Hetman sat on a black steed; his mace shone in his hand; the body-guards stood around him, and on each side moved the red sea of the Zaporozhians. The Hetman began to speak—and all stood as though rooted to the ground. The old man wept when he told us of bygone raids and battles. Ah, Katerina, if only you knew how we fought in those days with the Turks! The scar on my head shows even now. Four bullets pierced me in four places and not one of the wounds has quite healed. How much gold we took in those days! The Cossacks filled their caps with precious stones. What horses—if you only knew, Katerina, what horses we drove away with us! Ah, I shall never fight like that again! One would think I am not old and am strong in body, yet the sword drops out of my hand, I live doing nothing and know not what I live for. There is no order in the Ukraine; the colonels and the captains quarrel

like dogs; there is no chief over them all. Our gentry have
changed everything after the Polish style, they have copied
their sly ways; they have sold their souls, accepting the Unia
faith. The Jews are oppressing the poor. Oh, those days! those
days that are past! Whither have you fled, my young years?
Go to the cellar, boy, and bring me a jug of mead! I will drink
to the past, to the years that have gone!"

"How shall we receive our guests, my lord? The Poles are
coming from the side of the meadow," said Stetsko, entering

"I know what they are coming for," said Danilo, rising
"Saddle the horses, my faithful men! Put on your harness
Bare your swords! Don't forget to take your rations of lead
we must do honour to our guests!"

But before the Cossacks had time to saddle their horse
and load their guns, the Poles covered the hill-side as leaves
cover the ground in autumn.

"Ah, here we have foes to try our strength with!" said Danilo
looking at the stout Poles swaying gravely on their gold
harnessed steeds in the front ranks. "It seems it is our lot to
have one more glorious jaunt! Take your pleasure, Cossack soul
for the last time! Go ahead, lads, our festival has come!

And the festival was kept on the hills and the merry-making
was great: swords were playing, bullets flying, horses neighing
and stamping. The shouting dazed the brain; the smoke blinded
the eye. All was confusion, but the Cossack felt where was friend
where was foe; whenever a bullet whistled a gallant rider dropped
from the saddle, whenever a sword flashed a head fell to the
ground, muttering incoherent words.

But the red crest of Danilo's Cossack cap could always be
seen in the crowd; the golden girdle of his dark blue tunic
gleamed bright, and the mane of his black steed fluttered in the
breeze. Like a bird he flew hither and thither, shouting and wav

ing his damascus sword and hacking to right and to left. Hack away, Cossack, make merry! Comfort your gallant heart; but look not at the golden trappings and tunics: trample underfoot the gold and jewels! Stab, Cossack! Wreak your will, Cossack! But look back: already the godless Poles are setting fire to the huts and driving away the frightened cattle. And like a whirlwind Danilo turned back, and the cap with the red crest gleamed now by the huts while the crowd about him scattered.

Hour after hour the Poles fought with the Cossacks; there were not many left of either; but Danilo did not slacken; with his long spear he thrust mounted Poles from the saddle and his spirited steed trampled those on foot. Already his yard was almost cleared, already the Poles were fleeing; already the Cossacks were stripping the golden tunics and rich trappings from the slain; already Danilo was setting off in pursuit and looked round to call his men together, and was overwhelmed with fury; he saw Katerina's father. There he stood on the hill-side aiming his musket at him. Danilo urged his horse straight upon him. Stop, Cossack, you are going to your ruin! Then came the crack of a shot, and the wizard vanished behind the hill. Only the faithful Stetsko caught a glimpse of the wizard's red tunic and queer cap. The Cossack staggered and fell to the ground. The faithful Stetsko flew to his lord's aid: Danilo lay stretched on the ground, his bright eyes closed, while the crimson blood spurted from his breast. But he was evidently aware of his faithful servant's presence; slowly he raised his eyelids and his eyes gleamed: "Farewell, Stetsko! Tell Katerina not to forsake our son! And do not you, my faithful servants, forsake him either!" And he ceased. His gallant soul flew from his noble body; his lips turned blue; the Cossack slept, never to wake again.

His faithful servant sobbed and beckoned to Katerina. "Come, lady, come! Your lord has been carousing; in drunken sleep he lies on the damp earth; and it will be long before he awakens!'"

Katerina wrung her hands and slumped down on the dead body. "Husband, is it you lying here with closed eyes? Rise up, my beloved, stretch out your hand! Stand up! Look, if only once, at your Katerina, move your lips, utter one word! But you are mute, you are mute, my noble lord! You have turned dark as the Black Sea. Your heart is not beating! Why are you so cold, my lord? It seems my tears are not hot enough—they have no power to warm you! It seems my weeping is not loud enough—it cannot waken you! Who will lead your regiments now? Who will gallop on your black steed, calling loudly, and lead the Cossacks, waving a sabre? Cossacks, Cossacks, where is your honour and glory? Your honour and glory is lying with closed eyes on the damp earth. Bury me, bury me with him! Throw earth upon my eyes! Press the maple boards upon my white bosom! My beauty is useless to me now!'"

Katerina grieved and wept, while the distant horizon was covered with dust: the old Captain Gorobets was galloping to the rescue.

X

Lovely is the Dnieper in calm weather when, freely and smoothly, its waters glide through forests and hills. Not a sound is heard, not a ripple stirs. As you look at it you cannot tell whether its majestic expanse moves or not; it might be of molten crystal, and like a blue road of plate-glass, immeasurably broad, endlessly long, it winds its way through green regions. It is sweet then for the burning sun to peep at itself from the heights and to dip its beams into the cool of its glassy waters, and for the wooded banks to watch their bright reflections in the water. Wreathed in green, the woods press with the wild flowers close to the river's edge, and bending over, look in and are never tired of admiring their vivid reflection, and smile and greet it with their nodding boughs. In mid-Dnieper they dare not look: none but the sun and the blue sky gaze into it; rarely a bird flies to the middle of the river. Glorious Dnieper! There is no river like it in the world! Lovely too is the Dnieper on a warm summer night when all are sleeping—man, beast, and bird, while God alone majestically surveys earth and heaven and majestically shakes His garment. The stars are scattered from His garment; they glow and shine above the world, and all are reflected together in the Dnieper. All of them the Dnieper holds in its dark bosom; not one escapes it till quenched in the sky. The black forests dotted with sleeping crows and the hills cleft asunder in ages past strive, hanging over, to conceal the river in their long shadows, but in vain! Nothing in the world could hide the Dnieper. Deep, deep blue, it flows spreading its waters far and wide and at midnight as at midday it is seen far, far away, as far as the eye of man can see. Shrinking from the cold of night and pressing closer to the bank, it leaves behind a silver trail gleaming like the blade of a damascus sword, while the deep blue water slumbers again. Lovely then, too, is the Dnieper, and no river is like it in the world. But when dark blue storm-clouds pile in the sky, the dark forest totters to its roots, the oaks creak, and the lightning, zigzagging through the clouds, suddenly lights up the whole world, terrible then is the Dnieper. Then its mountainous billows roar and fling themselves against the hills, and flashing and moaning rush back and wail and lament in the distance. So an old mother laments as she lets her Cossack son go to war. Bold and reckless, he rides his black steed, arms akimbo and jaunty cap on one side, while she, sobbing, runs after him, seizes him by the stirrup, catches the bridle, and wrings her hands over him, shedding bitter tears.

Strange and black are the burnt tree-stumps and stones on the jutting bank between the warring waves. And the landing boat is beaten against the bank, thrown upwards and flung back again. What Cossack dared row out in a boat when the old Dnieper was raging? Surely he did not know that the river swallows men like flies.

The boat reached the bank, and the wizard stepped out. He was in no happy mood: the funeral feast which the Cossacks had kept over their slain master was bitter to him. The Poles had paid heavily for it: fourty-four of them in all their harness and accoutrements and thirty-three servants were hacked to pieces, while the others were captured with their horses to be sold to the Tatars.

He went down stone steps between the burnt stumps to a place where he had a cave dug deep in the earth. He went in softly, not letting the door creak, put a pot on the table that was covered with a cloth, and began throwing into it some strange herbs with his long hands; he took a jug made of some rare wood, scooped up some water with it and poured it out, moving his lips and repeating an incantation. The cave was flooded with rosy light and his face was terrible to look upon: it seemed covered with blood, only the deep wrinkles showed black upon it and his eyes were as though on fire. Foul sinner! His beard was grey, his face was lined with wrinkles, he was shrivelled with age, but still he persisted in his godless design. A white cloud began to hover in the cave and something like joy flashed across his face; but why did he suddenly stand motionless with his mouth open, not daring to stir, why did his hair rise up on his head? The features of a strange face gleamed upon him from the cloud. Unbidden, uninvited, it had come to visit him; it grew more distinct and fastened its eyes immovably upon him. The features—eyebrows, eyes, lips—all were unfamiliar; never in his life had he seen them. And there was nothing terrible, seemingly, about it, but he was overwhelmed with horror. The strange marvellous face still looked fixedly at him from the cloud. Then the cloud vanished, but the unfamiliar face was more distinct than ever and the piercing eyes were still riveted on him. The wizard turned white as a sheet; he shrieked in a wild voice and overturned the pot. Everything disappeared.

XI

"Take comfort, my dear sister," said the old Captain Gorobets, "rarely do dreams come true!"

"Lie down, sister," said his young daughter-in-law, "I will fetch an old dame, a wise woman; no evil spirit can stand against her, she will help you."

"Fear nothing!" said his son, touching his sword. "No one shall wrong you!"

Dully and with dim eyes Katerina looked at them all and found no word to say. "I myself brought about my ruin: I let him out!" she thought.

At length, she said:

"He gives me no peace! Here I have been ten days with you in Kiev and my sorrow is no less. I thought that at least I could bring up my son in peace to avenge. He looked so terrible in my dream, so terrible! God forbid that you should ever see him like that! My heart is still throbbing. 'I will cut down your child, Katerina,' he shouted, 'if you don't marry me!'" She flung herself sobbing on the cradle; and the frightened child stretched out its little hands and cried.

The captain's son was boiling with anger as he heard those words. Captain Gorobets himself was roused.

"Let him try to come here, the accursed antichrist; he will
learn whether there is still strength in the old Cossack's arm.
God knows," he said, turning his keen eyes to heaven, "I
hastened to give a hand to brother Danilo. It was His holy will!
I found him lying on the cold bed upon which so many Cossacks
have been laid. But what a funeral feast we had for him! We
did not leave a single Pole alive! Be comforted, my child! No
one shall dare to harm you, so long as I am alive, or my son."

As he finished speaking the old Cossack captain approached
the cradle and the child saw hanging from a strap his red pipe
set in silver and the pouch with flint and flashing steel, and stretched out its arms towards him and laughed. "He takes after his
father," said the old captain, unfastening the pipe and giving
it to the child. "He is not out of the cradle, but he is thinking of
a pipe already!"

Katerina heaved a sigh and fell to rocking the cradle. They
agreed to spend the night together and soon afterwards they
were all asleep; Katerina, too, dropped asleep.

All was still in the courtyard and the house; everyone slept
but the Cossacks who were keeping watch. Suddenly Katerina
woke with a scream, and the others woke, too. "He is slain, he is
murdered!" she cried, and rushed to the cradle. All surrounded
the cradle, and were numb with horror when they saw that the
child in it was dead. None uttered a sound, wondering at the unheard-of crime.

XII

Far from the Ukraine, beyond Poland and the populous
town of Lemberg, stretch ranges of high mountains. Mountain
after mountain, like chains of stone flung to right and to left
over the land, they fetter it with layers of rock to keep out the

resounding, turbulent sea. The stone chains stretch into Wallachia and Transylvania, and tower like a huge horseshoe between the Galician and Hungarian peoples. There are no such mountains in our parts. The eye shrinks from viewing them, and no human foot has climbed to the peaks of some of them. They are a strange sight. It might have been some angry sea that broke away from its wide shores in a storm and threw its monstrous waves aloft and they turned to stone and remained motionless in the air. Or perhaps heavy storm-clouds fell from heaven and cumbered up the earth. For the mountains have the same grey colour and their white crests flash and sparkle in the sun.

Up to the Carpathian Mountains one may hear Russian speech, and just beyond the mountains there are still here and there echoes of our native tongue; but further beyond, faith and speech are different. The numerous Hungarian people live there; they ride, fight, and drink like any Cossack, and do not grudge gold pieces from their pockets for their horses' trappings and costly tunics. There are great wide lakes among the mountains. They are still as glass, and as mirrors they reflect the bare mountain-tops and the green foot-hills.

But who rode through the night on a huge black steed whether stars shone or not? What hero of superhuman stature galloped under the mountains, above the lakes, was mirrored with his giant horse in the still waters and threw his vast and awesome shadow on the mountains? His plated armour glittered, a lance rested on his shoulder, his sabre rattled by the saddle; his helmet was tilted forward; his moustaches were black; his eyes were closed; his eyelashes were dropping—he was asleep and drowsily held the reins; and on the same horse rode a small boy, a page, and he, too, was asleep and drowsily held on to the hero. Who was he, where was he going, and why? Who knows! He had been travelling over the mountains for more than one day. The day broke, the sun shone, and he was seen no more; only from time to time the mountaineers beheld a long shadow flitting over the mountains, though the sky was bright and there was no cloud upon it. But as soon as night brought back the darkness, he appeared again and was reflected in the lakes, and his quivering shadow followed him. Already he had crossed many mountains, and at last he reached the Krivan. There is no mountain in the Carpathians higher than this one; it towers like a monarch above the others. There the horse and its rider halted and sank into even deeper slumber, and the lowering clouds hid them from view.

XIII

"Hush! don't knock like that, nurse: my child is asleep. My baby cried a long time, now he is asleep. I am going to the forest, nurse. But why do you look at me like that? You are terrible: there are iron pincers coming out of your eyes. Oh, how long they are! And they glow like fire! You must be a witch! Oh, if you are a witch, go away! You will steal my son. How absurd the captain is; he thinks I enjoy living in Kiev. No, my husband and my son are here. Who will look after the house? I went out so quietly that even the dog and the cat did not hear me. Do you want to grow young again, nurse? That's not hard at all; you have but to dance. Look how I dance."

And having uttered this wild speech, Katerina set to dancing, rolling her insane eyes and putting her arms akimbo. With a scream she tapped with her feet, her silver heels clanked out of time and tune. Her black tresses floated loose about her white neck. Like a bird she flew round without resting, waving her hands and nodding her head, and it seemed as though she must

ither fall helpless to the ground or soar away to the next
world.

The old nurse stood mournfully, her wrinkled face wet with
tears; the trusty Cossacks' hearts were heavy with sorrow as they
looked at their mistress. At last she was exhausted and languidly
tapped with her feet on the same spot, fancying she was dancing
round. "I have a necklace, lads," she said, stopping at last,
"and you have not! Where is my husband?" she cried suddenly,
drawing a Turkish dagger out of her girdle. "Oh, this is not the
knife I need." With that, tears of grief came into her eyes. "My
father's heart lies deep inside; this blade will not reach it. His
heart is wrought of iron; it was forged by a witch in the furnace
of hell. Why does not my father come? Doesn't he know it is
time to stab him? He wants me to come myself, it seems—"
And breaking off, she laughed uncannily. "A funny story came
into my mind: I remembered how my husband was buried. He
was buried alive, you know. It did make me laugh! Listen,
listen!" But instead of speaking she began to sing:

> *A blood-stained cart races on,*
> *A Cossack lies upon it,*
> *Shot through the breast, stabbed to the heart;*
> *In his right hand he holds a spear,*
> *And blood is trickling from it,*
> *A stream of blood is flowing.*
> *A plane-tree stands over the river,*
> *Above the tree a raven croaks.*
> *The mother is weeping for the Cossack.*
> *Weep not, Mother, do not grieve!*
> *For your son is married:*
> *He chose a lady for his bride,*
> *A mound of earth in the bare fields*

Without a door or window.
And this is how my story ends.
A fish was dancing with a crab.
And may an ague take the mother
Of him who will not love me!

This was how she muddled lines from different songs together
She had been living two days already in her own house and
would not hear of Kiev. She would not say her prayers, refused
to see anyone, and wandered from morning till night in th
dark oak thickets. Sharp twigs scratched her white face and
shoulders; the wind fluttered her loose hair; the autumn leave
rustled under her feet, but she heeded nothing. At the hour when
the glow of sunset dies away, and before the stars come ou
or the moon shines, it is fearful to walk in the forest; unbaptized
infants clamber up the trees and clutch at the branches; sobbing
and laughing, they roll along the roads and the wastes of net
tles; maidens who have lost their souls rise up one after the
other from the depths of the Dnieper; their green tresses stream
over their shoulders, the water drips sonorously to the ground
from their long hair; and a maiden shines through the water
as through a veil of crystal; her lips smile mysteriously, her
cheeks glow, her eyes bewitch the soul, as though she might
burn with love, as though she might kiss one to death. Flee
Christian! Her lips are ice, her bed—cold water; she will tickle
you to death and drag you into the river. Katerina looked
at no one, in her frenzy she had no fear of the mermaids; she
wandered at night with her knife, seeking her father.

In the early morning a visitor of a handsome appearance
clad in a red coat, arrived at the house and inquired for Danilo
He listened to the story, wiped his tear-stained eyes with
his sleeve, and shrugged his shoulders. He said that he had

fought side by side with Burulbash; side by side they had done battle with the Turks and the Crimeans; never had he thought that Danilo would meet with such an end. The visitor told them many other things and wanted to see Katerina.

At first Katerina heeded nothing of what the guest said; but afterwards she began to listen to him as though understanding. He told her how Danilo and he had lived together like brothers; how once they had hidden under a dam from the Crimeans. Katerina listened and kept her eyes fixed upon him.

"She will recover," the Cossacks thought, looking at her, "this guest will heal her! She is listening like one who understands."

The visitor began meanwhile describing how Danilo had once in a confidential conversation said to him: "Mind, brother Kopryan, when it is God's will that I be gone, you take Katerina —take her for your wife."

Katerina looked piercingly at him. "Ah!" she shrieked, "it is he, it is my father!" And she flew at him with her knife.

For a long time he struggled, trying to snatch the knife from her; at last he snatched it away, raised it to strike— and a terrible deed was done: the father killed his mad daughter.

The astounded Cossacks dashed at him, but the wizard had already leapt upon his horse and was gone.

XIV

An unheard-of marvel appeared beyond Kiev. All the nobles and the Hetmans assembled to see the marvel: in all directions the far distance had become visible. Far off was the dark blue of the mouth of the Dnieper and beyond that the Black Sea. Men who had travelled recognized the Crimea rising mountainous out of the sea and the marshy Sivash. On the right could be seen Galicia.

"And what is that?" people asked the old men, pointing to white and grey crests looming far away in the sky, looking more like clouds.

"Those are the Carpathian Mountains!" said the old men. "Among them are some that are for ever covered with snow, and the clouds cling to them and pass the night there."

Then a new miracle happened: the clouds vanished from the highest peak and on the top of it appeared a horseman, in full knightly accoutrements, with his eyes closed, and he was distinctly seen as though he had been standing close to them.

Then, from among the marvelling and fearful people, a man leapt on a horse, and looking wildly about him as though to see whether he were pursued, hurriedly set his horse galloping at full tilt. It was the wizard. Why was he so terrified? Looking in terror at the marvellous knight, he had recognized the face which had appeared to him when he was working his spells. He could not have said why his soul was thrown into confusion at this sight, and, looking fearfully about him, he raced till he was overtaken by night and the stars came out. Then he turned homewards, perhaps to ask the Evil One what was meant by this marvel. He was just about to leap with his horse over a stream which lay across his path when his horse suddenly stopped in full gallop, looked round at him—and, marvellous to relate! laughed aloud! Two rows of white teeth gleamed horribly in the darkness. The wizard's hair stood up on his head. He uttered a wild scream and wept like a madman and turned his horse straight for Kiev. He felt as though he were being pursued on all sides: the trees that surrounded him in the dark forest strove to strangle him, nodding their black beards and stretching out their long branches; the stars seemed to be racing ahead of him and pointing at the sinner; the very road seemed to be flying after him. The despairing wizard fled to the holy places in Kiev.

XV

A holy hermit sat alone in his cave before a little lamp and did not take his eyes off the holy book. It was many years since he had first shut himself up in his cave; he had made himself a coffin of planks in which he lay down to sleep instead of a bed. The holy man closed his book and fell to praying. Suddenly there ran in a man of a strange and terrible aspect. The holy hermit was astounded and stepped back, seeing such a man. He was trembling all over like an aspen leaf; his eyes wandered wildly, a light of terror gleamed in them; his hideous face made one shudder.

"Father, pray! Pray!" he shouted desperately. "Pray for a lost soul!" And he sank to the ground.

The holy hermit crossed himself, took up his book, opened it and stepped back in horror, dropping the book.

"No, incredible sinner! There is no mercy for you! Begone! I cannot pray for you!"

"No?" the wizard cried frantically.

"Look—the letters in the holy book are dripping with blood! There has never been such a great sinner in the world!"

"Father, you are mocking me!"

"Hence, accursed sinner! I am not mocking you. I am overcome with fear. It is not good for a man to be with you!"

"No, no! You *are* mocking—don't deny it! I see that your lips are smiling and the rows of your old teeth are gleaming white!"

And like one possessed he flew at the holy hermit and killed him.

A terrible moan was heard and echoed through the forest and the fields. Dry withered arms with long claws rose up from beyond the forest; they trembled and disappeared.

And now he felt neither fear nor anything else. All was confusion: there was a noise in his ears, a noise in his head as though he were drunk, and everything before his eyes was veiled as though by spiders' webs. Leaping on to his horse, he rode straight to Kanev, thinking thence to go through Cherkasi direct to the Crimean Tatars, though he did not know why he went. He rode one day and another, and still Kanev was not in sight. The road was the right one, he ought to have reached Kanev long before, but there was no sign of it. Far away there gleamed the cupolas of churches; but that was not Kanev but Shumsk. The wizard was amazed to find that he had travelled quite the wrong way. He turned back towards Kiev, and a day later a town appeared—not Kiev but Galich, a town further from Kiev than Shumsk, and not far from Hungary. At a loss what to do he turned back, but felt again that he was going backwards as he went on. No one in the world could have told what was in the wizard's soul; and had anyone seen and known, he would not have slept at night, or laughed ever again in his life. It was not malice, not terror, and not fierce anger. There is no word in the world to say what it was. He was burning and boiling, he would have liked to trample the whole world and to take the whole country from Kiev to Galich with all the people and everything in it and drown it in the Black Sea. But it was not from malice he would do it; he did not know why he wanted it. He shuddered when he saw the Carpathian Mountains and the lofty Krivan, its crest capped with a grey cloud; the horse galloped on and now was racing among the mountains. The clouds suddenly lifted, and the horseman appeared facing him in his terrible immensity. The wizard tried to halt, he tugged at the reins; but the horse neighed wildly, tossed its mane, and dashed towards the knight. The wizard felt everything freeze within him, while the motionless horseman stirred and suddenly opened his eyes, saw the wizard flying towards him and laughed. The wild laugh echoed through the mountains like a clap of thunder and resounded in the wizard's heart, setting his whole body throbbing. He felt as though some mighty being had taken possession of him and were moving within him, hammering on his heart and his veins—so fearfully that laugh resounded within him!

The horseman stretched out his terrible hand, seized the wizard, and lifted him into the air. The wizard died instantly and opened his eyes after his death: but he was dead and looked out of dead eyes. Neither the living nor the risen from the dead have such a terrible look in their eyes. He turned his dead eyes from side to side and saw dead men rising up from Kiev, from Galicia, and the Carpathian Mountains, exactly like him.

Pale, very pale, one taller than another, one bonier than another, they thronged round the horseman who held his awful prey in his hand. The horseman laughed once more and flung the wizard into a precipice. And all the corpses leapt into the precipice and dug their teeth into the dead man's flesh. Another, taller and more terrible than all the rest, tried to rise from the ground but could not—he had not the power because he had grown so immense underground; and if he had risen out of the earth he would have overturned the Carpathians and Transylvania and Turkey. He only stirred slightly, but that set the whole earth quaking, and overturned many houses and crushed many people.

And often in the Carpathians a sound is heard as though a thousand mills were churning up the water with their wheels:

it is the sound of the dead men gnawing a corpse in the fatal precipice which no man has seen yet, for none dare pass it. It often happens that the earth trembles from one end to another; learned men say that is due to a mountain near the sea, from which flames issue and hot streams flow. But the old men who live in Hungary and Galicia know better, and say that it is the dead man, who has grown so immense in the earth, trying to rise and making the earth quake.

XVI

A crowd had gathered round an old *bandura*-player in the town of Glukhov and had been listening for an hour to the blind man's playing. No *bandura*-player sang so well and such marvellous songs. First he sang of the rule of the Hetmans in the old days, of Sagaidachny and Khmelnitsky. Times were different then: the Cossacks were at the height of their glory, they trampled their foes underfoot and no one dared to mock at them. The old man sang merry songs, too, and looked about at the crowd as though his eyes could see, and his fingers with little plates of bone fixed on them danced like flies over the strings, and it seemed that the strings themselves were playing; and the crowd, the old people looking down and the young staring at the singer, dared not even whisper among themselves.

"Stay," said the old man, "I will sing to you of what happened long ago." The people pressed closer and the blind man sang:

"In the days of Stepan, Prince of Transylvania, who was also King of the Poles, there lived two Cossacks: Ivan and Petro. They lived together like brothers. 'See here, Ivan,' said Petro, 'whatever you gain, let us go halves; when one is merry, the other is merry, too; when one is sad, the other is sad, too; when one wins booty, we share it; when one gets taken prisoner, the other sells everything to ransom him, or else goes himself into captivity.' And, indeed, whatever the Cossacks gained they shared equally; whether they drove away herds of cattle or horses, they halved them.

"King Stepan made war on the Turks. He had been fighting with the Turks three weeks and could not drive them out. And the Turks had a pasha who with a few janissaries could cut down a whole regiment. So King Stepan proclaimed that if a brave warrior could be found to bring him the pasha dead or alive, he would give him a reward equal to the pay of the whole army.

"'Let us go and catch the pasha, brother,' said Ivan to Petro. And the two Cossacks set off, one one way and the other the other.

"There is no telling whether Petro would have been successful or not; but Ivan led the pasha with a lasso round his neck to the King. 'Brave fellow!' said King Stepan, and he commanded that he should be given a sum equal to the pay of the whole army, and that he should be given land wherever he chose and cattle as many as he pleased. As soon as Ivan received the reward from the King, he shared the money with Petro. Petro took half of the King's money, but could not bear the thought that Ivan had been so honoured by the King, and he hid deep in his heart desire for vengeance.

"The two Cossacks were journeying to the land beyond the Carpathians that the King had granted to Ivan. Ivan had set his son on the horse behind him, tying the child to himself. Night fell, and still they rode on. The boy had fallen asleep; Ivan, too, began to doze. Do not sleep, Cossack, the mountain paths are perilous! But the Cossack had a horse which knew the way; it would not slip or stumble. There is a precipice between the mountains; no one has ever seen the bottom of it; it is as deep as the sky is high. The road passed just above the precipice; two men could ride abreast on it, but for three it was too narrow. The horse began stepping cautiously with the slumbering Cossack on its back. Petro rode beside him; he trembled all over and was breathless with joy. He looked round and pushed his adopted brother into the precipice; and the horse with the Cossack and the child fell into the abyss.

"But Ivan caught at a branch and only the horse dropped to the bottom. He began scrambling up with his son upon his back. He looked up when he was nearly at the top and saw that Petro was holding a lance ready to thrust him back. 'Merciful God! I wish I could never raise my eyes again rather than see my own brother holding a lance, ready to thrust me back! Dear brother, stab me if that is my fate, but take my son: what has the innocent child done that he should be doomed to so cruel a death?' Petro laughed and thrust at him with the lance; the Cossack fell with his child to the bottom. Petro took all his wealth and began to live like a pasha. No one had such droves of horses as Petro; no one had such flocks of sheep. And Petro died.

"After he was dead, God summoned the souls of the two brothers, Ivan and Petro, to the judgement seat. 'This man is a great sinner,' said God. 'Ivan, it will take me long to find a punishment for him; you choose him a punishment!' For a long time Ivan pondered what punishment to fix and at last he said:

"'This man did me a great injury; he betrayed his brother like a Judas and robbed him of his honourable kin and offspring. And a man without honourable kin and offspring is like a seed of wheat dropped into the earth and wasted in vain. If it does not sprout, no one knows that the seed has been dropped into the earth.

"'Let it be, O Lord, that none of his descendants may be happy upon earth; that the last of his race may be the worst criminal that has ever been seen, and that at every crime he commits, his ancestors, unable to rest in their graves and suffering torments unknown to the world of the living, should rise from their tombs! And that the Judas, Petro, should be unable to rise and that hence he should suffer pain all the more intense; that he should bite the earth like a madman and writhe underground!

"'And when the time comes when that man's wickedness has reached its full measure, let me, O Lord God, rise on my horse from the precipice to the highest mountain peak, and let him come to me and I will throw him from that mountain into the deepest abyss. And let all his dead ancestors, wherever they lived in their lifetime, come from various parts of the earth to gnaw him for the sufferings he inflicted upon them, and let them gnaw him for ever, so that I may rejoice looking at his sufferings. And let the Judas, Petro, be unable to rise out of the earth, let him lust to gnaw too, but be forced to gnaw himself, and let his bones grow bigger and bigger as time goes on, so that his pain may be the greater. That torture will be worse for him than any other, for there is no greater torture for a man than to long for revenge and be unable to take it.'

"'A terrible punishment thou hast devised, O man!' God said. 'All shall be as thou hast said; but thou shalt sit for ever on thy horse there and shalt not enter the Kingdom of Heaven!' And all was fulfilled accordingly; the strange horseman still sits on his steed in the Carpathians and sees the dead men gnawing the corpse in the bottomless abyss, and feels how the dead Petro grows larger underground, gnaws his bones in dreadful agony, and sets the earth quaking fearfully."

The blind man had finished his song; he began thrumming the strings again and singing amusing ballads about Foma and Yerema, and Stklyar Stokoza. But his listeners, old and young, could not rouse themselves from reverie; they still stood with bowed heads, pondering on the terrible story of long ago.

IVAN FYODOROVICH SHPONKA AND HIS AUNT

There is a story about this story; we were told it by Stepan Ivanovich Kurochka, who came over from Gadyach. You must know that my memory is incredibly poor: you may tell me a thing or not tell it, it is all the same. It is like pouring water into a sieve. Being aware of this failing, I purposely begged him to write the story down in a notebook. Well, God give him good health, he was always kind to me; he set to work and wrote it down. I put it in the little table; I expect you know it; it stands in the corner as you come in by the door. But there, I forgot that you had never been in my house. My old woman, with whom I have lived thirty years, has never learnt to read—no use hiding it. Well, I noticed that she baked the pies on paper of some sort. She bakes pies beautifully, dear readers; you will never taste better pies anywhere. I happened to look at the underside of a pie—and what do I see? Written words! I went to the table as though my heart had told me to do so; only half the book was there! All the other pages she had carried off for the pies! What could I do? It would be silly to fight at our age!

Last year I happened to be passing through Gadyach. Before I reached the town I purposely tied a knot in my handkerchief that I might not forget to ask Stepan Ivanovich about it. That was not all; I vowed to myself that as soon as ever I sneezed in the town I would be sure to think of it. It was all no use. I drove through the town and sneezed and blew my nose, too, but still I forgot it; and I only thought of it about six versts after I had passed through the towngate. There was no help for it, I had to print it without the end. However, if anyone particularly wants to know what happened later on in the story, he need only go to Gadyach and ask Stepan Ivanovich. He will be glad to tell the story, I daresay, all over again from the beginning. He lives not far from the brick church. There is a little lane close by, and as soon as you turn into the lane it is the second or third gate. Or better still, his yard is where you will see a big pole with a quail on it and where a stout peasant woman in a green skirt (it may be as well to mention that he is a bachelor) will come out to meet you. However, you may meet him in the market, where he is to be seen every morning before nine o'clock, choosing fish and vegetables for his table and talking to Father Antip or the Jewish contractor. You will know him at once, for no one else has trousers of coloured linen or a yellow cotton coat. And another thing you may know him by—he always swings his arms as he walks. Denis Petrovich, the late assessor, used to say when he saw him in the distance, "Look, here comes our windmill!"

I

IVAN FYODOROVICH SHPONKA

It is four years since Ivan Fyodorovich retired from the army
and came to live on his Vitrebenki farmstead. When he was still a
boy and was accordingly called Vanyusha, he went to the Gadyach district school, and I must say he was a very well-behaved
and industrious boy. Nikifor Timofeyevich Deyeprichastiye,*
the teacher of Russian grammar, used to say that if all the boys
had been as anxious to do their best as Shponka, he would not
have brought into the class-room the maple-wood ruler with
which, as he owned himself, he was tired of hitting the lazy and
mischievous boys' hands. His exercise book was always neat,
with a ruled margin, and not the tiniest blot anywhere. He always sat quietly, with his arms folded and his eyes fixed on the
teacher, and he never used to stick scraps of paper on the back
of the boy sitting in front of him, never cut the form, and never
played at shoving the other boys off the form before the master
came in. If anyone wanted a penknife to sharpen his pen, he
immediately applied to Ivan Fyodorovich, knowing that he
always had a penknife, and Ivan Fyodorovich—at that time
simply Vanyusha—would take it out of a little leather case
attached to a buttonhole of his grey coat, and would only re-
quest that the sharp edge should not be used for scraping the
pen, pointing out that there was a blunt side for the purpose.
Such good conduct soon attracted the attention of the Latin
master himself, whose cough in the passage was enough to reduce
the class to terror, even before his frieze coat and pock-marked
countenance had appeared in the doorway. This terrible master,
who always had two bundles of birch lying on his desk and half

* Russian for verbal adverb.—*Ed.*

of whose pupils were always on their knees, made Ivan Fyodorovich monitor, although there were many boys in the class of much greater ability.

At this point I cannot omit an incident which had an influence on the whole of his future life. One of the boys entrusted to his charge tried to induce his monitor to write *scit* on his report, though he had not learnt his lesson, by bringing into class a pancake soaked in butter and wrapped in paper. Though Ivan Fyodorovich was usually conscientious, on this occasion he was hungry and could not resist the temptation; he took the pancake, and holding a book up before him, began eating it, and he was so absorbed in this occupation that he did not observe that a deathly silence had fallen upon the class-room. He only came to with horror when a terrible hand reaching from a frieze overcoat seized him by the ear and dragged him into the middle of the room. "Hand over that pancake! Hand it over, I tell you, you rascal!" said the terrible master; he seized the buttery pancake in his fingers and flung it out of the window, sternly forbidding the boys running about in the yard to pick it up. Then he proceeded to whack Ivan Fyodorovich very painfully on the hands; and quite rightly: the hands were responsible for taking the pancake and no other part of the body. Anyway, the timidity which had always been characteristic of him was more marked from then on. Possibly the same incident was the reason why he never felt a desire to enter the civil service, having learnt by experience that one is not always successful in covering up one's misdeeds.

He was very nearly fifteen when he moved up into the second form, where instead of the four rules of arithmetic and the abridged catechism, he went on to the longer one, the book on the duties of man, and fractions. But seeing, as they say, that the further you went into the forest the thicker the wood became, and receiving the news that his father had departed this life, he stayed only two years longer at school, and with his mother's consent joined an infantry regiment.

The regiment in question was not at all of the class to which many infantry regiments belong, and although it was for the most part stationed in country places, it was in no way inferior to many cavalry regiments. Most of the officers drank neat spirit and were quite as good at dragging about Jews by their curls as the hussars; some of them even danced the mazurka, and the colonel of the regiment never missed an opportunity of mentioning the fact when he was talking to anyone in society. "Among my officers," he used to say, patting himself on the belly after every word, "a number dance the mazurka, quite a number of them, a very great number of them." To show our readers the degree of culture of the regiment, we must add that two of the officers were passionately fond of playing cards and used to gamble away their uniforms, caps, overcoats, sword-knots, and even their underclothes, which is more than you could find even in a cavalry regiment.

Contact with such comrades did not, however, diminish Ivan Fyodorovich's timidity; and as he did not drink neat spirit, preferring to it a glassful of ordinary vodka before dinner and supper, did not dance the mazurka or play cards, he was naturally bound to be always left alone. And so it came to pass that while the others were driving about on hired horses and visiting the less important landowners, he sat at home and spent his time in pursuits peculiar to a mild and gentle soul: he either polished his buttons, or read a fortune-teller's book, or set mousetraps in the corners of his room, or he took off his uniform and lay on his bed.

On the other hand, no one in the regiment was more punctual

in his duties than Ivan Fyodorovich, and he drilled his platoon
in such a way that the commander of the company always
held him up as a model to the others. Consequently in a short
time—eleven years after becoming an ensign—he was promoted
to be a second lieutenant.

During that time he had received the news that his mother
was dead, and his aunt, his mother's sister, whom he only
knew from her bringing him in his childhood—and even sending
him when he was at Gadyach—dried pears and extremely nice
honey-cakes which she made herself (she was on bad terms
with his mother and so Ivan Fyodorovich had not seen her in
later years), this aunt, in the goodness of her heart, undertook
to look after his little estate and in due time informed him of
the fact by letter.

Ivan Fyodorovich, having the fullest confidence in his aunt's
good sense, continued to perform his duties as before. Some
men in his position would have grown conceited at such pro
motion, but pride was a feeling of which he knew nothing, and
as a lieutenant he was the same Ivan Fyodorovich as he had
been when an ensign. He spent another four years in the re
giment after the event of so much consequence to him, and
was about to leave Mogilyov Province for Great Russia with
his regiment when he received a letter as follows:

"My dear Nephew, Ivan Fyodorovich,

I am sending you some linen: five pairs of thread socks and
four shirts of fine linen; and what is more, I want to talk to you
of something serious; since you have already a rank of some
importance, as I suppose you are aware, and have reached a
time of life when it is fitting to take up the management of
your land, there is no reason for you to remain any longer in
military service. I am getting old and can no longer see to

everything on your farm; and in fact there is a great deal that I want to talk to you about in person.

"Come, Vanyusha! Looking forward to the real pleasure of seeing you, I remain your very affectionate aunt,

"Vasilisa Tsupchevska."

"P.S.—There are wonderful turnips in our kitchen-garden, they look very strange, more like potatoes than turnips."

A week after receiving this letter Ivan Fyodorovich wrote an answer as follows:

'Honoured Madam, Auntie Vasilisa Kashporovna,

Thank you very much for sending the linen. My socks especially were very old; my orderly had darned them four times and that had made them very tight. As to your views in regard to my service in the army, I completely agree with you, and the other day I sent in my papers. As soon as I get my discharge I will engage a chaise. As to your commission in regard to the seed wheat of the Siberian variety, I cannot carry it out; there is none in all Mogilyov Province. As regards pigs here, they are mostly fed on brewers' mash together with a little beer when it has grown flat.

"With the greatest respect, honoured Madam and Auntie, I remain your nephew,

"Ivan Shponka."

At last Ivan Fyodorovich received his discharge with the rank of lieutenant, hired for forty rubles a Jew to drive from Mogilyov to Gadyach, and set off in the chaise just at the time when the trees were clothed with young and still scanty leaves, the whole earth was bright with fresh green, and there was the fragrance of spring in the fields.

II

THE JOURNEY

Nothing of great interest occurred on the journey. They
were travelling a little over a fortnight. Ivan Fyodorovich
might have arrived a little sooner than that, but the devout
Jew kept the Sabbath on the Saturdays and, putting his horse-
cloth over his head, prayed the whole day. Ivan Fyodorovich
however, as I have already had occasion to mention, was a man
who did not give way to being bored. During these intervals
he undid his trunk, took out his underclothes, inspected them
thoroughly to see whether they were properly washed and folded
carefully removed fluff from his new uniform, which had been
made without epaulettes, and repacked it all in the best possible
way. He was not fond of reading; and if he did sometimes
look into a fortune-teller's book, it was because he liked to meet
again what he had already read several times. In the same
way one who lives in the town goes every day to the club, not
for the sake of hearing anything new there, but in order to
meet there friends with whom it has been one's habit to chat
at the club from time immemorial. In the same way a government clerk will read a directory of addresses with immense
satisfaction several times a day with no ulterior object but
merely because he is entertained by the printed list of names
"Ah! Ivan Gavrilovich So-and-so!" he murmurs to himself
"And here am I! H'm!" And next time he reads it over again
with exactly the same exclamations.

After a fortnight's journey Ivan Fyodorovich reached a little
village about a hundred versts from Gadyach. This was on
a Friday. The sun had long set when with the chaise and the
Jew he reached an inn.

The inn differed in no respect from other little village inns.
As a rule the traveller is zealously regaled in them with hay
and oats, as though he were a post-horse. But should he want
to lunch as decent people do lunch, he would keep his appetite
intact for some future opportunity. Ivan Fyodorovich, knowing
all this, had provided himself beforehand with two bundles
of bread-rings and a sausage, and asking for a glass of vodka,
of which there is never a shortage in any inn, he began his
supper, sitting down on a bench before an oak table which was
fixed immovably in the clay floor.

Meanwhile he heard the rattle of a chaise. The gates creaked,
but it was a long while before the chaise drove into the yard.
A loud voice was engaged in scolding the old woman who kept
the inn. "I will drive in," Ivan Fyodorovich heard someone
say, "but if I am bitten by a single bug in your inn, I will beat
you, on my soul I will, you old witch! And I will give you
nothing for your hay!"

A minute later the door opened and there walked, or rather
squeezed himself in a stout man in a green frock-coat. His head
rested immovably on his short neck, which seemed even thicker
because of the double chin. To judge from his appearance, he
belonged to that class of men who have never bothered about
trifles and whose whole life has passed easily.

"I wish you good day, sir!" he pronounced on seeing Ivan
Fyodorovich.

Ivan Fyodorovich bowed in silence.

"May I ask to whom I have the honour of speaking?" the
stout new-comer continued.

At this Ivan Fyodorovich involuntarily got up and stood at
attention, as he usually did when the colonel asked him a question.

"Retired Lieutenant Ivan Fyodorovich Shponka," he answered.

"And may I ask what place you are bound for?"

"My own farm, Vitrebenki."

"Vitrebenki!" cried the stern interrogator. "Allow me, sir, allow me!" he said, going towards him and waving his arms as though someone were hindering him, or as though he were making his way through a crowd; coming up to Ivan Fyodorovich, he folded him in an embrace and kissed him first on the right cheek and then on the left and then on the right again. Ivan Fyodorovich greatly enjoyed the osculation, for the stranger's large cheeks felt like soft cushions to his lips.

"Allow me to introduce myself, sir!" the stout man continued: "I am a landowner of the same district of Gadyach and your neighbour. I live not more than five versts from your Vitrebenki, in the village of Khortishche; and my name is Grigory Grigoryevich Storchenko. You really must, sir, you really must pay me a visit at Khortishche. I won't speak to you if you don't. I am in haste now on business. Why, what's this?" he said in a mild voice to his postilion, a boy in a Cossack jacket with patched elbows and a bewildered expression, who came in and put bags and boxes on the table. "What's this, what's the meaning of it?" And by degrees Grigory Grigoryevich's voice grew more and more threatening. "Did I tell you to put them here, my good lad? Did I tell you to put them here, you rascal? Didn't I tell you to heat the chicken up first, you scoundrel? Get out!" he shouted, stamping. "Wait, you monkey-face! Where's the basket with the bottles? Ivan Fyodorovich!" he said, pouring out a glass of liqueur, "I humbly beg you to take some cordial!"

"Oh, really, I cannot—I have already had occasion—" Ivan Fyodorovich began hesitatingly.

"I won't hear a word, sir!" The landowner raised his voice. "I won't hear a word! I won't budge till you take it!"

Ivan Fyodorovich, seeing that it was impossible to refuse, emptied the glass not without pleasure.

"This is a fowl, sir," said the fat Grigory Grigoryevich, carving it in a wooden box. "I must tell you that my cook Yavdokha is fond of a drop at times and so she often dries up things. Hey, lad!" He turned to the boy in the Cossack jacket, who was bringing in a feather bed and pillows. "Make my bed on the floor in the middle of the room! Mind you put plenty of hay under the pillow! And pull a bit of hemp from the woman's distaff to stop up my ears for the night. I must tell you, sir, that I have the habit of stopping up my ears at night ever since the damnable occasion when a cockroach crawled into my left ear in a Russian inn. The confounded long-beards, as I found out afterwards, even eat their soup with cockroaches in it. Impossible to describe what happened to me; there was such a tickling, such a tickling in my ear—it almost drove me crazy! I was cured by a simple old woman in our parts, and can you imagine how she did it? She charmed it out simply by whispering. What do you think, sir, about doctors? I think they just hoax us and make fools of us. Sometimes an old woman knows a dozen times as much as all those doctors."

"Indeed, what you say is perfectly true, sir. There certainly are cases—" Here Ivan Fyodorovich paused as though he could not find the right word.

It may not be amiss to mention here that he was at no time lavish of words. This may have been due to timidity, or to a desire to express himself elegantly.

"Shake up the hay properly, shake it up properly!" said Grigory Grigoryevich to his servant. "The hay is so bad about here that you may come upon a twig in it any minute. Allow me, sir, to wish you a good night! We shall not see each other tomorrow. I am setting off before dawn. Your Jew will keep the Sabbath because tomorrow is Saturday, so you need not get up early. Don't forget my invitation; I won't speak to you if you don't come to see me at Khortishche."

At this point Grigory Grigoryevich's servant pulled off his coat and high boots and pulled his dressing-gown on him instead, and Grigory Grigoryevich stretched on his bed, and it looked as though one huge feather bed were lying on another.

"Hey, lad! Where are you, rascal? Come here and arrange my quilt. Hey, lad, prop up my head with hay! Have you watered the horses yet? Some more hay! Here, under this side! And arrange the quilt properly, you rascal! That's right, more! Oof!"

Then Grigory Grigoryevich heaved two sighs and filled the whole room with a terrible whistling through his nose, snoring so loudly at times that the old woman, who was snoozing on the stove-couch, suddenly woke up and stared about her wide-eyed, but seeing nothing, subsided and went to sleep again.

When Ivan Fyodorovich woke up next morning, the stout landowner was gone. That was the only noteworthy incident that occurred on the journey. Two days later he drew near his little farm.

He felt his heart begin to throb when the windmill waving its sails peeped out and, as the Jew drove his hacks uphill, the row of willows came in sight below. The pond shone brightly through them and a breath of freshness rose from it. Here he used to bathe in old days; in this pond he used to wade with the peasant lads up to his neck after crayfish. The chaise mounted the dam and Ivan Fyodorovich saw the little old-fashioned house thatched with reeds, and the apple and cherry trees which he used to climb on the sly. He had no sooner driven into the yard than dogs of all kinds—brown, black, grey, spotted —ran up from every side. Some flew under the horse's hoofs, barking, others ran behind the cart, discovering that the axle was smeared with bacon fat; one, standing near the kitchen and keeping his foot on a bone, uttered a volley of shrill barks; and another gave tongue in the distance, running to and fro, wagging his tail, and seeming to say: "Look, good Christians, what a fine young fellow I am!" Boys in grubby shirts ran out to stare. A sow who was strolling in the yard with sixteen little pigs lifted her snout with an inquisitive air and grunted louder than usual. In the yard a number of hempen sheets were lying on the ground, covered with wheat, millet, and barley drying in the sun. A good many different kinds of herbs, such as wild chicory and swine-herb, were drying on the roof.

Ivan Fyodorovich was so occupied in scrutinizing all this that he was roused only when a spotted dog bit the Jew on the calf of his leg as he was getting down from the box. The servants, that is, the cook and another woman and two girls in woollen petticoats, ran out and after the first exclamations: "Why, it's our young master!" informed him that his aunt was sowing sweet corn together with the girl Palashka and Omelko the coachman, who also often performed the duties of a gardener and watchman. But his aunt, who had seen the chaise in the distance, was already on the spot. And Ivan Fyodorovich was astonished when she almost lifted him from the ground in her arms, hardly able to believe that this could be the aunt who had written to him of her old age and infirmities.

III

AUNTIE

Auntie Vasilisa Kashporovna was at this time about fifty. She had never been married, and usually declared that she valued her maiden state above everything. However, to the best of my memory, no one had ever courted her. This was due to the fact that all men felt a certain timidity in her presence, and never had the spirit to propose to her. "A girl of great character, is Vasilisa Kashporovna!" all the young men used to say, and they were quite right, too, for there was no one Vasilisa Kashporovna could not get the whip hand of. With her own manly hand, tugging every day at his scalp-lock, she could, unaided, turn the drunken miller, a worthless fellow, into a perfect treasure. She was of almost gigantic stature and her corpulence and strength were fully in proportion. It seemed as though nature had made an unpardonable mistake in condemning her to wear a dark brown gown with little flounces on week-days and a red cashmere shawl on Easter Sunday and on her name-day, though a dragoon's moustaches and top-boots would have suited her better than anything. On the other hand, her pursuits completely corresponded to her appearance: she rowed the boat herself and was more skilful with the oars than any fisherman; shot game; supervised the mowers all the while they were at work; knew the exact number of the melons in the kitchen garden; took a toll of five kopeks from every waggon that crossed her dam; climbed the trees and shook down the pears; beat lazy vassals with her terrible hand and with the same formidable hand bestowed a glass of vodka on the deserving. Almost at the same moment she was scolding, dyeing yarn, racing to the kitchen, brewing kvass, making jam with honey; she was busy all day long and managed to get everything done on time. The result of all this was that Ivan Fyodorovich's little estate, which had consisted of eighteen souls at the last census, was flourishing in the fullest sense of the word. Moreover, she had a very warm affection for her nephew and carefully accumulated kopeks for him.

From the time of his arrival at his home Ivan Fyodorovich's

life was completely transformed and took an entirely different turn. It seemed as though nature had designed him expressly for looking after an estate of eighteen souls. Auntie herself observed that he would make an excellent farmer, though she did not yet permit him to meddle in every branch of the management. "He's but a child yet," she used to say, though Ivan Fyodorovich was, as a matter of fact, not far off forty. "How should he know it all!"

However, he was always in the fields with the reapers and mowers, and this was a source of unutterable pleasure to his gentle heart. The sweep of a dozen or more gleaming scythes in unison; the sound of the grass falling in even swathes; the occasional carolling songs of the reapers, now joyous as the welcoming of a guest, now mournful as parting; the calm pure evening—and what an evening! How free. and fresh the air was! How everything revived: the steppe flushed red, then turned dark blue and glowed with colours; quails, bustards, gulls, grasshoppers, thousands of insects whistling, buzzing, chirring, calling, and all of it suddenly blending into a harmonious chorus; nothing silent for an instant. Meanwhile the sun set and disappeared. Oh, how fresh and delightful it was! Here and there in the fields fires were built and cauldrons set over them, and round the fires the moustached mowers sat down; the steam from the dumplings floated upwards; the twilight turned greyer... It is hard to say what passed in Ivan Fyodorovich at such times. When he joined the mowers, he forgot to try their dumplings, though he liked them immensely, and stood motionless, watching a gull drop out of sight in the sky, or counting the sheaves of corn dotting the field.

Before long Ivan Fyodorovich was spoken of as a great farmer. Auntie was never tired of rejoicing over her nephew and never missed an opportunity of boasting of him. One day—it was just after the end of the harvest, that is, late in July—Vasilisa Kashporovna took Ivan Fyodorovich by the arm with a mysterious air, and said she wanted to speak to him of a matter which had long been on her mind.

"You are aware, dear Ivan Fyodorovich," she began, "that there are eighteen souls on your farm, though, indeed, that is by the census register, and in reality they may reckon up to more; there may be twenty-four. But that is not the point. You know the copse that lies beyond our estate, and no doubt you know the broad meadow beyond it; there are very nearly twenty dessiatines in it; and the grass is so good that it is worth a hundred rubles every year, especially if, as they say, a cavalry regiment is to be stationed at Gadyach."

"To be sure, Auntie, I know: the grass is very good."

"You needn't tell me the grass is very good, I know it; but do you know that all that land is by rights yours? Why do you stare like that? Listen, Ivan Fyodorovich! You remember Stepan Kuzmich? But how can I ask? You were so little then that you couldn't even pronounce his name. Yes, indeed! When I came on the very eve of Christmas Fast and took you in my arms, you almost ruined my dress; luckily I was just in time to hand you to your nurse, Matryona; you were such a horrid little thing then! But that is not the point. All the land beyond our farm, and the village of Khortishche itself belonged to Stepan Kuzmich. I must tell you that before you were in this world he used to visit your mamma—though, indeed, only when your father was not at home. Not that I say it in blame of her— God rest her soul!—though your poor mother was always unfair to me. But that is not the point. Be that as it may, Stepan Kuzmich made a deed of gift to you of the estate I am speaking about. But your poor mamma, between you and me, was a very strange character. The devil himself—God forgive me for the nasty word!—would have been unable to make her out. What she did with that deed of gift God only knows. I think it must be in the hands of that old bachelor, Grigory Grigoryevich Storchenko. That pot-bellied rascal has got hold of the whole estate. I'd bet anything you like that he has hidden that deed."

"Allow me to ask, Auntie: isn't he the Storchenko whose acquaintance I made at the inn?"

Thereupon Ivan Fyodorovich described his meeting with Storchenko.

"Who knows," said his aunt after a moment's thought, "perhaps he is not a rascal. It's true that it's only six months since he came to live in these parts; you cannot come to know a man so soon. The old lady, his mother, is a very sensible woman, so I hear, and a great hand at pickling cucumbers. Her serf girls can make capital carpets. But as you say he gave you such a friendly welcome, you must go and see him—perhaps the old sinner will listen to his conscience and will give up what is not his. If you like you can go in the chaise, only those confounded brats have pulled out all the nails at the back. I must tell the coachman, Omelko, to nail the leather on better everywhere."

"What for, Auntie? I will take the trap that you sometimes go out shooting in."

There the conversation ended.

IV

THE DINNER

It was about dinner-time when Ivan Fyodorovich drove into the village of Khortishche, and he felt a little timid as he approached the manor-house. It was a long house, not thatched with reeds like the houses of many of the neighbouring land-owners, but with a wooden roof. Two barns in the yard also had wooden roofs: the gate was of oak. Ivan Fyodorovich felt like a dandy who, on arriving at a ball, sees everyone more smartly dressed than himself. He stopped his trap by a barn as a sign of respect and walked to the front door.

"Ah, Ivan Fyodorovich!" cried the fat man Grigory Grigoryevich, who was crossing the yard in his coat but without cravat, waistcoat and braces. But apparently even this attire weighed oppressively on his bulky person, for the perspiration was streaming down him. "Why, you said you would come as soon as you had seen your aunt, and all this time you have not been here!" After these words Ivan Fyodorovich's lips found themselves again in contact with the same cushions.

"Chiefly being busy looking after the farm—I have come just for a minute, as a matter of fact, on business."

"For a minute? Well, that won't do. Hey, lad!" shouted the fat gentleman, and the same boy in the Cossack jacket ran out of the kitchen. "Tell Kasyan to shut the gate tight—do you hear?—make it fast! And take this gentleman's horse out of the shafts this minute. Please come indoors; it is so hot out here that my shirt's soaked."

On going indoors Ivan Fyodorovich made up his mind to waste no time and in spite of his shyness to act with decision.

"My aunt had the honour—she told me that a deed of gift of the late Stepan Kuzmich—"

It is difficult to describe the unpleasant grimace made by the broad countenance of Grigory Grigoryevich at these words.

"Oh dear, I can't hear anything!" he responded. "I must tell you that a cockroach got into my left ear. Those bearded Russians breed cockroaches in their huts. No pen can describe

what agony it was, it kept tickling and tickling. An old woman
cured me by the simplest means—"

"I meant to say," Ivan Fyodorovich ventured to interrupt,
seeing that Grigory Grigoryevich was trying to change the
subject, "that in the late Stepan Kuzmich's will mention
is made, so to speak, of a deed of gift. According to it I ought—"

"I know; so your aunt has told you that story already. It's
a lie, upon my soul it is! My uncle made no deed of gift. It is
true, some such deed is referred to in the will, but where is it?
No one has produced it. I tell you this because I sincerely
wish you well. Upon my soul it is a lie!"

Ivan Fyodorovich said nothing, thinking that his aunt really
might be mistaken.

"Ah, here comes Mother with my sisters!" said Grigory
Grigoryevich. "So dinner is ready. Let us go!"

Thereupon he drew Ivan Fyodorovich by the hand into
a room in which vodka and savouries were standing on the
table.

At the same time a short old lady, a regular coffee-pot in
a cap, with two young ladies, one fair and one dark, came
in. Ivan Fyodorovich, like a well-bred gentleman, went up to
kiss the old lady's hand and then the hands of the two young
ladies.

"This is our neighbour, Ivan Fyodorovich Shponka, Mother,"
said Grigory Grigoryevich.

The old lady looked intently at Ivan Fyodorovich, or perhaps it only seemed so. She was good-natured simplicity itself,
though; she looked as though she would like to ask Ivan Fyodorovich: "How many cucumbers have you pickled for the winter?"

"Have you had some vodka?" the old lady asked.

"You mustn't have slept enough, Mother," said Grigory
Grigoryevich. "Whoever asks a visitor whether he has had

anything. You offer it to us, that's all: whether we've had any or not, that's our business. Ivan Fyodorovich, will you have centaury vodka or the Trofimov brand? Which do you prefer? And you, Ivan Ivanovich, why are you standing there?" said Grigory Grigoryevich, turning round, and Ivan Fyodorovich saw the gentleman so addressed approaching the vodka, in a frock-coat with long skirts and an immense stand-up collar, which covered the whole back of his head, so that his head sat in it, as though in a chaise.

Ivan Ivanovich went up to the vodka and rubbed his hands, carefully examined the wineglass, filled it, held it up to the light, and poured all the vodka at once into his mouth. He did not, however, swallow it at once, but rinsed his mouth thoroughly with it before finally swallowing it, and then, after eating some bread and pickled mushrooms, he turned to Ivan Fyodorovich.

"Is it not Ivan Fyodorovich Shponka I have the honour of addressing?"

"Yes, sir," answered Ivan Fyodorovich.

"You have changed a great deal since I saw you last. Why," he continued, "I remember you this high!" He held his hand a yard from the floor. "Your poor father, may he rest in peace, was a rare man. He used to have melons such as you never see anywhere now. Here, for instance," he went on, drawing him aside, "they'll set melons before you on the table—melons indeed! You won't care to look at them! Would you believe it, sir, he used to have water-melons," he pronounced with a mysterious air, flinging out his arms as if he were about to embrace a stout tree-trunk, "as big as this, honest to God!"

"Come to dinner!" said Grigory Grigoryevich, taking Ivan Fyodorovich by the arm.

The company went to the dining-room.

Grigory Grigoryevich sat down in his usual place at the end
of the table, draped with an enormous table-napkin which
made him resemble the heroes depicted by barbers on their
signs. Ivan Fyodorovich, blushing, sat down in the place as-
signed to him, facing the two young ladies; and Ivan Ivanovich
did not let slip the chance of sitting down beside him, inwardly
rejoicing that he had someone to whom he could impart his
various items of information.

"You shouldn't take the bishop's nose, Ivan Fyodorovich!
It's a turkey!" said the old lady, addressing Ivan Fyodorovich,
to whom the rustic waiter in a grey swallow-tail patched with
black was offering a dish. "Take the back!"

"Mother! No one asked you to interfere!" commented Grigory
Grigoryevich. "You may be sure our visitor knows what to
take himself. Ivan Fyodorovich, take a wing, the other one
there with the gizzard! But why have you taken so little?
Take a leg! Why do you stand gaping with the dish? Ask
him! Go down on your knees, rascal! Say, at once, 'Ivan Fyodorovich, take a leg!'"

"Ivan Fyodorovich, take a leg!" the waiter with the dish
bawled, kneeling down.

"H'm! do you call this a turkey?" Ivan Ivanovich muttered
in a low voice, turning to his neighbour with an air of disdain.
"Is that what a turkey ought to look like? If you could see
my turkeys! I assure you there is more fat on one of them
than on a dozen of these. Would you believe me, sir, they
look disgusting when they walk about my yard, they are so
fat!"

"Ivan Ivanovich, you are lying!" said Grigory Grigoryevich,
overhearing these remarks.

"I tell you," Ivan Ivanovich went on to tell his neighbour,
affecting not to hear what Grigory Grigoryevich had said,

"last year when I sent them to Gadyach, they offered me fifty kopeks apiece for them, and I wouldn't take even that."

"Ivan Ivanovich! You are lying, I tell you!" said Grigory Grigoryevich, stressing each syllable for greater distinctness, and speaking more loudly than before.

But Ivan Ivanovich behaved as though the words could not possibly refer to him; he went on as before, but in a much lower voice: "Yes, sir, I would not take it. There is not a gentleman in Gadyach—"

"Ivan Ivanovich, you are a fool, and that's the truth," Grigory Grigoryevich said in a loud voice. "Ivan Fyodorovich knows all about it better than you do, I'm sure he won't believe you."

At this Ivan Ivanovich was really offended; he said no more, but fell to stowing away the turkey, even though it was not so fat as those that looked disgusting.

For a while the clatter of knives, spoons, and plates took the place of conversation, but loudest of all was the sound made by Grigory Grigoryevich as he sucked the marrow out of the mutton bones.

"Have you," inquired Ivan Ivanovich after an interval of silence, poking his head out of his chaise-like collar, "read *Travels of Korobeinikov to the Holy Land?* It's a real delight to heart and soul! Such books aren't published nowadays. I very much regret that I did not notice in what year it was written."

Ivan Fyodorovich, hearing mention of a book, applied himself diligently to taking sauce.

"It is truly marvellous, sir, when you think that a humble townsman visited all those places: over three thousand versts, sir! over three thousand versts! Truly it was by divine grace that it was vouchsafed him to reach Palestine and Jerusalem."

"So you say," said Ivan Fyodorovich, who had heard a great deal about Jerusalem from his orderly, "that he visited Jerusalem?"

"What are you saying, Ivan Fyodorovich?" Grigory Grigoryevich inquired from the end of the table.

"I had occasion to observe what distant lands there are in the world!" said Ivan Fyodorovich, genuinely gratified that he had succeeded in uttering so long and difficult a sentence.

"Don't you believe him, Ivan Fyodorovich!" said Grigory Grigoryevich, who had not quite caught what was said. "He's always telling fibs!"

Meanwhile dinner was over. Grigory Grigoryevich went to his own room, as his habit was, for a little nap; and the visitors followed their aged hostess and the young ladies into the drawing-room, where the same table on which they had left vodka when they went out to dinner was now, as though by some magical transformation, covered with little saucers of jam of various sorts and dishes of cherries and different kinds of melons.

The absence of Grigory Grigoryevich was perceptible in everything: the old lady became more disposed to talk and, of her own accord, without being asked, revealed a great many secrets in regard to the making of apple cheese, and the drying of pears. Even the young ladies began talking; though the fair one, who looked some six years younger than her sister and who was apparently about five-and-twenty, was rather silent.

But Ivan Ivanovich was more talkative and active than anyone else. Feeling secure that no one would snub or contradict him, he talked of cucumbers and of planting potatoes and of how much more sensible people were in old days—no comparison with what people are now!—and of how as time goes on everything improves and the most intricate inventions are discovered. He was, indeed, one of those persons who take great pleasure in uplifting conversation and will talk of anything that possibly can be talked about. If the conversation touched upon grave and pious subjects, Ivan Ivanovich sighed after each word and nodded his head slightly; if the subject was of a more homely character, he would pop his head out of his chaise-like collar and make faces from which one could almost, it seemed, read how to make pear kvass, how large were the melons of which he was speaking and how fat were the geese that were running about in his yard.

At last, with great difficulty and not before evening, Ivan Fyodorovich succeeded in taking his leave, and although he was usually ready to give way and they almost kept him for the night by force, he persisted in his intention of going— and went.

V

AUNTIE'S NEW PLAN

"Well, did you get the deed of gift out of the old sinner?" Such was the question with which Ivan Fyodorovich was greeted by his aunt, who had been expecting him for some hours on the steps and had at last been unable to resist going out to the gate.

"No, Auntie," said Ivan Fyodorovich, getting out of the trap, "Grigory Grigoryevich has no deed of gift."

"And you believed him? He was lying, the confounded fellow! Some day I shall come across him and I will give him a drubbing with my own hands. Oh, I'd get rid of some of his fat for him! Though perhaps we ought first to consult our court assessor and see if we couldn't get the law on him. But that's not the point now. Was the dinner good?"

"Very—it was excellent, Auntie."

"Well, what did you have? Tell me. The old lady, I know, is a great hand at cooking."

"Curd fritters with sour cream, Auntie; stuffed pigeons in a sauce—"

"And a turkey with prunes?" asked his aunt, for she was herself very skilful in the preparation of that dish.

"Yes, there was a turkey, too! Very handsome young ladies—Grigory Grigoryevich's sisters—especially the fair one."

"Ah!" said Auntie, and she looked intently at Ivan Fyodorovich, who dropped his eyes, blushing. A new idea flashed upon her mind. "Come, tell me," she said eagerly and with curiosity, "what are her eyebrows like?"

It may not be amiss to observe that Auntie considered fine eyebrows the most important item in a woman's looks.

"Her eyebrows, Auntie, are exactly like what you said you had when you were young. And there are little freckles all over her face."

"Ah!" commented his aunt, well pleased with Ivan Fyodorovich's observation, though he had not at all meant to pay her a compliment. "What sort of dress was she wearing? Though, indeed, it's hard to get good material nowadays, such as I have here, for instance, in this gown. But that's not the point. Well, did you talk to her about anything?"

"Talk! How do you mean, Auntie? Perhaps you are imagining—"

"Well, what of it, there would be nothing strange in that. Such is God's will! It may have been ordained at your birth that you should make a match of it."

"I don't understand how you can say such a thing, Auntie. That shows that you don't know me at all."

"Well, well, now he is offended," said his aunt. "He's still only a child!" she thought to herself. "He knows nothing. I must bring them together—let them get to know each other."

Thereupon Auntie went to have a look at the kitchen and left Ivan Fyodorovich alone. But from that time forward she thought of nothing but seeing her nephew married as soon as possible and fondling his little ones. Her mind was absorbed in making preparations for the wedding, and it was noticeable that she bustled about more busily than ever, though the work was the worse rather than the better for it. Often when she was making a cake, a job which she never left to the cook, she would forget everything, and imagining that a tiny grand-nephew was standing by her asking for some cake, would absently hold out her hand with the nicest bit for him, and the yard-dog, taking advantage of this, would snatch the dainty morsel and by its loud munching rouse her from her reverie, for which it was always beaten with the poker. She even abandoned her favourite pursuits and did not go out shooting, especially after she shot a crow by mistake for a partridge, a thing which had never happened to her before.

At last, four days later, everyone saw the chaise brought out of the carriage-house into the yard. The coachman Omelko—he was also the gardener and the watchman—had been hammering from early morning, nailing on the leather and continually chasing away the dogs which licked the wheels. I think it my duty to inform my readers that this was the very chaise in which Adam used to drive; and therefore, if anyone gives out that some other chaise was Adam's, it is an absolute lie, and his chaise is certainly not the genuine article. There is no telling how it survived the Deluge. It must be supposed that there was a special coach-house for it in Noah's ark. I am very sorry that I cannot give a living picture of it for my readers. Suffice it to say that Vasilisa Kashporovna was very well satisfied with its structure, and always expressed regret that the old style of carriages had gone out of fashion. The chaise had been constructed a little on one side, so that the right half stood much higher than the left, and this pleased her particularly, because, as she said, a short person could climb up on one side and a tall person on the other. Inside the chaise, however, there was room for five small persons or three such as Auntie herself.

About midday Omelko, having finished with the chaise, brought out of the stable three horses which were but a little younger than the chaise, and began harnessing them with cord to the magnificent vehicle. Ivan Fyodorovich and his aunt stepped in—he on the left side and she on the right—and the chaise drove off. The peasants they met on the road, seeing this sumptuous turn-out (Vasilisa Kashporovna rarely drove out in it), stood respectfully, taking off their caps and bowing low.

Two hours later the chaise stopped at the front door—I think I need not say—of Storchenko's house. Grigory Grigoryevich was not at home. His old mother and the two young ladies came into the dining-room to receive the visitors. Auntie walked in with a majestic step, with great skill put one foot forward, and said in a loud voice:

"I am delighted, Madam, to have the honour to offer you my respects in person, and at the same time to thank you for your hospitality to my nephew, who has been warm in his praises of it. Your buckwheat is very good, Madam—I saw it as we drove into the village. May I ask how many sheaves you get to the dessiatine?"

There followed kisses all round. As soon as everybody was seated in the drawing-room, the old lady began:

"About the buckwheat I cannot tell you: that's Grigory Grigoryevich's department. It is long since I have had anything to do with that; indeed, I could not do it—I am old now. In old days I remember the buckwheat stood waist-high; now goodness knows what it is like, though they say everything is better now." The old lady heaved a sigh, and some observers would have heard in that sigh the sigh of a past age, of the eighteenth century.

"I have heard, my lady, that your maids can make excellent carpets," said Vasilisa Kashporovna, and with that touched on the old lady's most sensitive chord; at those words she seemed to brighten up, and she talked readily of the way to dye the yarn and prepare the thread.

From carpets the conversation drifted easily to the pickling of cucumbers and drying of pears. In short, before the end of an hour the two ladies were talking together as though they had known each other all their lives. Vasilisa Kashporovna had already said a great deal to her in such a low voice that Ivan Fyodorovich could not hear what she was saying.

"Yes, would not you like to have a look at them?" said the old lady, getting up.

The young ladies and Vasilisa Kashporovna also got up and all moved towards the maids' room. Auntie made a sign, however, to Ivan Fyodorovich to remain and said something in an undertone to the old lady.

"Mashenka," said the latter, addressing the fair-haired young lady, "stay with our visitor and talk with him, that he may not be dull!"

The fair-haired young lady sat down on the sofa. Ivan Fyodorovich sat on his chair as though on thorns, blushed and cast down his eyes; but the young lady appeared not to notice this and sat unconcernedly on the sofa, scanning the windows and the walls, or watching the cat running timorously round under the chairs.

Ivan Fyodorovich grew a little bolder and would have begun a conversation; but it seemed as though he had lost all his words on the way. Not a single idea occurred to him.

The silence lasted for nearly a quarter of an hour. The young lady went on sitting as before.

At last Ivan Fyodorovich plucked up his courage.

"There are a great many flies in summer, Madam!" he brought out in a half-trembling voice.

"A very great many!" answered the young lady. "My brother has made a flapper out of an old slipper of Mamma's to kill them, but there are lots of them still."

Here the conversation ran out, and Ivan Fyodorovich was utterly unable to find anything else to say.

At last the old lady came back with his aunt and the dark-haired young lady. After a little more conversation, Vasilisa Kashporovna took leave of the old lady and her daughters in spite of their entreaties that they should stay the night. The three ladies came out on the steps to see the visitors off, and continued for some time nodding to the aunt and the nephew, as they looked out of the chaise.

"Well, Ivan Fyodorovich, what did you talk about when you were alone with the young lady?" Auntie asked him on the way home.

"A very discreet and well-behaved young lady, is Marya Grigoryevna," said Ivan Fyodorovich.

"Listen, Ivan Fyodorovich, I want to talk seriously to you. Here you are over thirty-seven, thank God; you have obtained a good rank in the service—it's time to think about children. You must have a wife."

"What, Auntie!" cried Ivan Fyodorovich in fright. "A wife! No, Auntie, for goodness' sake! You make me quite ashamed. I've never had a wife. I shouldn't know what to do with her!"

"You'll find out, Ivan Fyodorovich, you will," said his aunt, smiling. "Why, he is a perfect baby—he knows nothing!" she thought to herself. "Yes, Ivan Fyodorovich," she went on aloud, "we could not find a better wife for you than Marya Grigoryevna. Besides, you are very much attracted by her. I have had a good talk with the old lady about it; she'll be delighted to see you her son-in-law. It's true that we don't know what that reprobate Grigory Grigoryevich will say to it; but we won't consider him, and if he takes it into his head not to give her a dowry, we'll have the law on him."

At that moment the chaise drove into the yard and the ancient nags grew more lively, feeling that their stable was not far off.

"Mind, Omelko! Let the horses have a good rest first, and don't take them down to water the minute they are unharnessed—they are overheated."

"Well, Ivan Fyodorovich," his aunt went on as she got out of the chaise, "I advise you to think it over well. I must run to the kitchen: I forgot to tell Solokha what to get for supper, and I expect the wretched woman won't have thought of it herself."

But Ivan Fyodorovich stood as though thunderstruck. It was true that Marya Grigoryevna was a very nice-looking young lady; but to get married! It seemed to him so strange, so peculiar, he couldn't think of it without horror. Living with a wife! Unthinkable! He would not be alone in his own room, but they would always have to be two together! Perspiration came out on his face as he sank more deeply into meditation.

He went to bed earlier than usual, but in spite of all his efforts he could not go to sleep. But at last sleep, that universal comforter, came to him; but what sleep! He had never had such incoherent dreams. First he dreamed that everything was whirling with a noise around him, and he was running and running, as fast as his legs could carry him. Now he was at his last gasp.

All at once someone caught him by the ear. "Ouch! Who is it?"

"It is me, your wife!" a voice resounded loudly in his ear, and he woke up. Then he imagined that he was married, that everything in their little house was so peculiar, so strange: a double bed stood in his room instead of a single one; his wife was sitting on a chair. He felt queer: he did not know how to approach her, what to say to her, and then he noticed that she had the face of a goose. He happened to turn aside and saw another wife, also with the face of a goose. Turning again, he saw yet another wife; and behind him was a fourth. Then he was seized by panic; he dashed away into the garden, but there it was hot; he took off his hat, and saw a wife sitting in his hat. Drops of sweat came out on his face. He put his hand in his pocket for his handkerchief and in his pocket, too, there was a wife; he took some cotton wool out of his ear—and there, too, sat a wife. Then he suddenly began hopping on one leg, and Auntie, looking at him, said with a dignified air: "Yes, you must hop on one leg now, for you are a married man." He went towards her, but his aunt was no longer an aunt but a belfry, and he felt that someone was dragging him by a rope up on the belfry. "Who is it pulling me?" Ivan Fyodorovich asked plaintively. "It is me, your wife. I am pulling you because you are a bell." "No, I am not a bell, I am Ivan Fyodorovich," he cried. "Yes, you are a bell," said the colonel of the infantry regiment, who happened to be passing. Then he suddenly dreamed that a wife was not a human being at all but a sort of woollen material; that he went into a shop in Mogilyov. "What sort of stuff would you like?" asked the shop-keeper. "You had better take a wife, that is the most fashionable material! It wears well! Everyone is having coats made of it now." The shopkeeper measured and cut off a wife. Ivan Fyodorovich put her under his arm and went off to a Jewish tailor. "No," said the Jew, "that is poor material. No one has coats made of that now."

Ivan Fyodorovich woke up in terror, not knowing where he was and dripping with cold perspiration.

As soon as he got up in the morning, he went at once to his fortune-teller's book, at the end of which a virtuous bookseller had in the goodness of his heart and disinterestedness inserted an abridged dream-book. But there was absolutely nothing in it that remotely resembled this incoherent dream.

Meanwhile a quite new design, of which you shall hear more in the following chapter, had taken shape in Auntie's brain.

A PLACE BEWITCHED

A True Story told by a Sacristan

Upon my word, I am sick of telling stories! Why, what would you expect? It really is tiresome; one goes on telling stories and there is no getting out of it. Oh, very well, I will tell you a story then; only mind, it is for the last time. Well, we were talking about a man's being able to get the better of the Evil One, as they call him. To be sure, if you come to that, all sorts of things happen in this world. Better not say so, though: if the devil wants to bamboozle you he will, upon my soul he will...

You see, my father had the four of us. I was only a silly child then, I wasn't more than eleven, or even less than that. I remember, as though it were today, when I started running on all fours and set to barking like a dog, my dad shouted at me, shaking his head: "Look here, Foma, you are old enough to be married but you are getting to be as foolish as a young colt." My grandfather was still living then and was fairly—may his hiccup be easier in the other world—strong on his legs. At times he would take a fancy.

But this is not the way to tell a story! One of you has been for the last hour raking an ember for his pipe out of the stove and another has run behind the barn for something. What's this, now! It would be all very well if I forced you to listen to me, but you kept pressing me for a story. If you want to listen, then listen properly!

Early in spring Dad carted some tobacco to the Crimea to sell, only I don't remember whether he loaded two or three waggons; tobacco fetched a good price in those days. He took my three-year-old brother along to train him as a dealer. Grandfather, Mother, and I, and a brother, and another brother were left at home. Grandfather had sown melons on a bit of ground by the roadway and went to stay at the shanty there; he took us with him to scare the sparrows and the magpies off the garden. I can't say it came amiss to us: sometimes we'd eat so many cucumbers, melons, turnips, onions, and peas that, upon my word, you would have thought there were cocks crowing in our stomachs. Besides, it was profitable: travellers jogged along the road, everyone wanted to treat himself to a melon, and, besides that, from the neighbouring farms they often brought us fowls, turkeys, eggs, to exchange for our vegetables. We did very well.

But what Grandfather liked more than anything else was that some fifty waggoners would pass with their waggon-loads every day. Those are people who have seen the world; when anyone of them started telling a story you might well prick up your ears, and to Grandfather it was like dumplings to a hungry man. Sometimes there would be a meeting with old acquaintances— everyone knew Grandfather—and you know how it is when old folks get together: it is this and that, and so this happened and that happened. Well, they just run on. They remember things that happened God knows when.

One evening—why, it seems as though it had happened today— the sun had begun to set. Grandfather was walking about the garden taking off the leaves with which he covered the watermelons in the day to keep them from being scorched by the sun.

"Look, Ostap," I said to my brother, "there come some waggoners!"

"Where are the waggoners?" said Grandfather, as he put a mark on a big melon that the lads mightn't eat it.

There were six waggons trailing along the road; a waggoner, whose moustache had gone grey, was walking ahead of them. He was still—what shall I say?—ten paces off when he stopped.

"Good day, Maxim, so it has pleased God we should meet here."

Grandfather screwed up his eyes.

"Oh, good day! Where do you come from? And Bolyachka here, too! Good day, brother! What the devil! They are all here: Krutotrishchenko, too! and Pecheritsya! and Kovelek and Stetsko! Good day!" And they fell to kissing each other.

They unharnessed the oxen and let them graze; they left the waggons on the road and all sat down in a circle in front of the shanty and lighted their pipes. Though they had no thoughts for their pipes; what with telling stories and chattering, I don't believe they smoked a pipe apiece.

After dinner Grandfather began regaling his visitors with melons. So, taking a melon each, they peeled it neatly with a knife (they were all old hands, had been about a good bit, and knew how to eat in company—I daresay they would have been ready to sit down even at a gentleman's table); after peeling the melon well, everyone made a hole with his finger in it, drank the juice, began cutting it up into pieces and putting them into his mouth.

"Why are you standing there gaping, lads?" said my grandfather. "Dance, you puppies! Where's your reed pipe, Ostap? Now then, the Cossack dance! Foma, arms akimbo! Come, that's it! Now!"

I was a brisk lad in those days. Cursed old age! Now I can't step out as I used to; instead of cutting capers, my legs can only trip and stumble. For a long time Grandad watched us as he sat with the waggoners. I noticed that his legs wouldn't keep still, it was as though something were tugging at them.

"Look, Foma," said Ostap, "if the old chap isn't going to dance."

He had hardly uttered the words when the old man could resist it no longer. He longed, you see, to show off before the waggoners.

"I say, you brats, is that the way to dance? This is the way to dance!" he said, getting up, stretching out his arms, and tapping with his heels.

Well, there is no denying he couldn't have danced better if it had been with the Hetman's wife. We stepped aside and the old man went twirling his legs all over the smooth space beside the cucumber beds. But when he had got to the middle and wanted to do his best and cut some capers with his legs in a whirl— his feet wouldn't rise from the ground, whatever he did! What a plague! He moved backwards and forwards again, got to the middle—it just wouldn't go! He couldn't do it! His legs stood still as though made of wood. "Look you, the place is bewitched, it is a visitation of Satan! The Herod, the enemy of mankind, has a hand in it!"

Well, he couldn't disgrace himself before the waggoners like
that, could he? He made a fresh start and began cutting tiny
trifling capers, a joy to see; then he got to the middle, and again
he couldn't dance!

"Why, you rascally Satan! May you choke with a rotten melon,
may you have perished when you were little, son of a cur. See
what shame he has brought me to in my old age!" And indeed
someone did laugh behind his back.

He looked round; no melon garden, no waggoners, nothing;
behind, in front, on both sides was a flat field. "Well, I never!"
He began screwing up his eyes—the place did not seem quite
unfamiliar: on one side a copse, behind the copse some sort of
post sticking up which could be seen far away against the sky.
Dash it all! but that was the dovecote in the priest's kitchen
garden! On the other side there was something greyish; he looked
closer: it was the district clerk's threshing-barn. So this was where
the Evil One had dragged him! Going round in circles, he hit
upon a little path. There was no moon; instead of it a white
blur glimmered through a dark cloud.

"There will be a high wind tomorrow," thought Grandad.
All at once there was the gleam of a candle on a grave a little way
off the path. "Well, well!" Grandad stood still, put his arms
akimbo, and stared at it. The light went out; far away and a
little further yet, another twinkled. "A treasure!" cried Grandad.
"I'll bet anything if it's not a treasure!" And he was just about
to spit on his hands to begin digging when he remembered that
he had no spade with him. "Oh, what a pity! Maybe I have only
to lift the turf to see it lying there, the precious dear! Well,
there's nothing for it, I'll mark the place at least so as not to
forget it afterwards."

So pulling along a good-sized branch that must have been
broken off by the wind, he laid it on the little grave where the

candle gleamed, and walked along the path. The young oak copse grew thinner; he caught a glimpse of a fence. "There, didn't I say it was the priest's plot ?" thought Grandad. "Here's his fence; now it is less than a verst to the melon patch."

It was pretty late, though, when he came home, and he wouldn't have any dumplings. Waking my brother Ostap, he asked him whether it was long since the waggoners had gone, and then rolled himself up in his sheepskin. And when Ostap asked him: "Where did the devils keep you today, Grandad ?"— "Don't ask," he said, wrapping himself up still tighter, "don't ask, Ostap, or your hair will turn grey!"

And he began snoring so loudly that the sparrows which had been flocking together at the melon patch took off in a fright. But how could he sleep ? He was a sly old fellow—may he rest in peace—he could always get out of any scrape. Sometimes he would pitch such a yarn that our hair would stand on end.

Next day, as soon as it began to get dark, Grandad put on his jacket, fastened his belt, took a spade under his arm, put on his cap, drank a mug of kvass, wiped his lips with his skirt, and marched straight to the priest's kitchen garden. He passed both the fence and the low oak copse, and there was a path winding between the trees and coming out into the open country; it seemed like the same. He came out of the copse and the place seemed exactly the same as yesterday: he saw the dovecote sticking out, but he could not see the threshing-barn. "No, this isn't the place, it must be a little further; it seems I must turn a little towards the threshing-barn!" He turned back and walked along another path—then he could see the barn but not the dovecote. Again he turned, and a little nearer to the dovecote the barn was hidden. As though to spite him it began drizzling with rain. He ran again towards the barn—the dovecote vanished; towards the dovecote—the barn vanished.

"You damned Satan, may you never live to see your children!" he cried.

Now it was raining cats and dogs. So, taking off his new boots and wrapping them in a handkerchief that they might not be warped by the rain, he ran off like a regular ambler. He crept into the shanty, drenched to the skin, covered himself with his sheepskin and set to grumbling between his teeth, and calling the devil names such as I had never heard in my life. I should really have blushed if it had happened in broad daylight.

Next day I woke up and saw Grandad walking about the melon patch as though nothing had happened, covering the melons with burdock leaves. At dinner the old chap got talking again and began scaring my young brother, saying he would swop him, instead of a melon, for a fowl; and after dinner he made a pipe out of a bit of wood and began playing on it; and to amuse us gave us a melon which was twisted in three coils like a snake; he called it a Turkish one. I don't see such melons anywhere nowadays; it is true he got the seed from somewhere far away.

In the evening, after supper, Grandad went with the spade to dig a new bed for late pumpkins. As he was passing that bewitched place he couldn't help muttering, "Cursed place!" He went into the middle of it, to the spot where he could not finish the dance the day before, and in his anger struck it a blow with his spade. In a flash that same field was all around him again: on one side he saw the dovecote sticking up, and on the other— the threshing-barn. "Well, it's a good thing I thought of bringing my spade along. And there's the path, and the grave! And there's the branch lying on it, and yonder is the candle! If only I have made no mistake!"

He ran up stealthily, holding the spade in the air as though he were going to hit a hog that had poked its snout into a melon patch, and stopped before the grave. The candle went out. On the grave lay a stone overgrown with weeds. "I must lift up that stone," thought Grandad, and tried to dig round it. The damned stone was huge. But planting his feet firmly on the ground he shoved it off the grave. "O-o-o!" the valley echoed all round. "That's the right road for you to take! Now things will go more briskly!"

At this point Grandad stopped, took out his horn, sprinkled a little snuff in his hand, and was about to raise it to his nose when all at once something sneezed above his head, so that the trees shook and Grandad's whole face was spattered.

"You might at least have turned aside when you wanted to sneeze," said Grandad, wiping his eyes. He looked round—there was no one there. "It seems the devil doesn't like the snuff," he went on, putting back the horn in his bosom and picking up his spade. "He's a fool! Neither his grandfather nor his father ever had a pinch of snuff like that!"

He began digging; the ground was soft, the spade simply sank into it. Then something clanked. Shovelling aside the earth he saw a cauldron.

"Ah, so there you are!" cried Grandad, thrusting the spade under it.

"Ah, so there you are!" piped a bird's beak, pecking the cauldron.

Grandad stepped aside and dropped the spade.

"Ah, so there you are!" bleated a sheep's head from the top of a tree.

"Ah, so there you are!" roared a bear, poking its nose out from behind a tree.

A shudder ran down Grandad's back.

"Why, one is afraid to say a word here!" he muttered to himself.

"One is afraid to say a word here!" piped the bird's beak.

"Afraid to say a word here!" bleated the sheep's head.

"To say a word here!" roared the bear.

"Hm!" said Grandad, and he felt terrified.

"Hm!" piped the beak.

"Hm!" bleated the sheep.

"Hum!" roared the bear.

Grandad turned round in a fright. God Almighty, what a night! No stars, no moon; pits all round him, a bottomless precipice at his feet, and a crag hanging over his head and looking as though it might break off any moment and come down on him. And Grandad fancied that a horrible face peeped out from behind it. "Oo! Oo!" A nose like a blacksmith's bellows. You could pour a bucket of water into each nostril! Lips like two logs! Red eyes starting out above and a tongue thrust out, jeering.

"May the devil take you!" said Grandad, letting go of the cauldron. "Damn you and your treasure! What a loathsome snout!" And he was just going to cut and run, but he looked round and stopped, seeing that everything was as before. "It's only the Evil One trying to scare me!"

He set to work at the cauldron again. It was too heavy! What was he to do? He couldn't leave it now! So, exerting himself to his utmost, he clutched at it.

"Come, heave ho! again, again!" He dragged it out. "Oof, now for a pinch of snuff!"

He took out his horn. Before shaking the snuff out, though, he took a good look round to be sure there was no one there. He fancied there was no one; but then it seemed to him that the trunk of the tree was gasping and blowing, ears showed; there were red eyes, puffing nostrils, a wrinkled nose and it seemed on the point of sneezing. "No, I won't have a pinch of snuff!" thought

Grandad, putting away the horn. "Satan will be spitting in my eyes again!" He made haste to snatch up the cauldron and set off running as fast as his legs could carry him; only he felt something behind him scratching on his legs with twigs. "Ouch! Ouch!" was all that Grandad could cry as he ran his utmost; and it was not till he reached the priest's kitchen garden that he took breath a little.

"Where can Grandad be gone?" we wondered, after waiting three hours for him. Mother had come from the farm long ago and brought a pot of hot dumplings. Still no sign of Grandad! Again we had supper without him. After supper Mother washed the pot and was looking where to throw the dish-water because there were melon beds all round, when she saw a barrel coming straight towards her! It was rather dark. She felt sure one of the lads was hiding behind it in mischief and shoving it towards her. "That's good, I'll throw the water into it," she said, and flung the hot dish-water out.

"Ouch!" boomed a voice. Fancy, it was Grandad! Well, who could have known it? Upon my word, we thought it was a barrel coming up! I must own, though it was rather a sin, we really thought it funny to see Grandad's grey head drenched in the dish-water and decked with melon peelings.

"You devil of a woman!" said Grandad, wiping his head with the skirt of his jacket. "What a hot bath she has given me, as though I were a pig before Christmas! Well, lads, now you will have something for bread-rings! You'll go about dressed in gold tunics, you puppies! Look what I have brought you!" said Grandad, and opened the cauldron.

What do you suppose there was in it? Come, think well, and make a guess. Eh? Gold? Well now, it wasn't gold—it was dirt, filth, I am ashamed to say what it was. Grandad spat, flung away the cauldron, and washed his hands.

And from that time forward Grandad made us too swear never to trust the devil.

"Don't you believe him!" he would often say to us. "Whatever the foe of our Lord Christ says, he is always lying, the son of a cur! There isn't a kopek's worth of truth in him!"

And if ever the old man heard that things were not right in some place he would say, "Come, lads, let's make the sign of the cross over him. That's it! That's it! Properly!" and he would begin making the sign of the cross. And that accursed place where he couldn't finish the dance he fenced in and bade us dump there all the rubbish, all the weeds and litter which he raked off the melon patch.

See how the Evil One takes a man in? I know that bit of ground well; later on some neighbouring Cossacks hired it from Dad for a melon patch. It's capital ground and there is always a wonderful crop on it; but there has never been anything good grown on that bewitched place. They may sow it properly, but there's no saying what it is that comes up: not a melon—not a pumpkin—not a cucumber, the devil only knows what to make of it!

THE END

THE END